Praise for

I0663078

League of Love

This was such an emotionally filled story on so many
levels! Goodness and love win again... 5 STARS.
 ~ *Erzabet's Enchantments*

Total-E-Bound Publishing books by Donna Gallagher:

League of Love Volume One
Caitlin's Hero
Mandy's He-Man

League of Love Volume Two
Laura's Light
Pippa's Fantasy

LEAGUE OF LOVE
Volume Two

Laura's Light

Pippa's Fantasy

DONNA GALLAGHER

League of Love Volume Two
ISBN # 978-1-78184-604-9
©Copyright Donna Gallagher 2013
Cover Art by Posh Gosh ©Copyright 2013
Interior text design by Claire Siemaszkiewicz
Total-E-Bound Publishing

This is a work of fiction. All characters, places and events are from the author's imagination and should not be confused with fact. Any resemblance to persons, living or dead, events or places is purely coincidental.

All rights reserved. No part of this publication may be reproduced in any material form, whether by printing, photocopying, scanning or otherwise without the written permission of the publisher, Total-E-Bound Publishing.

Applications should be addressed in the first instance, in writing, to Total-E-Bound Publishing. Unauthorised or restricted acts in relation to this publication may result in civil proceedings and/or criminal prosecution.

The author and illustrator have asserted their respective rights under the Copyright Designs and Patents Acts 1988 (as amended) to be identified as the author of this book and illustrator of the artwork.

Published in 2013 by Total-E-Bound Publishing, Think Tank, Ruston Way, Lincoln, LN6 7FL, United Kingdom.

No part of this book may be reproduced, scanned, or distributed in any printed or electronic form without permission. Please do not participate in or encourage piracy of copyrighted materials in violation of the authors' rights. Purchase only authorised copies.

Total-E-Bound Publishing is an imprint of Total-E-Ntwined Limited.

If you purchased this book without a cover you should be aware that this book is stolen property. It was reported as "unsold and destroyed" to the publisher and neither the author nor the publisher has received any payment for this "stripped book".

.

LAURA'S LIGHT

Dedication

For anyone who has ever felt they needed help.

Chapter One

"This is pointless. What on earth was I thinking? Forty-two-year-old women do not accept dates from thirty-four-year-old men, especially when the man in question is a famous and mouth-wateringly hot television personality."

Laura Harris scolded her reflection in the full-length mirror she was standing before. "This is a nightmare. What *do* old, desperate women wear to this sort of thing?" she groaned as she took in her appearance grimly.

"Nope, too much cleavage," she said as she ruthlessly tossed aside the little black dress.

"Far too short..." was the decision that condemned the blue dress to the pile of discarded clothes that was becoming a mountain on the floor of her small, but usually tidy, bedroom.

"Yeah, okay... Maybe these black pants with this sweater—I do love the feel of the soft wool and these little pearl buttons are so sweet... Oh, my God—sweet. This is ridiculous! I'm too old for sweet. Sophisticated. Mature. That's what I need. How do people do this…dating thing?" She waved frantically at her dishevelled self in the mirror. "I'm terrified."

She took a deep breath, then shook her hands a few times to try to dispel the anxiety that was eating her up.

"No, Laura, get a grip. Terrified is finding yourself pregnant at twenty. Terrified is being kicked out of home by your unforgiving parents with no way of supporting yourself. This is just dinner, dinner with a man who presents a sports programme on TV. A man who knows your twenty-one-year-old, football-playing son."

Having now managed to turn down the panic level a few notches Laura perused the mess on the floor. The ruby colour caught her eye, and as she picked the knee-length, full-skirted dress with the tailored bodice from the floor, she thought, *What the heck, why not?*

It wasn't that bad a sight that greeted Laura in the mirror's reflection, once she had finished primping and pruning for the good part of an hour. Her blonde, almost white hair was in a loose updo and grey-and-silver eyeshadow highlighted her pale blue eyes. Happy with the way her dress fit tastefully over her trim body and noticing that her moderately high black pumps gave her calves a nice shape, Laura twirled one more time, reasonably pleased with the overall result, before picking up the small clasped handbag she had set aside.

"Well, as my mother used to say, 'That will do for the fella you're after and the chance you've got'." The sound of the snort she made in response to repeating one of her estranged mother's pearls of wisdom was not at all ladylike, in Laura's opinion. "Great, and now I'm turning into my mother," she mumbled as she headed towards her living room to await her date's arrival.

"Hey, Ma—did you say something? Wow, what's with the get-up? Where are you going?"

Laura hadn't heard her son come home but it was no shock to see him sitting on the couch with the TV on—probably a replay of the last year's winning Grand Final. She smiled to herself, noticing the surprised expression on his face when he saw her.

"What's wrong, Mitchell? Don't I look okay? Do you think I should change? Yes, you're probably right. It is a bit too much for dinner…" Laura had really got herself into a tether and rambled on until she felt her son's hands come down gently on top of her shoulders.

"Slow down, Mum, you look fantastic. Hot—which is quite awkward for me to notice." Mitchell Harris—known as 'the Rookie' to fans of rugby league—shuddered visibly in response. "What's got you into such a state, and all dressed up like that? Where are you going and who with?"

Laura would have laughed at the ridiculousness of the moment, if she hadn't already felt as if she were about to faint from the nerves caused by the quickly approaching dinner date. Her son had sounded just like her father in his demand to know her plans. *Nice turn of events,* she thought.

"Huh, not that it is any of your concern, young man—you are still the child in this relationship and me the mother—but to answer your question, I've been invited out to dinner. Pretty sure we've already had this conversation. Mitchell Harris, were you not listening to me…again?" Laura looked up into her tall son's face, trying to appear stern, but she couldn't hide her affection for her only child.

"I'm sorry, Ma, I didn't mean to sound nosey… But who *are* you going out with, again? I forgot."

Laura had always had a hard time not falling for that puppy dog look Mitch had perfected early on in his life when he'd really wanted something. Many a time it had broken Laura's heart to disappoint him, but money had always been tight back then. She thanked her lucky stars, every day, that their life had taken a turn for the better. Not that luck had had much to do with it. No, it was all Mitchell and his amazing sporting ability that had given their small family a leg-up in life.

"Trevor Hughes. He is taking me to Mia's. Caitlin James is singing tonight—it's the first time since the wedding that she's been back at Mia's. In fact, it was at Brodie and Caitlin's wedding that Trevor and I made the plans for tonight. You would have known all this if you ever listened to me, Mitchell."

Before her son could shut his now gaping mouth and respond to her, the sound of the front doorbell ringing interrupted them.

"Well, that will be Trevor now." Laura told her motionless, slightly horrified-looking son. "Don't wait up," she couldn't resist adding to further tease him as she opened the door.

All joking was immediately forgotten when Laura caught sight of the most enormous bunch of red roses she had ever seen blocking her doorway—and holding those roses, far outshining their spectacle, stood Trevor Hughes. The man was an Adonis, dressed to kill in an expensively tailored suit that emphasised his wide shoulders beautifully. His light brown hair was slightly mussed, as if he had run his fingers through it recently, but it was his dimpled smile that took Laura's breath from her lungs.

"My, you're gorgeous! I-I-I mean those roses—*they're* gorgeous," she stuttered, and wanted to die from embarrassment at her slip-up, certain her cheeks were as red as the flowers themselves. "Are they for me?" she asked in a small voice as a sudden wave of shy apprehension stole over her.

"Yes, they are for you, Laura, but they fade in comparison to how beautiful you look tonight. You look amazing." The smooth, rich tones of Trevor's voice and compliment did nothing to extinguish the burning in her cheeks. As Laura reached to take the offered roses, the door was thrust all the way open and Mitchell almost knocked her aside as he stood, his stance tense, glaring daggers at Trevor.

"G'day, Rookie," Trevor said, using Mitchell's footy nickname.

Just about everyone but Laura called her son Rookie, much to her horror. It only made things worse when she caught herself using the name, which was happening more often lately.

"Was just telling your Mum how amazing she looks. Really beautiful, don't you think, Rookie?" Trevor continued. Laura wasn't sure whether Trevor had picked up on her son's animosity, but he was doing a good job of ignoring it if he had.

"Let me just put these in water and then we can head off. Mitchell, move out of the way so Trevor can come in off the front step." Laura gave her son a firm shove to get him to move as she made the request. "Come in, Trevor. Welcome—make yourself at home while I fix these. Mitchell, see if Trevor would like something to drink. I think there is some beer in the fridge, or I do have wine if you'd prefer, Trevor? Just let Mitchell know your preference."

I'm rambling again, Laura thought and caught herself, stopped talking, and stood awkwardly in her family room, not sure what to do first. She had never really entertained a man in her house before, especially not with her son hovering about, trying his best to act intimidating.

"Thanks, but I'm good, driving and all that. I'll save it up and have a glass or two over dinner. Go do what has to be done with the roses, I'll sit and watch the replay with Rookie." Trevor, after graciously declining her offer of a drink, turned towards her son. "I see we've interrupted your viewing. This was such a great game. You played your socks off, as I recall."

Laura, thankful for the change in subject, hurried off to find a vase big enough to set the flowers in. She ended up just sitting them in a large saucepan full of water, eager to get back to her living room and make sure Mitchell had not thrown Trevor out of the door while she'd been busy in the other room. Not that Laura could see her son—as big and fit as he was— achieving the task. Trevor was also a prime specimen of manhood, all tall and muscled.

She giggled girlishly, the sound a shock to her system, making her shake her head. Her palms were moist and her heart was beating double-time in her chest.

"Oh, my… You are in way over your head this time, Laura Harris," she told herself as she took a moment to smell the heavenly scent of the roses. "These roses must have cost a small fortune—such an extravagant gesture. Please don't let Mitchell have scared him off."

Chapter Two

Trevor was trying to ignore Rookie's blatant hostility. It was a bit of a blow to his ego that the kid didn't think Trevor was good enough for his mother, but he couldn't blame Rookie. Trevor did not want to contemplate the thought of his own mother dating. But then again, his mother had nowhere near the beauty of Laura Harris, and she was still married to his father, albeit unhappily.

"So are you looking forward to the new season, Rookie? How do you think the Jets will cope with the double retirement? JT and Brodie are sure to be missed."

"What, you doing an interview with me or something, Hughes?"

Rookie's response was full of sarcasm, but Trevor tried his best to get the kid to calm down. "No, buddy, just makin' conversation while I wait for your mother. But if you don't feel like talking, that's okay—I'll just sit and watch the game."

"Why are you taking my mum out, anyway?"

The kid's question was so out of line that Trevor wouldn't have bothered to answer if not for the sulky tones in which it had been delivered. God, if Rookie had stood up and stamped his foot in a temper tantrum it wouldn't have surprised Trevor.

"Do you really need me to answer that question, Rookie? Your mother is single and an adult, and so am I. We are going out to dinner to get to know one another. I wasn't kidding when I said how beautiful Laura looks tonight, mate." Trevor was trying to be diplomatic but the faces Rookie was pulling were beginning to get on his nerves. "Be assured I will treat your mother with the dignity she deserves, okay, Rookie? Stop worrying. It's not like I'm kidnapping her or anything. It's dinner."

"Yeah, right—you just want dinner and nothing else. Give me a break, Hughes. I'm not an idiot, you know. I know what you'll be wanting after dinner."

"Mitchell John Harris, how dare you say something like that?"

Trevor hadn't noticed Laura had come back into the room until she confronted her son and his comments. The blaze in her eyes as she took her cantankerous son to task was glorious. Her cheeks had a flush to them that Trevor imagined would resemble the effects of a post-orgasmic glow, and he hoped he would have the chance to test his theory one day. Her eyes sparkled with fury, making her face come alive. She was a magnificent sight, and Trevor stood captivated.

"I will have you know, young man, that I do not appreciate your rudeness to a guest in my house. I raised you better than that. What I do and who I choose to have dinner with is my business, Mitchell. And son, if want to have sex, I will have sex with whomever I deem fit."

"Oh, God, Mum! Don't say things like that — I'll have nightmares. It's sick."

Trevor was dumbfounded by the turn of conversation, but he had to admit he liked where Laura was heading. He sure as hell would be happy and willing to oblige her in the sex department. God, his cock was at half-mast already, and seeing Rookie squirm at his mother's comment was one sight he would remember for a long time. He could only imagine the talented halfback's opponents' faces if they could see Rookie Harris being put back in his place by his mother. They could only wish they could control him that way.

"What, Mitch? At twenty-one, you're still a virgin? Or is it just okay for men to have sex, but not women? Apologise to Trevor so I can go. I'm so upset with you right now."

Trevor felt it was time he stepped in and tried to calm the situation down. He certainly didn't want Laura to be worrying about her son's behaviour during dinner, and really, Rookie was just protecting his mother. Trev could understand that.

"Laura, no need for an apology. I'm sure Rookie just had your best interests at heart. No harm done. I respect him for his protectiveness. Would expect nothing less, from what I hear of your son's outstanding character. JT certainly holds him in high regard after he stood up to protect Mandy from that madman she was having all those problems with. What say we just forget all about this and go to Mia's? What do you say, Rookie? Shake hands and move on?"

"That's very generous of you, Trevor, but Mitchell still treated you — my guest — rudely and I won't stand for that. Mitchell, do you have something to say?"

Trevor fought back the grin that was threatening as he watched Rookie shuffling his feet like a small child who had been caught out being naughty. What was it about mothers that could bring grown men to their knees?

"Sorry." Rookie's apology was quiet and quick. Trevor nearly missed it altogether.

"Sorry for what, Mitchell?" Laura really wasn't letting her son off the hook anytime soon, and Trevor was actually starting to feel sorry for the kid. No wonder Rookie Harris was such a respectable and mature young man — Laura wouldn't let him be any other way.

"I'm sorry for being rude, Hughes. Is that better, Mum? You're really embarrassing me here, you know." Rookie's plea apparently fell on deaf ears, as Laura still did not let up.

"Trevor or Mr Hughes, please, Mitchell. You know how much I hate you just using surnames when addressing another human being. Politeness is free, you know. And if you are embarrassed by my attempts at teaching you some manners, then perhaps you can understand how I felt over your behaviour."

Trevor did get to shake hands with a very meek Rookie before finally getting Laura strapped safely in his car so they could be on their way. The trip to Mia's was filled with her apologising over Rookie's attitude, and the more he tried to convince her it was all forgotten the more she apologised. He really had to get her off the subject or the date would be a disaster.

"I hear on the grapevine you have a cleaning company, Laura. So you're a businesswoman as well as being beautiful." Trevor hoped distracting Laura with a question about her work might get her onto another topic — usually people had a lot to say about their careers, Trev had found, and he just hoped it was the case with Laura.

"I'm not expecting any write ups in the *Australian Financial Review* anytime soon." Laura's laugh at her own expense was warm and throaty. Trevor found the sound enticing, sexy, as it caressed over him, and he wanted to hear it again.

"I clean houses for busy people and have been fortunate enough to get to the stage where I can employ a small staff, as well. It's nothing grandiose — just hard menial work. But it pays the bills and in the beginning I could schedule my time around Mitchell's needs, so it worked well for me. Growing to become my own company is something I only dreamed of. In the beginning it was just a way a young, uneducated woman could make a living."

"Laura, don't sell yourself short. You own a business, have clients and staff — it's something to be proud of. You have obviously worked hard to get where you are now. Hey, I just talk for a living. Now *that's* shallow."

Trevor was glad to finally start up a normal conversation with Laura, get her thoughts away from her son. He loved the humble way she'd described what she did to make a living. She might have been short of a formal education, but Trevor could tell Laura was no brainless blonde. She had guts, that was clear, and the few conversations they'd had previously had all been highly entertaining.

Trevor couldn't wait to find out more about what made the attractive woman tick — he wanted to know her favourite food, what music she listened to, the movies she preferred, what the score was with Rookie's father... He wanted to know everything there was about Laura. And that alone should have had him running for the hills. Trevor preferred to keep a comfortable distance from relationships.

As they walked through the door of Mia's, Trevor knew he had made a mistake. What had he been thinking when he'd offered to bring Laura here on a date? There would be no chance of sharing an intimate dinner and getting to know her better when more than half of the restaurant's patrons were people he knew, all probably in attendance to enjoy listening to the beautiful sounds of Caitlin James' voice. Caitlin's husband, Brodie James, was already waving them over to join his table, a table also occupied by another of the Jets stalwarts—Jon 'JT' Thompson and his fiancée, Mandy.

His fate was sealed with the sound of Laura's happy gasp at the sight of the very pregnant Mandy.

"Oh, look, Trevor—there's Mandy and JT, as well as Brodie, and Caitlin's little brother, Riley! We should go over and say hello." Laura shot off in their direction, leaving him to follow.

"Well, would you look who we have here?" Brodie James' voice held a touch of smugness, Trevor thought, as he shook hands with the newly retired player, now assistant coach of the Jets. Trevor and Brodie went way back and he really enjoyed hanging out with Brodie, but it hadn't been what he'd had in mind for tonight.

His face must have shown his thoughts because Brodie laughed, a deep guffawing that rumbled from the giant of a man's chest. "What's wrong Trevor? Did you not realise that we would all be here for Cate's first night back?" The man added, too aware of Trevor's mind for his liking, "If you wanted a quiet night with Rookie's mother, maybe this was the last place you should have come, mate."

"Yeah, right, smart-arse—maybe I wanted to have you all around so you could give me some pointers. Hey, look at you and JT, wrapped around your women's fingers. The once big, tough Jets front-row forwards reduced to bending and scraping to please the little women…" Trevor's teasing was just that—he actually envied Brodie's and JT's newfound happiness. He could see for himself how much Caitlin and Mandy had enhanced his mates' lives. Not that he was ever likely to have that sort of relationship.

"What's that rubbish you're spouting, Hughes? No-one tells JT what to do. I'm a man's man, and don't you forget it." When JT welcomed someone, he often nearly smothered them in a bear hug or knocked them over with a punch to the arm. In this case, Trevor found he was the recipient of both, and as he rubbed at the painful repercussion of JT's friendship he shook his head.

"Dare you to say that again when Mandy's not distracted talking to Laura. You, JT, my friend, are a lost cause and you know it. How are you both? Hope the honeymoon was *nice*, Brodie." Trevor gave a smirk as he mentioned Brodie and Caitlin's honeymoon, knowing that there was no way Brodie would divulge any information in front of his new young brother-in-law. Riley Walters had quickly become a part of everyone's hearts. The poor kid and his sister had had a hard life after losing both their parents in a tragic car accident, before Brodie had walked into their lives and changed them for the better.

"Do you want to join us for dinner, Trev? You're welcome, but I'll understand if you would rather not," Brodie added diplomatically. But the decision was taken out of Trevor's hands as Mandy and Laura both made very feminine squealing noises in response to the idea.

"Would you mind terribly, Trevor? I really would love to chat some more with Mandy about the pregnancy." Laura leaned towards him and, with a wisp of air blowing gently over his ear and neck, she whispered, obviously not wanting to be overheard, "Mandy doesn't really have anyone to talk to about that sort of thing. She's estranged from her own mother and Caitlin's not experienced with this sort of thing, either."

Trevor would have given Laura the world at that moment as the feel of her breath on his neck took all rational thought from his brain. Not only was she the sexiest woman he had ever laid eyes on, but that innocent caress of exhaled air on his skin filled him with a sense of need so urgent he wanted to sweep her into his arms and carry her away to some secluded spot and ravish her for hours, days…maybe even years. Laura also had a heart of gold, he was discovering.

"Sure, gorgeous. This table is as good as any, but I'm not sharing my meal with these apes. I'm ordering my own dish—you got that, JT?"

As everyone settled back into their seats and Angelo, the owner of Mia's, fussed over them, taking orders and returning with drink selections, Trevor smiled. He was happy. Laura looked so comfortable sitting amongst his friends. They chatted easily back and forth with her. It might not have been the romantic night of seduction he had planned, but Laura was enjoying it, and that was what was important to make a first date successful, he supposed.

Chapter Three

Laura was having the time of her life. After such an uncomfortable start to the evening, thanks to her son's well-meaning but embarrassing intervention, she and Trevor were having a wonderful time. Okay, so the fact they weren't alone wasn't the best prelude to the night of debauchery she'd been hoping for, but catching up with the Jets gang was so much fun. JT and Brodie were fantastic men and had been such great mentors to Mitchell. Mandy was just a delight. Apart from the fact that they looked totally different, and that Mandy was an artist and Laura a cleaner, Mandy reminded Laura of her younger self. Mandy had had problems with her family, just as her own family had had issues. Mandy had struggled to overcome her problems, resulting in some bad life choices—just as Laura had dealt with being left confused, alone and pregnant by a man she had too innocently trusted. Laura loved the young woman's determination.

Listening to Caitlin sing was a joy. Laura thought Caitlin had a voice like an angel—which was her devoted husband's nickname for her. Laura mused over the fact that Aussie men seemed to require a nickname for everyone, but 'angel' was at least a term of endearment and very sweet. It was a good feeling to sit amongst friends, enjoying the entertainment—and having such a handsome companion did not hurt, either.

It was easy for Laura to forget that she was the mother of one of the Jets team. That she was at least half as old again as the young woman singing, and a good many years senior to the rest of the table's occupants. At the moment, she felt like a normal woman on a date, surrounded by friends. That in itself was an unusual feeling for Laura. She was so used to being a mother first and a woman second.

Relaxed and happy, Laura found there were no uncomfortable silences or gaps in conversation—the night just flowed easily along. The food was delicious and the champagne cold, sweet and bubbly. Trevor was attentive and just the sound of his voice in conversation was doing incredible things to her. His smooth commentator's voice was like a warm breeze over her body, evoking new and unusual sensations, and on more than one occasion she found herself just staring at his profile in a sort of hypnotic trance.

"Like what you see, Laura?" Mandy giggled to her softly, so as not to be heard by the rest of the table. "I may not have known him long, but Trevor seems like a stand-up sort of guy. Have you been seeing him long, Laura?"

"Well, apart from a few casual conversations at Mitchell's games and again at Caitlin and Brodie's wedding, this is the first time we have spent any real length of time together. This is our first date...so to speak. God! That sounds ridiculous at my age. Dating," Laura replied.

"Rubbish, Laura! You are definitely not too old to go on a date. You don't look any older than the rest of us. You're so beautiful and you have way less wrinkles than me — you have to tell me your skincare secrets. Just looking at your sexy figure has me green with envy...and you know me and my colours! I really hope it works out for you and Trevor. You and he would make a brilliant addition to our little group of happy couples, and it would be lovely to have you around more. You know, to talk about motherhood and stuff."

Laura swallowed the lump in her throat, bought on by Mandy's heartfelt and lengthy welcome, not to mention her acceptance of the fact Laura was on a date with Trevor.

"You are too kind, Mandy. Thanks for the pep talk — I think I needed it! To be honest with you, I'm a bit terrified of what I'm feeling at the moment. I've never had the desire to rip off anyone's clothes and rub myself over every inch of their extremely hot body. I'm finding it hard to believe I'm actually here with him at all."

"Laura, what are you talking about? Why wouldn't you be here with Trevor? You're a goddess, just look at you. Not to mention how accomplished you are and what a doll Rookie is — thanks to you, I'm sure. Trevor would be nuts not to find you attractive. What man wouldn't?" Laura hadn't noticed Caitlin sit down, and was surprised by the angelic redhead's compliments.

If anyone was accomplished, it was Caitlin — just twenty-one and already so much responsibility thrust into her life, what with looking after her brother and all. Not to mention having dealt with that nasty experience with Brodie's ex-wife, and the embarrassing media attention it had caused. No— Laura thought if anyone was a goddess and accomplished, it was the emerald-eyed, angel-voiced beauty speaking to her.

"Caitlin, you are a honey, thanks. But I think maybe you are all those things you just mentioned, and more. That voice of yours is divine—I could listen to you all night. How was the honeymoon? And by the way, your wedding was beautiful. Thank you so much for the invitation. Mitchell and I had a lovely night."

"The honeymoon was…oh, there are no words to describe how perfect it was, Laura. Brodie was just…" Caitlin gushed, her cheeks pinking up a little.

"No, don't let her get started on 'hero' talk—she'll gush all night," Mandy joked, cutting off Caitlin's reply.

"Hero? I don't understand…?" Laura looked at Mandy in confusion before a growling reply from JT explained his fiancée's comment.

"Laura, don't get these two lovebirds started—she is his angel and he is her hero. It's pathetic, the way they carry on." JT's tone was full of sarcasm but the smile that went with it let Laura in on the fact he was teasing the newlyweds.

"You are just jealous, JT, 'cause all you could come up with for me was a car term. 'Mags'—it's not very imaginative, He-Man, and now I *look* like a big, black tyre with this belly of mine," Mandy added, giving her burly husband a lingering kiss. Laura had to look away, the kiss was so passionate.

The conversation flowed on around Laura with more light-hearted teasing, mostly at Brodie's and Caitlin's expense. It was about this time that Trevor started rubbing his hand up and down Laura's thigh, occasionally massaging her leg gently, his fingers dancing all over her skin, before resuming the nerve-tingling, mind-blowing journey. She could feel her nipples grow hard and push against the cups of her bra as her core ached and throbbed in response. He moved farther and farther under the now elevated skirt, closer to her throbbing heat.

When the little moan involuntarily escaped Laura's lips, she quickly jammed them together, her gaze immediately going in young Riley's direction as she prayed he had not heard her, or noticed Trevor's explorations. Thankfully, the boy was absorbed in his hand-held computer game, obviously bored by the adult conversations around him, and was none the wiser when it came to her lustful behaviour. Laura breathed a sigh of relief and pushed Trevor's hand back more modestly back towards her knee, and away from the needy, hot and increasingly moist junction between her legs.

"You are distracting me from the conversation, Trevor. I can't think straight when you touch me like that, and I'm a bit concerned over what Riley might think if I climb into your lap and ravish you," Laura whispered in Trevor's direction, hoping no-one was listening, her voice breathless. She particularly enjoyed the look on Trevor's face as he absorbed her words. The man's eyes widened and his nostrils flared as a look of sexual hunger stole over his features. At least, that was what Laura assumed was behind Trevor's reaction.

"I think we need to move this date somewhere a little more private." Trevor's voice sounded a little huskier than his normal smooth tones, and Laura's heart raced at the thought of being alone with him and what that might entail.

"Yes, let's go. Umm… Maybe it would be better if we didn't go straight back to my place, though. You know, Mitchell and all that…" Laura felt a little bold at suggesting that Trevor not take her home yet, and hoped she hadn't scared him off by being so forward. But from the look on his face she didn't think that was the case.

His urgent reply of, "My place," left her in no doubt.

It was as if Laura's world was spinning—she did not have the chance to overthink her hasty, blatant suggestion, as it seemed only a fraction of time before Trevor had them back in his car and speeding away from Mia's. Goodbyes and well wishes had trailed behind them as they had rushed out of the door.

* * * *

Trevor could not get away from Mia's fast enough. He had never wanted anything as much as he wanted to feel Laura's body writhing under his, and his rock-hard cock buried to the hilt inside her. He could not believe his lucky stars that this amazing woman wanted him, and he certainly wasn't going to give her time to change her mind. Trevor gave his steadfast attention to getting her back to his place in the shortest possible time.

He couldn't help his sigh of relief as he finally pulled into the driveway of his house. He jammed his foot down on the brake and reefed the handbrake up to stop the car. Switching the ignition off, her turned to face her, and was grateful to see she was smiling back at him.

"Well, I think that broke the land speed record— who knew you could get from Ashfield to Summer

Hill so quickly?" Laura's raised eyebrow made him grimace.

"I swear I was under the speed limit the whole way. It's just I know a few short cuts that make the trip seem faster." He grinned sheepishly. "Would you still like to come in, have a drink or coffee? If you'd rather not, I could drop you home. Whatever you want." Trevor put the keys back in the ignition, ready to restart the car to take her home—hoping that this would not be the case, but willing to do anything to make Laura happy.

But he did say a quick prayer of thanks when she took his hand in hers and replied that a drink sounded good to start with.

Chapter Four

Trevor was out of the car and around to the passenger door in a flash, his bung knee—the knee that had ruined his rugby league-playing days—no issue, not a hindrance in his haste to help Laura from the car. He was full of nervous energy, excited to finally have Laura to himself, but it wasn't the usual deep paralysing dread that Trevor often found swamped him. This nervousness was filled with a bright anticipation of what was to come. Light filled his heart and brain as the touch of Laura's hand in his sparked a current of energy to race up his arm. The heat caused by her touch travelled immediately to his cock, leaving it throbbing against the fastening of his pants, wanting freedom.

He fumbled with the key to unlock his front door, taking three attempts to engage the lock. As he pushed the door closed behind them, Laura forcefully shoved him back against it. She placed her arms around his neck and pulled his head down towards her face. He went eagerly, and as their lips connected Trevor was lost for all time. The sensation of her soft lips against him was so electric, yet so soothing at the same time. Trevor could not gentle his response. He growled, the sound muffled between their lips as he greedily plundered her mouth with his tongue.

Her taste was unique. Trevor could not compare the kiss to any that had come before it. She tasted sweet, hot, and refreshing all at once. Addictive — he couldn't get enough of her. He felt her tongue mingle with his — their first kiss and yet it was as if they'd kissed a thousand times before.

He grabbed her by the backside and drew her up his body until she wrapped her legs around his hips. She was so slight and weighed almost nothing at all. He moved towards his bedroom, all the while keeping them joined at the lips as he continued to devour her mouth. He wasn't sure which of them was in control of the kiss, but didn't care as long as it never ended.

Finally, he stumbled into his bedroom and although the thought of ending their kiss was not appealing to Trevor, the thought of getting Laura naked was. He drew away from her and carefully set her down on the bed, ignoring the little mewling sound she made, signalling her displeasure at his actions.

"I want you naked. Tell me you want the same thing, Laura, before I go mad with need." He groaned the thought of her rejecting him to terrifying to consider.

"I'm so out of control I can hardly think. I have never felt this hot before, this needy. Trevor, please help me." Laura's response to him, her plea, drove Trevor's insanity to new levels. His desire was also all-consuming.

In a frenzy of arms and hands they undressed, Laura unbuttoning his shirt as he unzipped the back of her dress. Trevor finished removing the remainder of this clothes, his shoes and pants, as Laura threw his shirt behind her and stepped from her dress. Standing in nothing but his boxers, now tented by his rigid cock, he gazed at her. He was struck motionless by her beauty, the way she thrust her breasts towards him. Her nipples pressed against the fabric of her bra — he could see the berry-coloured temptations and needed to taste them. His gaze roamed over her taut, toned skin, down to her slightly flared hips. There was a small swell to her belly, a womanly softness that begged to be worshipped, and as his gaze lingered on the sheer fabric of her panties, he could clearly see the blonde patch of hair that covered her pussy. His mouth watered — he hungered for her.

Slowly he reached out towards her, the movement hesitant. He was trying not to scare her, still half expecting her to change her mind, refuse his advances, still not quite believing she was here with him.

As his hands made contact with the skin on either side of Laura's hips, she moaned, the sound a melody to his ears. He dropped to his knees and carefully removed the slip of material that stood between him and his hunger. After she had stepped away from the dainty underwear, Trevor encouraged Laura to sit on the edge of his bed. He pushed her thighs apart and ran a fingertip over the curls above her pussy. Trevor preferred his women with a more natural covering — the manicured, sculpted look wasn't a turn-on for him, too fake for his liking. He could feel the heat emanating from Laura's pussy, could see a glistening of moisture under her soft, blonde covering.

"Trevor, please…"

Trevor lowered his head between her thighs and with a deliberate, strong swipe of his tongue he licked her from vagina to clit. The taste of her juices was sweet nectar to his tastebuds. Her hips jerked in response and she moaned again. He adjusted his position so his arms were now holding down her legs, immobilising her, as he went to work feasting on her.

Like the first rainfall on a drought-parched land, her juices quenched him, seeped into his body. Gently holding apart her wet pussy lips with his thumbs, he sucked and ravished her, left nothing untouched, unexplored as he worshipped her with his tongue, lips and mouth. As she writhed, moaned and begged, he took her up higher and higher, then backed off just in time to not let her peak, loving the sounds she made— her frenzied gasps, her pleas, the thrash of her head from side to side—as she strove for completion. When Trevor felt she could take no more, he clamped his lips around her unhooded bud and sucked as he plunged two fingers into her depths, the rhythm fast and deliberate. Trevor felt her tense, felt her push herself hard against his face, and tasted the cream from her orgasm as she shuddered, screamed, then went still beneath his onslaught.

"I could eat you all night. You taste so sweet, look so delicious lying naked on my bed," Trevor said as he lavished little kisses on her inner thighs, before remembering that he still had not tasted her berry-coloured nipples. In fact, Laura was not completely naked as she was still wearing her bra.

"Mmmm. My mistake—you're not naked, but let me take care of that oversight immediately."

Trevor lifted Laura to a sitting position, chuckling at her limp form, and leaning her against his chest, he reached around her back and unclasped the hooks of the offending piece of clothing. He drew the straps down her arms and put a modicum of space between their bodies to free her breasts. He tenderly rolled a nipple between his fingers, savouring the feel of her tight bud, but before he could wrap his lips around the temptation he felt a nip on his shoulder.

"I need you inside me now, Trevor. It's been so long since I've had a man inside me... I can't wait any longer."

Even though the sentiment was exactly what Trevor wanted, the thought of her with any other man left a sour taste in his mouth. Which he knew was a ridiculous train of thought. The woman was a siren. Of course she would have been with other men — Rookie was a tangible testament to that fact — but still he couldn't stop the jealousy from turning his stomach.

"Honey, you can have me, all of me, right now. Move up a little on the bed while I grab a condom. I just hope I can control myself. You make me so hot and horny I'm afraid I'll come the second I bury my cock in you."

He tore the condom packet with a ferocity he didn't know he had, sheathed himself and positioned the rounded head of his erection at her opening. With his arms locked at either side of her head, his palms flat on the mattress, he looked into her pale blue eyes. They reminded him of icebergs — Trevor was not sure why that comparison had popped into his mind, as she certainly was far from cold beneath him. The heat from her body rose to touch his skin even before they were joined.

"Look at me, Laura. Look while I enter you. Look into my eyes while my body joins with yours."

Chapter Five

Laura looked into Trevor's eyes, stared at him as he slowly entered her. Saw the tension in his face, the clenched set of his jaw as her body swallowed him tightly, her inner muscles grasping at his shaft, holding it in the wet warmth of her pussy. She could tell he was fighting for control, and loved the knowledge that it was her doing. She was desirable, able to make a man struggle to control himself. Trevor was well-endowed—Laura had noticed his manhood jutting out proudly just before he had sent her world flying apart with his talented mouth and tongue, her body screaming in delight. She was glad of his girth, glad it filled her sheath, had been worried that due to childbirth she might not be as snug as the average woman.

Her worries had been unfounded. As she relished that fullness that Trevor, fully seated inside her, created, he stretched her. The sensation was so intense, the desire so consuming, her emotions so highly strung that Laura could not stop the lone tear escaping from the corner of her eye. She felt so overwhelmed. So good.

"Honey, what's wrong? Am I hurting you?" Trevor stilled over her, caught the escaping tear with his fingertip, his expression a mixture of concern and fear.

"No, you feel so good, Trevor. It was a happy tear. A tear of pure joy at what you make me feel, how you feel inside me. Don't stop — please, don't stop." She kissed him deeply, lifted her hips up to meet his, trying to urge him to move again.

The sensations caused by Trevor's continued motions — in and out, back and forward, as she caught and joined in the rhythm of his hips — were so overpowering. A tidal wave of pleasure was building, swamping her senses. Streaks of sizzling pleasure crested and rolled higher and higher, soaring. Every nerve, every cell of Laura's being waited for her orgasm to reach its peak. Trevor moaned, growled her name. A grimace crossed his sweat-streaked face as he tried to hold back. Laura could tell he was close and it was that sight, that knowledge of his impending orgasm, that thrust her mercilessly into the abyss, her body quivering, shaking uncontrollably as she screamed his name.

"I'm coming, oh, I'm coming, Trevor!"

"Fuck, yeah, honey, break apart for me, do it now! I'm holding on by a thread. Oh, yeah, here it is, it's all for you."

Trevor thrust hard, pounded into her relentlessly. The muscles she clung to in his back tensed, and even though he was wearing a condom Laura swore she could feel his seed, the warmth of it as it flooded into the protective latex skin that covered his penis, buried deep inside her. She drew her fingernails down his back, knew that the scratch mark would mar his skin, but she didn't care. She wanted to mark him. Claim him. And it was that thought that brought her crashing back to reality. She had just had sex with a relative stranger on a first date. No promises made.

"My God, I'm acting like a tramp." Laura didn't realise she had voiced her thought until Trevor raised his prone body, placed his hands on either side of her face as he took his own weight on his elbows.

"Never. Don't say that. I refuse to let you think like that. I've wanted you from the first time I set eyes on you, Laura. You were at the club after Rookie's first-grade debut. It was the colour of your hair that caught my eye. You were standing next to Rookie, then you smiled — it shone like a beacon, lighting up the room. At first I thought you were *with* Rookie. It wasn't until Brodie mentioned later on that you were his mother that I knew any different. Even then, I couldn't believe that you were anywhere near old enough to be his mother. I still don't. You must have been just a babe yourself when you gave birth. You are not a tramp. This is not dirty. What we just experienced, Laura, is something special. *You* are special, and I will never think of you any other way."

Laura was so moved by Trevor's words that her heart nearly burst with joy, but in her mind a niggling voice cautioned her. Trevor had mentioned her age — well, not specifically, but the fact she was no spring chicken was not lost on her. How long could she expect him to desire her when he was so many years younger, still had his life ahead of him? She was certain Trevor would never find himself short of younger female attention, even without the notoriety of his career. The man was sin on two legs. What right-minded woman wouldn't want him between her thighs?

Laura would have to be careful that she didn't do or say anything that would portray her as the needy, clingy type, that she didn't do anything to scare Trevor away. She thought that maybe if she remained aloof, in it for the joy of sex with no strings attached, she could keep Trevor interested for a while longer. It was up to her to protect her heart along the way.

"Stop over-thinking it, honey," Trevor added, giving a small tug on her hair, which he was twisting around his fingers. "Just let this, whatever it is between us, live, grow. Let's just see where it goes."

She could do that, she thought, and nodded in agreement. Reached up and stroked a finger around his jawline, savouring the texture and roughness of the stubble, the masculine feel of him, the warmth of his skin to her touch as she gazed into his dark eyes, eyes that seem to storm with unsaid emotion. Trying not to let her imagination run away with her, portray sights that might not really exist, she shut her eyes and pressed her mouth to his. She whispered, her lips moving against his, "Take me again, Trevor. Make me feel like a desirable woman once more. Let me feel your hardness inside me."

As Laura felt Trevor's shaft lengthen, harden against her, she opened her legs in invitation. Banished any fears to the back of her mind. She would make the most of tonight, relish her younger lover's experience, his endurance. She deserved it, had lived life modestly since that night of her son's conception. Tomorrow would come soon enough and she would deal with consequences then.

Chapter Six

Laura awoke, startled. Her surroundings were confusing, unfamiliar. Then the reality sank in as she felt the weight and warmth of the masculine arm weighing her down. She had fallen asleep in Trevor's bed after their third mind-blowing, earth-shattering coupling. She didn't know what time it was and panicked that the consequences of her previous night's indiscretions would now need to be faced head-on. She could only imagine the state she was in — smudged makeup, hair resembling a bird's nest… *Not my finest moment.*

"Way to go, Laura. If he didn't notice how old you looked last night, now you're this rumpled it will be undeniable — probably a shock to his ego. It's a wonder he hasn't chewed off his own arm to get away." She was lying on one of Trevor's arms, trapping him beneath her, while his other was resting over her hip.

Laura didn't realise that she had spoken the thought out loud until she heard the rumbling of his voice.

"That's never gonna happen, honey. I'm right where I want to be," he whispered in her ear, and she felt the slight sting as Trevor nipped her earlobe playfully.

"I didn't mean to fall asleep. I'm sorry... I should have left hours ago. This isn't what is supposed to happen these days, I suspect." Laura caught sight of the light shining from the corner of the closed drapes.

"The sun is up! I have no idea what time it is. What on earth is Mitchell going to think?" Laura started to struggle in an attempt to free herself from Trevor's hold, tried to remove herself from his arms, his bed. Then, realising she was naked, she froze. How the hell was she going to make a gracious exit when she would have to hunt, completely naked in front of him, for her clothing? Any chance of her maturing body's flaws remaining hidden in the room's darkness was now fading as the sun rose. Not to mention the walk of shame she was facing, going home in the probably now rumpled clothing that she'd left home in last night. Laura groaned.

"Oh, this is so embarrassing. I'm not really up on the etiquette this sort of thing involves. You know, the morning after the night before. What the hell was I thinking?" Laura buried her face into the pillow, thinking that hiding from the world might magically make all her uncertainty and embarrassment go away.

She heard Trevor chuckling next to her, and anger was the first emotion to take hold.

"This might seem funny to you, but I'm not some young bunny that hops from bed to bed. This is my first one-night stand and I'm a mother, for goodness' sake. What will I tell my son? 'Yes, Mitchell, it's okay for me to stay out all night without letting you know, but heaven help you if you do the same to me—I'm the only one allowed to worry in this family.' Not to mention the fact I've never stayed away from home before. No, I'm sure Mitchell is feeling just fine that his accusations proved correct, that we did end up in bed together. My God, what must he think of me?" And if the embarrassment of admitting her lack of a sex life hadn't been enough to completely humiliate her, then bursting into tears left her in no doubt.

"C'mon now, don't do that. Don't cry." Trevor's voice soothed her as he tightened his arms around her. "We will face Rookie together, and this is no one-night stand, Laura. Stop fretting — everything will work out fine. Look, if you want to we can stop off at the shops, grab you something else to wear. Anything to make you feel more comfortable, honey."

Laura finally pulled herself together with a very ungraceful final sniff. "Really, would you do that for me? I could just duck in quickly and grab a new dress before we head home, just in case the neighbours are up and about. I would just rather not telegraph to all and sundry what we've been up to — facing Mitchell will be bad enough."

"Honey, nothing is too much trouble for you. While you pick something to buy I'll grab us some takeaway coffees and maybe a few breakfast burgers, and we can try and bribe Rookie into forgiving us. What do you say?"

"Sounds like a plan. My boy does like his food. I'm pretty sure he doesn't have an early training session this morning, so he's probably still in bed anyway," Laura replied, feeling a little cheered up by Trevor's understanding of her feelings, his take-charge attitude. She had always tried to set a good example, to not bring any unwanted gossip her way. She had worried that being a single parent was enough of a stigma, enough of a burden for her son to live with, without adding to the problem by acting loose in the morality department.

"Don't you have somewhere else to be, though?" Laura added quickly, worrying now that she was just compounding the drama, causing so much trouble and keeping Trevor from his day. *So much for keeping it light and fun*, she thought ruefully.

"Nope, lucky for me I have the next few days off and my sports show is all set to go straight to taping next week. My day is your day, beautiful."

The kiss Trevor delivered left Laura in no doubt that he was happy to have her with him. In fact, the immediate reaction of her body to his kiss left little doubt in her mind as to how they felt about each other. 'Smouldering' and 'hot' were some of the words that flitted through Laura's mind as she relaxed into Trevor's kiss, and a now familiar, throbbing need consumed her body. She wanted him again. Of that, she had no doubt.

To hell with morals, Laura thought with a contented sigh, as she realised that she'd had more sex in one night with Trevor than she'd had in the last few years. And not just sex. No—it had been the best sex of her life.

* * * *

Trevor had spent a great amount of the time it had taken Laura to shop praying that Rookie would not cause him too much grief. He knew that any future he hoped to have with Laura would depend heavily on her son's acceptance of him. Which was ludicrous, considering Rookie was twenty-one, and a heartbreaker himself with the girls—or so Trevor believed, making his judgements based on the amount of female attention that swarmed around the young man after a Jets game. So he continued his prayers as he waited for the coffee and assorted versions of bacon and eggs on white and brown bread, various rolls and foccacia bread, just so he had every base covered. And he was definitely not spending any time examining why this sudden concern for a future with Laura had entered his thoughts at all.

Sunshine poured off Laura as she rejoined him, her new brightly-coloured dress showing off the toned skin of her arms and legs perfectly. The memory of those shapely limbs draped over his shoulders as he pounded into her pussy gave Trevor half an erection, making the simple act of walking a discomfort, but hell—a discomfort he was willing to withstand any day of the week. Laura made his heart full. Trevor had no idea if it was possible to fall in love so soon. He had shied away from the whole idea of being in any kind of relationship for so long that the depth of what he was feeling blindsided him.

The smile Laura graced him with brightened the world around her as she walked towards him, a fresh, bright skip in her step. Trevor could not help but return her smile in response.

"You are breathtaking, honey. The world seems full of light around you." Trevor could not keep from kissing her right there in the middle of the shopping centre—to hell with the consequences. In fact, he was feeling rather proud and possessive to be in Laura's company.

"Skim latte, just as you requested, my lady." Trevor handed Laura a cup from the cardboard tray that housed the coffee and the large bag of food.

"Well, thank you, sir," Laura replied with a little curtsey, adding to the frivolous feeling of the moment.

"How many people are we feeding this morning? That bag must hold a ton of food."

"I didn't know what to get Rookie. I'm hoping to win him over with bribes of food, so I got one of everything. We should get going before it all gets cold."

Trevor moved the bag of food from one hand to the other so that he could take hold of Laura's free hand. The simple act of returning to the car was a heart-warming experience. Trevor noticed the attention Laura gained from other male shoppers and even though he disliked their interest, he did take pleasure in the fact it was he who held her hand in his.

* * * *

They made quick time back to Laura's house — it was still reasonably early, so there was not much Sydney traffic around to deal with. As Trevor pulled up in the driveway, he could feel the tension radiating from Laura. Before they left the car he turned to face her.

"Would it be easier if I didn't come in? I'll do whatever you think is best. You can take the food in either way." He really hoped that Laura would let him join her in facing Rookie. Trevor felt his readiness to face any animosity from her son would make a better impression than if he looked as if he was running away or had something to hide.

Trevor waited anxiously for Laura's answer — he needed to do this right and he just hoped she wouldn't shut him out. Either way, he was prepared to do as she wished, but if he had to leave now it would not be forever. He and Laura would be seeing each other again if Trevor had anything to say about it.

"Why? Don't you want to come inside?" Laura asked, but Trevor could hear a little tremor of something in her voice. He hoped it was disappointment that he might leave, because that would confirm she wanted him around.

"Of course I want to come in, honey. I bought this breakfast to share with you. I'm also not ready to bring our date to an end before you promise to see me again. Trust me, Laura, there is nothing I want more than to spend more time with you. I just didn't want to intrude or cause you any grief with your son." Trevor leaned over the middle console of his car and proved his intentions with a lingering kiss. Laura's lips softened under his and the little moan she gave made his heart race, but he quickly pulled back, aware that Laura was concerned enough about her neighbours' reactions. Seducing her in the car would only have her worrying later.

"Let's go face the music, shall we?" Trevor was delighted when Laura put her hand in his and together they walked up the path to her door.

Just as Laura had guessed, Rookie was not about, which meant he was still upstairs sleeping. Trevor headed towards the kitchen to lay out the food while Laura went to rouse her son. He had no trouble finding crockery and cutlery, only taking a few attempts to pick the correct cupboard. He was so lost in his own endeavours that he didn't hear mother and son enter the kitchen. As he made one last trip from bench to table, the tray he had hunted up full of his food choices, he was startled to see Rookie seated at the table. The Jets star recruit was still rumpled from sleep, hair-mussed and pyjama-clad.

"Mornin', Rookie. Hope you're hungry, 'cause there's plenty of food. You're not on any diet restrictions, are you?" Trevor tried to sound lighthearted and friendly as he put the platter of food down in front of the one person who could impact on his plans regarding Laura.

"Nope, Trev—starving and no diet restrictions. Not sure about taking bribes from the press, though—have to check on that with the coach—but might as well not waste any of this good food. After all, there are all those starving people in the world. Isn't that right, Mum?"

When Rookie smiled at his mother, before piling food on the empty plate in front of him, Trevor could see Laura's shoulders drop in relief. *They have the same smile*, Trevor thought as he reached for his own food, not quite believing that he was sitting having breakfast with a woman and her grown son. He'd never envisaged he would partake in such a domestic picture, but an enormous feeling of contentment settled over him.

Breakfast was going really well. Trevor enjoyed the light banter between Rookie and Laura. It was clear that they were incredibly close—there was an abundance of love between the pair. He enjoyed being a part of something so good and easy, so honest, right up until the moment Rookie touched on the subject of Laura's arrival home. Trevor spluttered, nearly choked on a hard piece of bacon that he swallowed whole in a nervous response to the enquiry.

"How was Mia's last night, Mum? Were Brodie and JT around? I waited up for you for a while but ended up going to bed and falling asleep watching a movie on my laptop. I must have been dead to the world 'cause I didn't even hear you come in. What time did you get home?"

Trevor's eyes flew to Laura to judge her reaction to the question, wondering whether she would flat-out lie or if she would admit that she had fallen asleep at his place—which would, of course, lead to Rookie coming to the correct conclusion as to what had occurred between them. There was a pause, silence filling the room as both Rookie and Trevor stared at Laura, waiting for her response.

Chapter Seven

"Well, you wouldn't have heard me come in last night, Mitchell, because I didn't come home until this morning."

Laura held her breath, waiting for her son to explode. Waited for his disapproval of her behaviour, which really should not have been a concern — she was the mother, but that knowledge did not quell the uneasiness, the sick feeling down deep in the pit of her stomach. This was the first time that Mitchell would understand that she was also a woman. A woman with needs, healthy needs. A woman who had sex.

How her son reacted to this newfound knowledge might not be pretty, but Laura was not going to compound the situation by lying to him. He was old enough to understand, if he thought about it rationally.

"Hmmm, is that right?" Mitchell's reply was flat. Laura could not judge his emotions by those few words so she remained still waiting for him to continue. She was not going to start making any excuses for her actions, well not yet anyway.

"So what you're telling me is…that not only did you stay out all night without ringing home—you know, so I wouldn't worry—but you stayed out all night with Trevor, here? Considering you both seem quite refreshed and not drunk, I can assume you slept at some stage during the night. Now being that I am a grown-up and all, I assume that sleep was not all that would have occurred last night. So, Mother…I hope you used protection."

Laura did not believe she could feel any more mortified than she did right at that moment. Here was her son—the son she had lectured on more than one occasion about responsibilities and safe sex, not to mention dragging him over hot coals when he had forgotten to let her know his movements, causing her to worry over his safety—and he was throwing her own words back at her. And she deserved every one of them. She was about to apologise to him for acting like a hypocrite when, to her absolute surprise, he burst out laughing, as he shook his head and rocked on his chair, clearly finding the confronting moment full of amusement.

"Oh, Mum, you should see the look on your face…on Trevor's face. You both look like kids that have been caught with their hands in the cookie jar…so to speak. Don't sweat it, Mum."

It was Mitchell's next words that left Laura feeling more relaxed, finally calm and back in control of her emotions. And proud of her son.

"Look, Trev, about last night… I was way out of line. I'm sorry, man. After you guys left I sat around feeling a whole heap of things—angry, confused and maybe a bit jealous. I actually had the thought that you were stealing my mum away from me. It was that ridiculous accusation that brought me to my senses.

I'm twenty-one, but I was acting like a spoilt child. You're a good bloke, I suppose, Trev—if Brodie James is any judge, and he certainly has a high opinion of you. And what can I say, you must have great taste in women, 'cause Mum's one in a million."

With an endearing and cheeky grin, her son continued, "Hope there's no hard feelings between us, Trev. But I couldn't help making Mum squirm a little bit. I knew she wouldn't try and cover it up—Mum's no liar, that's for sure. Hah, you guys are so cute. Love it. Thanks for the breakfast, guys, but I gotta go. Doing a weights session with the boys in a few. Love you, Mum."

Laura sat at a loss for words as her son jumped from the table, shook hands with an equally stunned Trevor, kissed her on the cheek and continued to laugh as he left the room. She didn't even admonish him about leaving his dirty plate on the table.

"Well, that went better than I had anticipated. Remind me to buy Brodie a drink next time I see him."

Trevor's voice broke Laura from her frozen, bewildered state. She shook her head and stood, then started to collect and clean up the remnants of their breakfast, trying to clear her head and take stock of what had just occurred and the ramifications that had on her life. Her son had, in his own way, just given her the go-ahead to have a sexual relationship, to get on with her own life. Laura dissected that as she rinsed dishes, aware that she had yet to utter a word to Trevor about the situation.

Her life was about to change. Gone were the days when Mitchell had been the highest priority in any decision she made. He had just moved from boy to man in one conversation. He had shown her that he could make rational judgements and decisions about not only his life, but hers as well.

The whole reason for her being was now moving away from her, leaving her behind to find a life of her own. She knew her thoughts were way exaggerated—it wasn't like Mitchell was leaving her forever or even moving out—but he had made it clear to her that he no longer needed her protection, that all-consuming protection a mother felt for her child. He was a man. He would always be her child, but it was now fact that he could make his own way. Make his own choices. Choices thought over with a clear and mature outlook. And Laura was sad and happy at the same time. It had only felt like yesterday that she'd first held a squealing and squirming newborn Mitchell in her arms, so small, so precious. Those years had flitted by so quickly. It was incomprehensible that so much time had passed.

"Hello? Anyone home, honey? I thought you would be relieved that Rookie wasn't tearing me apart, but you look so sad. What is it, what's wrong?"

"Umm…did you say something?"

"Honey, you're miles away. What's up?"

"I'm sorry, Trevor, nothing is wrong. I am relieved that Mitchell took it all so well, that is the reason I'm sad. My little boy is all grown up and it has just hit me—he no longer needs me like he used to. What am I going to do with myself if I don't have Mitchell to worry about?" She couldn't help the little sob that formed as she voiced her concerns.

"Rookie will always need you, Laura. You two are so intertwined, no one will ever sever that connection. It's just time you both moved it on to the next level. You have raised a wonderful young man, Laura. Be proud of that achievement. Rookie loves you. I only wish I could have half of what you two have. I'm a continual disappointment to my parents."

As Trevor spoke he pulled her into his arms. Laura was glad for the comfort and his praise for her son, but Trevor's comments about his own family concerned her greatly. How could his parents not be proud of him? Trevor was a success in everything he touched. Not only had he represented Australia playing rugby league, which surely should make any parent burst with pride, but after his debilitating injury he had carved out a successful media career, his face on television more than once a week. Trevor's high intelligence was plain to see in his in-depth commentary and the ease with which he communicated to the masses week after week. She would question him more about his parents later. At this moment in time, she needed his comfort.

"Have I told you how yummy you smell? Woodsy, like the scent of a forest. It reminds me of my favourite room deodoriser, which may sound unromantic, but if you knew how much I loved that scent… I buy it by the truckload for my cleaning. You also remind me of strength and it does funny things to my tummy…and some other places, too!" Laura's words were light, fun-filled. She wanted to move away from the tension that had wavered there between them since her breakdown that morning. She wanted to make love to Trevor again before he left, and she was hoping she could convince him as soon as Mitchell left the house.

Trevor groaned in her ear, a throaty sound that connected directly to her nipples and made her labia throb and her clit pulse with longing. She felt his shaft pushed up against her lower back as he moved closer to her. His arms were still wrapped around her from before when he had tried to comfort her as she stood at the sink. Now, as he pressed up against her harder, she could feel herself coming to life, sparking from the feel of those arms that hugged her almost painfully tight.

"I'm so hot for you, Laura. I wish I could just lift your dress and tear off your panties so I could thrust my hard cock into you right here, right in this kitchen in this position. Slam into you from behind. Can you feel how hard I am for you right now?"

Laura was panting from Trevor's words, slightly crude and outrageous words that burned to her very core. She was physically trembling in response, the thought that Mitchell could enter the room not enough to distract her from her desires. She leaned her head back onto Trevor's chest, felt his heart beating, strong and rapid. Knew he was as consumed with need as she was.

"Catch ya later, Mum, I'm outta here. Should be back in a couple of hours, behave yourselves while I'm gone, guys." Laura heard her son's voice as he shouted to her from the hallway, then the bang of the door closing, confirming his departure.

"Shit, totally forgot Rookie was still here," Trevor gasped as he started to pull away from her.

Laura gripped his arms, stopping Trevor from moving from her, and she wiggled her bottom into his groin area. "Not so fast, you are not getting away from me after teasing me with such lust-filled words. I think you need to put that scenario you so eloquently described into action, and I think you should hurry… I'm about to spontaneously combust, I'm so hot for you."

She didn't have to wait long for Trevor to respond. His growl as he shoved her new sundress up over her hips, scrunching the fabric against her stomach with one hand as the other stripped her bare of her underwear, left her in no doubt that he liked her ideas. Laura felt the fabric being peeled down from her hips and she writhed and twisted her body to facilitate its quick removal. The heat between her legs was heading towards unbearable, her need intense. She wanted Trevor's hands on her as soon as possible.

Within moments Trevor was strumming her folds with magical fingers. She pressed against his hand, trapping it between her body and the cupboard door she was standing before. The pressure built quickly as her body strove to find release. She swayed her hips and thrust against his clever, dancing fingers as the intensity climbed, the peak of the moment within reach. Trevor nipped and laved at her ear, her neck, each sensation contributing to the orgasm that was rapidly approaching, threatening to take her sanity by force if she did not find that final ecstasy.

Trevor must have understood her desperation, must have been so in tune with her body's responses because his movements became more hurried, more forceful as he rubbed and circled her clit. Then, finally taking that sensitive nub between his thumb and forefinger, he gently squeezed, applied just the right amount of pressure, and Laura's world exploded.

Lightning flashes erupted behind her eyelids. Her body flew, felt freed as her release slammed home, from her little toes to the top of her head, every nerve sang with joy. Any tension, sadness or unsettling thought that had been left in her mind, body or soul was well and truly washed away with the force of her orgasm. She slumped against Trevor's chest, her body boneless, limp. If he had not had his arms around her she would have ended up a puddle of mush on the floor. But he held her to him. She felt the hardness of his manhood pressed against her. Laura recalled Trevor's original plan to take her from behind, but a wicked thought shot into her mind and she knew she just had to fulfil her own plan first.

Chapter Eight

The woman was a firebrand. The way she'd come apart in his arms, so honestly, holding nothing back... Trevor could wish for nothing more in life than to bring pleasure to this woman, over and over again. He was giving her just a little time to recover from her orgasm, then he would begin again. He would touch her, taste her, have her coming so hard and fast and often she'd be begging him to stop.

So he was unprepared for her onslaught. She had spun from his hold and swapped their positions before he could react, but as she dropped to her knees before him Trevor finally got the message. Yes, his dick had certainly got the message loud and clear as it hardened even more in anticipation of what was to come – him!

"Careful with the zipper, babe. I'm a bit worked up." He spoke the warning through clenched teeth, convinced the enamel on his molars was fast eroding, as he fought the urge to thrust towards her mouth. Just the thought of her lips wrapped around the head of his cock, stretched around him, her lips glistening with his pre-cum as she knelt before him in a generous and submissive posture had him about to blow his load. And that, to his mind, would be a terrible waste. He wanted to feel what was about to happen, not just think it. He shuddered, trying to control his body, as she carefully, slowly, lowered his zipper over his erection. As soon as his pants were undone his cock thrust fully upward, reaching a little above the elastic of his jocks.

"Mmmm! You are a big boy, Trevor, aren't you? I knew you were above average last night—I just didn't really appreciate how big, though."

Laura's voice was husky to his ears, or maybe his own lust clouded his hearing. Trevor did not care which as Laura wrapped her small hand around him, stroked him as her open mouth zeroed in on his cock. Her eyes never left his as she bent forward and took him between her lips, his cock disappearing into her open, wet, warm mouth. The sensation was incredible, indescribable, heavenly—there were not enough words to accurately describe the phenomenon.

Trevor locked his knees so as not to crumple to the floor, felt his eyes roll back into his head, and even though he wanted to watch Laura, wanted to watch her mouth ride him, her cheeks hollow as she sucked on him, he couldn't manage to focus his eyes. His balls tightened—he could feel the impending release about to spurt from him. God, he was about to come quicker than a virgin on prom night and there was nothing that could save him. He could not prolong the inevitable even though he wanted to feel the thrill of Laura's mouth on him for longer. *Let's see, eternity might be a good start*, he thought.

"I'm not going to last—this feels so fucking good, Laura, so fucking fantastic," he managed to moan. The words were hardly romantic and not nearly deserving of this amazing woman who knelt before him, but they were all he could manage. He would make it up to her later, when he could manage to think with something other than his cock.

The cock that was plunging in and out of her mouth—he felt the head of his shaft bump the back of her throat, felt her fight the gag reflex. She actually swallowed, the sensation mind-blowing. She was blowing his mind and body. Her teeth grazed his cock as she continued her actions, rolling her tongue over the slit in the end of his cock before sucking him back in greedily, all the way until he felt his balls slap her chin.

He tried to remain gentle but could not stop himself from reaching out to her. As his hands found either side of her head, he fisted her hair in his fingers, felt the softness of the strands as her head bobbed up and down over him. Encouraging Laura to find the rhythm he needed, Trevor forced his eyes to open, needed to take in the sight of Laura and what she was doing to him. And it was that view that caused the eruption. He tried to pull himself from her mouth in time but her hands clasped his hips and drew him closer. He spilled, spurted inside her and watched as she took all of his seed into her, watched as she swallowed every last drop. She was still lapping at his flaccid cock until he thrust her head away—it was too much.

Overwhelming.

He dragged her roughly by the shoulders to her feet—too roughly, probably, but the need to kiss her robbed Trevor of rational thought.

Laura's swollen, wet lips opened under his and their tongues duelled, competing in a dance of passion.

They stood embracing, kissing, looking dishevelled. Trevor's pants were around his ankles and his cock drooped, sated, from his body. Laura's discarded underwear was strewn beside them and her dress was creased and rumpled. Trevor drew his lips from hers, leaned his forehead against hers.

"Wow, that was unbelievable. You are unbelievable. We are unbelievable together."

His words came in a whisper, his emotions spinning out of control. Trevor did not want to scare her, did not want to come across too strong, but he could not stop himself. Laura filled a hole in his soul, made him feel complete. Touching her filled him with such a sense of contentment, a sensation that was so foreign to Trevor. In a moment of clarity so strong he could not ignore it, Trevor understood that Laura was the missing piece of the puzzle he had searched for his entire life.

And that thought scared the shit out of him. His life was not a life to share. It was a life that was not always easy to live. A life that had been filled with dark thoughts and, a short while ago, even darker days. It was not the sort of life he would wish upon anyone, least of all Laura.

Those dark days still haunted Trevor. He hadn't realised at the time that depression was an illness, had thought that this latest bout of black moods then decline into utter despair was due to the knee injury that had subsequently forced him into retirement. Just thinking back on those times made Trevor mentally shudder. It was still hard to put into words the depths of his struggle to regain some kind of perspective — sanity.

After months of counselling and with the help of prescription medication, Trevor now understood that he had been battling depression for a good chunk of his life. All those times when the world had seemed against him, it had felt as though he was being singled out, that people just didn't understand him. Those times, when he'd just locked himself away, struggled to get out of bed because facing the world and all that was expected of him had been too daunting a task, had been as a result of his ongoing battle with the misunderstood disease.

It had many names, his demon. Clinically, it was called depression but some called it 'black dog' or 'feeling blue'.

He remembered the times he had tried speaking to his mother about how unhappy he was, trying to get her to understand him, but she had put it all down to teenage angst. Told him to cheer up, stop worrying, be happy that he was good-looking, popular and such a great sportsman. She had told him to stop feeling sorry for himself, that there were many people out there so much worse off than him, with real problems. She'd spoken of how he had such a great future ahead of him, playing rugby league, and how proud his father would be if he signed with a first-grade team.

And Trevor had tried to just *cheer up*, but it had never seemed to work.

It hadn't been the thought of going through all the pain of another knee reconstruction, or the long rehabilitation again so soon after the first injury that had pushed him over the edge. It hadn't even been the knowledge that he would probably never play football again—in fact, that was almost a relief to Trevor, knowing that he wouldn't have to take the field each week, worrying about failure. No, what had really been the last straw, so to speak, was the unmistakeable look of disappointment on his father's face as the man had voiced his regret that because Trevor had injured himself again—as if it had been some intentional plan—his father would miss out on going to the games and sitting in the good seats.

The weeks that followed had been an endless nightmare, with Trevor not leaving his house—in fact, hardly leaving his bed unless it was completely necessary. The darkness that had filled his mind and soul was a living thing. It was as if the sun, although obviously in the sky, had not been able to brighten up the world. Everything, anything had seemed an unimaginable task, an insurmountable mountain to climb. Even the slightest of mundane acts like eating or bathing had been just too tiring to carry out.

But it was his own thoughts that scared Trevor to this day—it terrified him that one day they would return to him and he wouldn't have the strength or clarity of mind to fight them. For weeks back then, he had imagined ways to end his suffering, end his despair permanently. His consciousness was so persuasive in its belief that no one would care if he was not in this world. That perhaps everyone would be better off without him around to disappoint them. That the pain he was constantly in and the grief that ate at him and the darkness that consumed him would go. All he had to do was end his life.

To that Trevor, that depressed, broken Trevor, it had seemed the only alternative. Living was not an option, death the only solution. Then Brodie had barged into his blackness and forced a glimmer of light to appear.

How Brodie had known something was wrong, Trevor would never understand. How Brodie had known it was depression was something Trevor had never asked, but thankfully, Brodie had known what to do to help.

It had taken a long time, his recovery from his injured limb and depressed mind both painstakingly slow, but Trevor had recovered. He'd put his mind back on the right path, aligned it so that thoughts of sadness were just that—sadness that promptly disappeared, didn't fester, grow and swell into pools of blackness. Trevor, through counselling, had learnt ways of dealing with his anxiety, his fear of failure around every corner, and it worked to a point.

He found life a lot more enjoyable, found his new career as a sports commentator rewarding, and his being on television dimmed his father's disappointment.

But every now and again those niggling uncertainties popped up and Trevor had to fight them away. It was one of the reasons he had never entered into any serious long-term relationships—he had never really wanted anyone to know the demons he fought, the weakness inside him, or the shame of his past suicidal thoughts.

Laura was different somehow. He couldn't explain it, was not able to pinpoint when or how she'd got through his defensive emotional wall, but she had. Trevor had never felt so at ease with another living soul. Not even his saviour, Brodie James, could completely erase his own inner conflict. But Laura had.

Trevor felt nothing but peace as he pressed his forehead against Laura's. Felt her breath against his face. There was this easy way about her, so fresh, so happy and caring. Her honesty and openness. Her love for her son. They attracted him to her like a magnet to metal. Life had not been a breeze for Laura Harris, but she had not let it get to her. She was infectious with her joy and enthusiasm, and she was just what he needed.

Unfortunately, they were the same reasons Trevor feared he should walk away. How could he bring his darkness to her light? What if he sucked that light from her life? He would never forgive himself — but what if her light was strong enough to overcome his darkness?

Could that be possible? Could Trevor dare to dream? He was feeling selfish enough to try as he held Laura in his arms. And what sort of a man did that make him?

Chapter Nine

Laura couldn't remember the last time she had been in bed so late in the morning. Not that she had been sleeping—no, after their smoking hot session in her kitchen she and Trevor had moved to her bedroom, giggling and laughing all the way like lovestruck teenagers. There they'd made love. *It was definitely making love and not sex,* Laura mused as she lay staring at Trevor's handsome face, resting on the pillow beside her. Their most recent coupling had been slow, sensual, more of a worshipping of bodies than the heated sex they had previously shared. Trevor had left no inch of Laura undiscovered, had kissed and stroked every part of her body with intent, intimately, and she had done the same to his in return.

They had gazed deeply into each other's eyes as they'd joined their bodies as one. The rhythm they'd found had been more like a waltz, a gentle swaying of two bodies dancing together, back and forth, rocking and swaying in a calmer mating than the usual frantic pace one expected of sex.

Laura's orgasm had been slow and drawn-out, sweet — no crashing of waves or molten lava heat this time. This time her crescendo had slipped upon her, brushing over her like silk over skin, a tantalising, lingering pleasure that lasted for what had seemed an eternity. To Laura, it had felt as if their souls had merged — Trevor and Laura, one persona. It was a fanciful notion for a grown woman, but nonetheless her heart had opened. But Trevor had some hidden pain — she could see it buried deep behind his eyes. She remembered the way he'd spoken of his parents, his confession that they were disappointed in him, and wondered what had happened to make him feel that way. Trevor's life, in Laura's opinion, was filled with success. He was a renowned sportsman and journalist, highly regarded by his peers. And he was smoking hot and unbelievably giving in the bedroom. Laura could attest to that. He made her happy, filled her with hope of being loved. He had already convinced her she was desirable…more than once. She smiled at her own humour.

"This is the best Saturday I've had in way too long to remember. My muscles feel like jelly, I'm so relaxed right now." She stroked his stubbled cheek and cradled it in her hand, enjoying the warmth and texture of Trevor's skin. The maleness he exuded made her feel so feminine. Laura had not felt that particular way for an age. She had been mother and provider for so long that being a woman had come way after that. And feminine? Maybe never. Even though she knew she should keep her thoughts to herself, Laura couldn't.

"You make me feel things I thought were lost to me, Trevor. You have awakened a part of me that was missing, and I thank you for that. But I have to admit in all honesty, I'm a little terrified of what will happen next. I feel this connection to you, and it scares me. Should it be this quick, this intense? Is this real? Should I be feeling so much for you, so soon? Or are my hormones and emotions just confused because of the sex? But I do look forward to this new stage in my life and what happiness it will bring. Having someone to talk to and connect with. Sharing thoughts and dreams. Hopefully more of this — the sex is amazing. It's been so long for me I'd almost forgotten, and I want more, much, much more."

Laura saw the hesitation in Trevor's eyes as soon as she'd blurted out her hopes. She could have kicked herself for her stupidity.

"Laura, there has never been anyone that has connected to me as you have. I'm not sure if this is too fast. It's the first time I've ever felt so strongly for a woman, so complete. Just having you next to me fills my heart with joy. But I don't think you should count on me. I'm not what I appear to be on the outside. I have what some would say is 'too much baggage'. You deserve someone that will fill your life with joy and happiness, and I'm worried that I won't be that person. As much as I want to just stay here with you, forever, I also know that my personal demons will ruin us — ruin you — and just as I have everyone else that was of any importance to me, I will disappoint you in the end. You deserve someone better than me."

His words just confirmed what she had begun to suspect. She was making more of this than it deserved.

The pain that lanced through Laura's chest was sudden, excruciating. What was Trevor saying? She'd had to open her big mouth and scare him off. She knew she had said too much, so now he was backtracking away from her — and fast. Yes, his words were remorseful. He was pretending that it was for her own good, not to expect much from him, she was the best and so on, but it was the 'him not her' analogy that angered her the most. The bottom line was she had blown it, but the least he could do was be honest with her and just admit that it had never been meant to be anything but a quick fling, and stop all the guilty rhetoric.

She was a fool.

Of course he wouldn't want her long-term — she was old. He was still in his prime, probably wanted kids, a family, and she had already done that.

When had she forgotten about their age differences, social differences? She had known them last night, had reminded herself not to get attached. Why had she not heeded her own words? Why had she let herself get carried away by the moment? This wasn't some romantic novel where the hero fell for the heroine at first glance. This was real life. Laura shut her eyes, broke the connection that she had mistakenly felt was between them.

She needed to pull herself together. Her pride would not let her show him how much he had hurt her. How much she had *let* herself be hurt was probably fairer. She had made it through life without a man and one night was not going to change that. She was strong. She would survive, learn from this experience and maybe one day trust a man again. If she could be bothered!

She turned from him and rolled from the bed. As she stood, she snatched up the robe that lay over the chair, then quickly donned it, hoping that the fabric would help shield her from her pain. The idea of being nude when her heart was breaking was just too much for Laura to bear.

"That's okay, Trevor. I don't know what got into me. Of course I wouldn't expect anything from you. We had a lovely date and you have been very gallant, accompanying me home to face Mitchell. But you're right—we all have too much baggage in our lives to get into any messy kind of relationship." Laura could feel her heart tearing. The pressure on her chest was unbearable, the moisture behind her eyes had started to build. She had to get Trevor out of her house, and fast, before she broke down. Her humiliation was already a heavy burden and she wasn't about to add to the load.

"Well, I'm sure you have things to do. I know I have—paperwork, rosters and things like that. Maybe we should both get on with our days. Thanks for dinner and breakfast and everything. I'll see you around. I'm just going to grab a shower. Do you think you can let yourself out?"

She spared a quick glance towards her bed, could not stop herself from having one last look at the man lying there. He might have blindsided her with his words, but he was still a sight to behold, naked and sex-rumpled in her sheets.

She was surprised to see what appeared to be a look of uncertainty on his face. Trevor's mouth gaped open, as if he was trying to find the right words, but she didn't want to hear any more patronising excuses from him. Didn't think she could keep from weeping if he tried. So before he had a chance to speak, Laura fled from the room.

Once safely inside her bathroom, the door firmly closed behind her, Laura slid down to sit on the cold tiles of the floor, the chill nothing compared to the ice in her heart. She finally let go, let the misery and humiliation free, using a towel to muffle any sound of her distress.

She didn't hear any noise that indicated Trevor's departure from her home and heart, but considering her face had been stuffed against a towel that was not surprising. Finally, after the tears began to slow, then dry on her cheeks, Laura dragged her spent body from the floor. Turning on the shower, she stepped under the stream of warm water and tried to wash away some of the pain. Mitchell would be home soon, and the last thing she wanted was for her son to see her in such distress. Especially since her distress was of her own making. She had let romantic fantasies cloud reality. She didn't want Mitchell blaming Trevor or doing anything that might impact on his rugby league, and feuding with a reporter would probably not be a great career move.

It was sadly ironic that after years of censoring her life, making sure her actions did nothing to embarrass or negatively impact on her son, Laura had achieved that misery in one night.

Chapter Ten

He still did not know how it had all gone to hell so quickly. One minute he was gazing lovingly into Laura's iceberg-blue eyes, recovering from the single most awe-inspiring moment of his life. The next, he was in his car, driving back to his empty house. A house he had left with Laura only hours ago. And his bed would still smell of sex and Laura.

Trevor was so shaken up that he hadn't even had time for the blackness to take hold. But he was expecting it anytime now. As per usual, he had fucked up. He tried to recall what he had said that had sent Laura running. He'd been trying to explain his problems, his depression, but somehow the words had come out all wrong. He hadn't wanted her to go—he'd just been trying to warn her that eventually he would disappoint her. He had hoped that she would be strong enough, loving enough to work through the dark times with him. But he had been so wrong.

Laura had sprung from the bed as if she had been bitten.

She'd looked so panicked, obviously embarrassed that he had put his heart on the line when he had admitted that he felt for her like he had for no other. He must not have heard her correctly, because the only reason he'd opened up about his feelings had been in response to her claim that she felt a connection. But her gratitude that he had awoken her sex drive must have been just that—a 'thanks for the fuck'.

Anger simmered underneath his skin. How could he have been such an idiot, such a spineless, gullible fool? It had been a ridiculous notion that he was good enough for someone like Laura Harris. Trevor's dark side put him way out of her league.

Better yet, Trevor still had the disconcerting knowledge he would have to face Rookie Harris— both professionally and more than likely socially—on a regular basis, which would remind him of his mistakes, his loss. *What a clusterfuck.*

"Way to go. This time you have outdone yourself," he berated his reflection in the rear-view mirror of his car as he pulled into the driveway of his home—his cave, the place he hid from the world when the world felt too big, too hard to navigate. The place that had been filled with Laura just a few hours ago, but was now empty.

"Remember your pills. You really can't afford to lose it now. There is too much to do," he reminded himself as he dragged his body from his car. He wondered why his life had to be so difficult—he was always on the edge of despair, the precipice of doom.

"Well, at least I should be thankful this happened so quickly. Surely I can't have become that invested in her so quickly? My God, it was only one night, one fucking mind-blowing, passion-filled night." He dragged his fingers through his already mussed hair.

"C'mon, Trev, this isn't helping yourself, mate," he mumbled as he stumbled through the doorway, then closed the door, shutting the world out behind him. "Tough it out... Medicate and shower." Trevor spoke the words aloud, the emptiness of his house echoing the hollow sound of his voice back at him. "Change the sheets, get rid of every reminder of her."

He needed to wash the scent of Laura from his skin, as well. He could still smell her essence on him, and until that had been removed there was no way he could move forward.

Before he could put any of his plans in action, or even move, he was interrupted by the ringing of his phone.

Last thing I feel like doing is speaking to anyone, he thought, but really couldn't ignore the call. It might be about work, about his weekly sports show. Work was something he could focus on to keep his brain from thinking about Laura. So Trevor moved towards the intrusive, noisy device.

"Hughes," he grunted into the mouthpiece. And, as if by some divining stroke of luck, the voice on the other end of the phone belonged to Brodie James, Trevor's own personal guardian angel. How Brodie always seem to ring at the most important times in Trevor's life, Trevor had no clue, but that voice on the line, that familiar sound, connected to his spirit.

"Hey, Trev, it's Brodie. Glad I caught you. Was wondering if you feel like a gym session? A little birdie just told me that some of my Jets boys have been and gone. I know I'm just the assistant coach, but I feel like if I don't keep in some sort of shape the boys will get the better of me, and I haven't hit the gym in weeks."

"Brodes, don't know if I'm up for it, mate." Trevor's voice sounded flat and even though he tried to keep the darkness from his voice, he just knew Brodie would pick up on it straight away, so he tried to lighten his tone with some humour.

"The missus given you a leave pass or something? Where is your partner in crime? Wouldn't JT normally jump at the chance to show off his brawn at the gym?" Trevor added, trying to sound better than he felt. But Brodie had already picked up on his mood.

"Trev, you sound a bit flat. Everything okay, buddy? I thought you would be in a better frame of mind after your speedy exit from Mia's last night. Did it not go well? You and Laura, I mean."

"Huh, what is it with you, Brodie? Always so touchy-feely, and fretting all the time. Butting into everyone's business." Trevor's tone was sharp, but he couldn't help the bitterness aimed at his friend. He didn't really mean the words he had spoken.

"Wow, man, I didn't mean to upset you. I think a gym session is just what you need. I'm coming over and I'm not taking no for an answer. And just to clarify your disparaging remarks over my needing a leave pass from my wife, yep, you're spot on. Apparently I'm getting on her nerves, being underfoot all the time. She and Mandy are going shopping. JT is hitting the gym as well. We just thought maybe you'd like a session. And it is clear you need one." Brodie's dark chuckle filtered down the line. No matter what Trevor said, no matter how rudely he spoke, Brodie always managed to ignore it, managed to find some humour to lighten the mood.

"Sorry, mate, didn't mean to bite your head off. Yeah, you're probably right. No point sitting here feeling sorry for myself. Maybe a few rounds of boxing with the big fella might knock some sense into me. Appreciate the invite. I'll be ready when you get here."

"Goodo! And Trev, whatever it is that has you down, it'll pass. You've got support—you know that, right?"

After hanging up, Trevor felt slightly more with it. Brodie was right—no point dwelling on stuff that *had* happened. It was better to concentrate on the good things in his life. His mates, his job, the rugby league community—especially his old club, the Jets—those things were his lifelines. He could count on Brodie to have his back and not judge. Trevor needed his mate, and with Brodie's help he would not fall into that dark abyss that was always a lingering presence in his life.

Chapter Eleven

"Hey, Ma, you home? Is it safe to come in? You're not doing anything that might scar my young, impressionable mind, are you?"

Laura was sitting at the kitchen table when she heard her son come home, and she tried not to overact at his light-hearted jest. God, she was a mess. She needed to pull herself together for the sake of her son.

"Yeah, funny, Mitchell. I'm here in the kitchen, and yes, fully clothed and acting like a respectable mother should."

"Good to know, Mum." Mitchell said as he entered the room and made a beeline for the refrigerator, dropping his gear bag on the floor next to the table. "So I don't suppose this respectable mother has been cooking? You know, made something to eat for her starving son?"

When her son entered their home, his first mission was always about food. Laura smiled at the thought, reminiscing over all the home-baked cookies and milk the two had shared over the years at this very table.

But suddenly Laura felt a tiredness, an all-consuming weariness that seeped to the centre of her being.

"Mitchell, don't leave your gym bag there—put your dirty clothes in the washing basket. How many times do I have to tell you? You're an adult. I shouldn't even be *doing* your washing anymore."

"Sorry, Mum. I was on my way to the laundry. But you know how the fridge always calls to me," Mitchell said. Laura watched as her son closed the refrigerator door. He walked over and picked up his discarded bag, pulling a face as he opened the zipper. "My stuff reeks—what about I put this load on straight away, save your delicate nose from my sweaty stench?"

Mitchell's apology and thoughtfulness shook Laura from her bitter mood. She had spoken harshly and it wasn't her son's fault she was feeling low. She shouldn't take it out on him. Shaking herself from her gloom, she stood and headed towards the fridge. She would make Mitchell some lunch to make up for her grumpiness.

"Thanks, son. That sounds good. You start the washer and I'll throw something together for you. Wouldn't want you passing out from starvation, would we?"

Laura stared into her full refrigerator, trying to find some inspiration as to what to feed her son. She could hear him moving around the laundry room, then the water coming on to fill the washer. "Just a spoonful of the washing powder, Mitchell—it's concentrated." She shouted out the instructions as she began pulling foodstuffs from the fridge. "What about some grilled cheese, ham and tomato? How does that sound?" She didn't wait for Mitchell's response—she knew him well enough to know he loved her toasties.

"Awesome, Mum. Sounds great. Did Trev leave?" Mitchell's voice was closer — he had obviously returned to the kitchen. Laura was pleased her back was to him as she prepared the food, so she didn't have to mask her pain.

"He had things to do." Her response was clipped. Laura was not sure she could have said any more without giving away her distress.

"Well, I gotta tell you, Mum, the Jets gossipmongers have been out in full force — got ribbed by all the guys this morning about you and Trev having dinner at Mia's. Gosh, you can't sneeze these days without someone knowin' about it. Anyway, the guys were giving me shit about how now that my mum and Trevor had hooked up I'd be getting heaps of good press. They were sayin' stuff like I wouldn't even have to play all that good and my new daddy would edit the footage to make me look like a star. Pfft! As if I need any help to be a star — I'm a natural."

Laura was only just holding it together. Mitchell was confirming her worst fears. She had been gossiped about — his teammates all knew that she had been out with Trevor. The clichéd desperate older woman chasing a younger man — what did they call it, a pity fuck? And now that it was all over, they would also know that he had rejected her. More gossip. More gossip about Mitchell's single mother.

She was filled with shame, so caught up in her own thoughts that she not only hadn't picked Mitchell up on his swearing, but hadn't noticed she was burning the food.

"Mum... *Mum.* Are you okay? Umm, I think something is burning." Laura felt Mitchell push past her, watched as he removed the tray from under the heat. She blanched as she realised that he had probably burnt his hands on the hot tray because she was wearing the oven mitt.

"Ouch… Ouch… That's hot."

Laura turned the cold water tap on and grabbed her son's hands, pulling them under the water to ease the pain of his burns. They didn't seem to be bad, but she had to do something. *Hopefully the water will work better on his pain than the shower worked on mine*, she thought sadly. A sob escaped her mouth before she managed to get herself back under control.

"Mum, it's okay. I'm not burnt, the tray was just a bit hot. Don't cry." Mitchell's voice was full of concern as he stood looking down at her. Mitchell had grown taller than Laura at the age of thirteen. Her son, her beautiful boy. Her life. And she had just done something so stupid… She was an old fool.

"Mum, look at me. What is wrong? You're scaring me, Mum. Have I done something, have I upset you? Something has been wrong from the minute I got home. Tell me, Mum. Maybe I can help or fix whatever it is I've done to cause this."

"Oh, baby, you have done nothing wrong, sweetheart. It's me — I'm the one. I've been such a silly old woman. Shameful. I should never have let Trevor Hughes… Anyway, it's over now. Trevor has gone. Hopefully the gossip will fade. I'm sorry for embarrassing you, Mitchell. I didn't think. It wasn't my intention. I've been alone for so long…haven't dated for so long… I just didn't understand."

It was reprehensible that she stood crying in her son's arms, but she couldn't stop. What sort of mother was she, leaning on her own son this way? But she couldn't stop.

"Oh, Ma! I'm so sorry, Ma. I don't give a fuck about gossip, Mum. And neither should you. Fuck Trevor

Hughes—he wasn't good enough for you anyway. Scumbag. You're not alone, Mum. I'm here, always will be. The Dynamic Duo, you and me."

"Watch your language, young man. I may be a snivelling mess but I'm still your mother and you will not use those words in my home." Laura gave the admonishment lightly—she even managed an awkward smile as she let her son console her, let him hold her as she had held him so many times through his childhood. "You're a good boy, Mitchell. I love you, son. Please don't hold any animosity towards Trevor." Just saying his name made Laura's voice quiver. "He made me no promises. It was what it was—a one-night stand. It was me who misunderstood. I'm being silly and dramatic. Your mother had sex."

"Too much information, Mother."

"Well, you can rest assured that I'm unlikely to ever bother again, if that helps?" Laura's sad chuckle was muffled against the warmth of her son's chest. And with the realisation that it was a warm and rather pungent chest, Laura found that her distress was fading. She felt calmer. Soothed.

"So you didn't shower at the gym, then, Mitchell?" she said as she pulled herself from her son's embrace. Stood on her own two feet. Regained her composure. "You stink, son. Go shower and I will redo these toasties. This time I'll try not to burn them." She spun him towards the kitchen doorway and playfully swatted her six-foot-tall, muscular son's backside. "Just make it a quick shower, or your food will get cold and soggy."

"Mum. I love you. You're the best mother anyone could have. Don't for a second think I don't understand what you have sacrificed for me, given up for me. I know, I do."

"Mitchell, stop. Otherwise I'll be crying again and honestly, I'm all cried out. Darling, I gave nothing up because of you. What I did or didn't do was my own choice. You are the best thing in my life, my greatest achievement. There was never anything more important to me than you. Never will be. No matter who may or may not come into my life, you will always be my priority, always be my baby. So scoot — you are stinking up my kitchen."

Laura watched, full of emotion, as her son left the room. She could still feel the warmth lingering from the kiss he delivered to her cheek. He was her sunshine. Her life was good. She would be fine. And much to her surprise, she found herself humming as she set to work making something more edible than the blackened tray of food she left sitting in her sink.

Chapter Twelve

"Well, boys, gotta say that this is a sorry sight. Once the scourge of opposition forwards across the globe, and now here we sit, drinking juice from a bloody yuppie juice bar at the gym. What's next—sipping caramel lattes with the womenfolk?"

JT's gruff mocking tones had Trevor chuckling under his breath. Just the thought of the monster that was JT sitting around sipping fancy coffee was a sight he'd pay to see, and filming it would be even better.

"*Skinny* lattes, mate," Brodie added, laughing. "Honestly, think we're getting old, big guy. I'm exhausted—my body aches and it wasn't half the session we'd have been doing if we were still playing. At least we won't have to do the bloody Kurnell sand hills anymore. Pre-season training's the pits."

"Boys, come now, you've only been retired for a minute. Just wait till you have to sit through a game…just watching. Then you'll feel the pain of old age. You'll both be dinosaurs before you know it," Trevor added, feeling better than he'd thought he would, enjoying the laughter his comments caused from the men sitting with him. *True mates.*

"Dinosaurs. Huh. Just like we thought about the older blokes way back when we started out, hey, mate. Karma, Mandy would call it."

"God, JT, what has happened to you? Mandy is turning you into a metro—all this yuppie and karma shit. The JT I knew wouldn't have known what those words were, let alone used them in conversation."

"Fuck you too, Brodes."

Trevor laughed at the two-fingered salute JT gave Brodie.

"Good to hear you laughing, Trev. Wanna tell me what had you all in a spin earlier?"

"Here we go, touchy-feely Brodie comes a-calling." Trevor grinned as he used the same words that he had uttered in anger a short while ago.

"You might as well spill, mate," JT butted in. "Brodes is like an old woman when he gets a bee in his bonnet over something."

"It's not much really...just... I blew it with Laura Harris this morning. Everything was going great and then I had to open my big mouth—you know, mentioned how I would probably stuff up and disappoint her, said she probably shouldn't count on me. And the next thing I knew, she'd booted me to the kerb. I was just trying to look out for her, you know?"

"Mate, when it comes to women, they just don't get us. Just take me and Mandy. After she got hurt I tried to protect her by not having sex, didn't want to hurt her. Next thing I know, she's accusing me of going off her. Fuck, I'd walked around with a hard-on for days with wanting her. You can't win with women." JT shock his head, clearly frustrated.

"Yeah, but you can't live without them once they get under your skin," Brodie added, his tone serious.

Trevor would have laughed over their conversation if it hadn't been exactly how he was feeling.

"Thanks for that insight, JT," Trevor said, raising one eyebrow in JT's direction. "I'm sure Mandy will be pleased you shared it with us."

"Trevor, do you think you really blew it? Or are you using it as an excuse to hide away?" Brodie's directness caught Trevor off guard. "If you want something with her, don't give up. Laura's a top woman—solid, mate. Go back, try again. She doesn't strike me as the sort of woman that just wants a casual thing. You two really had chemistry last night. And before you make some smart-arsed remark, JT, I'm quoting your missus. Caitlin and Mandy were gushing about it for hours after you left last night, Trevor. And if I know anything, I know my wife and Mandy notice stuff like that."

Trevor liked the sound of that—chemistry, noticeable chemistry. The more he thought about what Brodie had said, the more positive he felt. Brodie was right. *Again.* He and Laura had a connection. She wasn't the sort of woman to have a fling. There had never been even a hint of her being involved with anyone, never any gossip surrounding Rookie's mother… *Up until now*, he thought grimly.

"Do you really think she could put up with me? You know, Brodie, that dark side of me." Trevor didn't really want to elaborate about his fight with depression in front of JT, didn't want his friend to think any less of him because of his weakness.

"It's a fucking illness, mate. Stop punishing yourself. You didn't cause it, it just happened. Do you think we would think less of you if you were a diabetic or suffered from some other disease? Depression is nothing to be ashamed of. You are surviving, not letting it get the better of you. You are actively fighting the disease and if you want to know, I'm fucking proud of you, mate," Brodie said, as he leaned towards Trevor and placed his hand on Trevor's shoulder. "It can't be easy for you – I can't pretend to understand what it feels like, just like I can't feel what a diabetic feels. Tell Laura. Explain that you fight the disease, take medication. She'll be sweet."

"Fuck yeah, Trev," JT added fervently. "Never understood why you try to hide it from me. We are your friends, and friends stand by you. You're the first to jump in if we ever need anything. You publicly crucified the jerk that falsely accused Brodie of adultery on your show. We might not take the field anymore but we will always be a team."

Trevor didn't think he'd ever heard JT so poignant. Mandy really had opened up the man emotionally. Trevor felt as though a heavy burden had been lifted from his shoulders. Brodie's and JT's words were a balm, and they were right. Not only did he now feel his confidence to fight for Laura growing, but it also dawned on him that he was in a position to help others who suffered the same way he did.

He needed to do what Brodie had done. He needed to tell others who suffered depression that they were not alone. He had a high profile – his big mug was always on the television, beamed into homes across the country. If he could help just one person, give one person a helping hand, he could show that mental illness was not something to be hidden away. It was something you could openly talk about, a disease that could be managed with the help of the right professionals and maybe medication, just as he was managing his. It was his bloody *duty*. He could pass on the gift that Brodie had given him—life.

"Brodie, JT... I think it's time I spoke up about mental illness. Time I owned it. I'm thinking a fundraiser, the money going to those groups already out there, especially the ones that help prevent youth suicide. Can I count you in? It may ruffle some feathers, cause you some uncomfortable press. My Dad's going to have a stroke when he hears. But stuff him."

"You couldn't stop me, Trev. In fact, I have just the venue, and can even hook you up with some first-class entertainment. Caitlin would be thrilled to help any way she could. My wife has a heart of gold."

"Count me in. Anything you need, mate. Guarantee I can hook you up with some of Mandy's artwork and jewellery, as well. Her stuff sells like hotcakes," JT quickly added.

"As long as it's not those nudes your old man told me about, JT." Brodie turned towards Trevor, an eyebrow raised in mock alarm as he whispered conspiratorially, "Apparently Mandy finds the big bugger's body artworthy—*urgh*! Each to their own, I suppose, but really—JT?"

"Yeah, you're a funny man, Brodes, fucking hilarious. But on a serious note, Trev, I was just thinking about *your* old man. Have you ever thought that maybe he has his own demons? Maybe the reason he is always so 'glass half empty' is that *he* has some type of depression? You know you probably inherited it from him."

Trevor was blown away by the support that Brodie and JT were showing. The thoughts of Caitlin singing—obviously at Mia's Restaurant—and having some of Mandy's creations available for him to sell—

probably not nudes, though — gave him a real lift. He could really do some good. If he reached out to some more of his mates he could come up with a really good money-earning night.

But it was JT's comments about his father that really had Trevor thinking. Could that be the reason his father was such a hard man to please? Why his mother spent so much time and put so much energy into making her husband happy? It all fitted, even down to his mother's reluctance to discuss his own fears with her. It must be a nightmare for his father. Trevor understood that people of his parents' generation, especially the men, would never dream of reaching out, or of showing any weakness. The world would have eaten his father alive when he'd been young. *But maybe if we had all spoken about it together as a family,* Trevor thought sadly, *my life might have been so much easier.*

Chapter Thirteen

Two weeks passed quickly for Laura. Life went on. Her business consumed a lot of her time and concentration, and Mitchell had even stopped hovering over her. The bitterness and empty feeling that had taken over from the jagged, lancing pain in her heart had receded to a manageable level—every now and again Laura would feel a sense of sorrow, but if she kept herself busy those moments were few and far between.

The worst times were at night, alone in her bed, when she would imagine Trevor's hands touching her. The feel of his lips on hers, their tongues exploring, the feel of him entering her, pushing past her slick folds as they'd joined together. The fullness he had created in her body as he'd become part of her. During these times, she relieved her own needs. At first she tried to ignore the desire, ignore the heat, but after a few sleepless nights of tossing and turning, she found it easier just to give in to the hunger.

So night after night as she lay remembering Trevor, Laura would touch herself. She would let her hands roam across her breasts, down past her abdomen to rest at the apex of her thighs. At first she would touch herself lightly, just a flutter of fingertips, circling, stroking timidly, but as the heat escalated and the memories of her single night and half a morning of passion consumed her thoughts, her movements would become stronger, more rapid. She would plunge her own fingers into her wet depths, her breathing becoming more rapid. She would sometimes roll to her stomach and ride her hand. Press her clit hard into the heel of her palm, muffle the sounds in her pillow as she pressed down on the sensitive nub until she could ease the ache.

The pleasure was never prolonged, never rivalled what Trevor had ignited in her, but it was a release, and once it was finished, as she lay silently weeping, she would finally drift off to sleep.

As much as Laura tried to convince herself that she was acting ridiculous, that she should grow up and act her age—as she reminded herself over and over that there was no way anyone could fall in love in one night—Laura found that her heart disagreed with her brain. She had never known love, per se. Mitchell's father had been more of a donation of sperm, a young girl's mistake, than anything more, but this deep emotion that consumed her when she thought of Trevor left her confused. If this was love, then it was painful and she wished she did not feel it. Her love for her son was completely different. Easy. Light-filled, happy, maybe a little frightening at times, but all in all a much better feeling than those she now associated with Trevor.

It was that love for her son that had her standing in front of her wardrobe, trying to decide what to wear. They were going to a fundraiser being held at Mia's, and Laura was terrified that she would run into Trevor. The thought made her stomach roll, caused goosebumps to cover her skin, but Mitchell had explained that he had been told by the Jets powers-that-be that his presence was required. He'd left Laura in no doubt that it was an order rather than an invite, but it still didn't explain why *she* had to go.

Mitchell had all but begged her, so Laura searched again for something to wear, her actions slow and unenthusiastic, her heart not in it.

"Jeans? A dress? I have no idea what to wear." She groaned.

"Here, Mum, I bought this for you."

Laura was startled by her son's voice, hadn't realised he had entered her room. He usually knocked. *Thank goodness I'm not in my underwear*, she thought before comprehending what he'd said. He had bought her an outfit. How? When? Why?

"You bought me something to wear? Why?"

"I just wanted to cheer you up. I know you don't really want to come tonight and I really appreciate the fact you are. Like I've said before, best mum ever! Here, take a look." Rookie pushed the bag out towards her.

Laura looked at the bag. It had a designer's name in gold on the fancy-coloured cardboard swing bag. *The bag alone looks expensive – goodness knows what Mitchell has spent buying anything from a shop as high-brow as this one*, she pondered, still clutching the unopened bag.

"Open it, Mum. If you hate it then that's okay, you can wear something else, but I think this will really suit you."

Laura could hear the apprehension in her son's voice, and knew — as any mother would — that she would be wearing this outfit, no matter what it looked like on her. There would be no disappointing her son on this and if he had taken the time, not to mention the expense, to buy her something then she would wear it and smile.

Laura opened the bag a little nervously, trying to stop her hand from shaking. The first thing she noticed was the fabric's unusual colour—it was not quite white, not quite toffee, but somewhere in between. She pulled the dress from the bag and let it fall to its full length. It was the most beautiful thing she had ever seen. It wasn't just the colour of the delicate fabric, but also the design.

"Mitchell Harris, this is the most gorgeous dress I have ever laid eyes on. My goodness, son, if I'd known you were this good with fashion I would have made you shop with me more often. In fact, I'm never buying another thing without your input."

"Mum! No! Don't say that!" He laughed. "I'm glad you like it. Put it on. I'll go get in my penguin suit. Can't have my mum outshine the famous and incredibly sexy Rookie, now, can we?"

He chuckled and left the room, leaving a stunned Laura clutching the dress.

"Well, here goes nothing. Let's hope it fits," she told her reflection. She undressed and stepped into the dress.

"Oh, my!"

Those were the only words that would come out as she looked at the sight before her. The dress fit as though it had been made especially for her, fell deliciously over her hips and body. The fabric felt heavenly against her skin. She did a little twirl in front of the mirror and watched as the dress swirled, the light catching a gold sparkle embedded in the material. She felt like a princess—a forty-two-year-old princess, but a princess nevertheless.

The gathered fabric over the bust enhanced her figure without being overly suggestive, and the straps were delicate over her shoulders. It was as if the dress was enchanted. Laura felt her spirits soar—she felt beautiful. She felt confident. She was now looking forward to her outing, and all because of a dress her son had so thoughtfully provided.

"Forty-two going on twenty-one." Laura laughed as she did another twirl. "You are totally ridiculous! Shoes—I need shoes." She started rummaging through her closet. "Stop it, Laura. It's a dress. It's still you underneath it—don't let it go to your head. Remember what happened last time you got caught up in a fantasy?" she admonished herself sternly, but was still unable to quash the beauty of the dress, and the thrill she felt at wearing it.

When Mitchell returned—this time Laura heard his knock on the door—she was ready to go. Her hair and makeup were done, and she had an appropriate pair of stilettos on her feet.

"Mum, you look amazing," Mitchell said as he entered her room. "Ready to go?"

Laura gazed upon her son, handsome—stunning, in fact—in his black dinner suit. He looked amazing, that was no lie, and not just because he was her son. He looked dressed to kill, all grown up, mature beyond his years.

"Son, you are by far the most handsome escort I've ever had." She felt a lump in her throat and refused to let the tears of pride ruin her makeup.

* * * *

The trip to Mia's Restaurant took no time at all. Laura was impressed that Mitchell drove carefully and slowly, not forgetting that it was his mother sitting next to him. As they pulled into a parking spot just a little down the road from their destination — the street was already packed with cars — Mitchell turned to her, his look as serious as his tone.

"Mum, do you trust me? Trust that I would never do anything to hurt you? Trust that I love you?" he said solemnly.

Laura couldn't help the panic that invaded her mind. Just the serious tone of her son's voice was enough to set alarm bells ringing in her ears. "Of course I do, Mitchell, why do you ask? What's wrong?" Her reply was immediate.

"I just want you to remember, okay? 'Cause I think in a few minutes you are going to need to remember that."

Mitchell's reply was unsettling. Laura didn't understand what her son was saying, but she knew without doubt that she did trust him.

No matter what.

It was just as well, because the second they entered the restaurant Laura understood her son's worry. Not only had the whole night been organised by Trevor Hughes, but she and Mitchell would be sitting at his table. Her only comfort was that she was buffeted from him by Caitlin and Brodie James on one side and Mitchell, JT Thompson and Mandy on the other. She was in such a state of shock over the nightmare that she missed Caitlin speaking to her and had to ask her to repeat what she had said.

"You look gorgeous, Laura. That dress is divine — where did you get it?"

It took Laura a few moments to gather her thoughts and answer, but finally the words came, her voice sounding calmer than she had expected. "Thank you, Caitlin. It *is* a beautiful dress — Mitchell gave it to me. You look quite stunning yourself, but then again, you always do, honey."

Her emotions were in such turmoil over the idea of spending the night in Trevor's company. She'd also had the horrifying thought of how she would cope if Trevor had a date, and her conclusion had been 'badly' — imagining some young, sexy catwalk model on his arm was enough to make her want to vomit. As Laura answered Caitlin she did a quick headcount of chairs and realised that there was a spare, which indicated her worst fears were highly possible.

"Seriously, are you telling me a man picked out *that* dress?" Caitlin asked. "My goodness, wait till I tell Brodie. Sit down, Laura — here, sit next to me. It's just the gang at this table. Oh, and Riley, of course — he's just running a few errands for Trevor. This is Trevor's show tonight. I'm so proud of him. He is very brave to speak up about his struggle with depression, don't you think?"

For Laura it was just one blow after another, while she was relieved, eternally grateful that the spare seat was for Caitlin's brother, Riley, and had not been set aside for some beauty queen of Trevor's, she was equally shocked by Caitlin's explanation of the night's purpose. *Trevor suffers from depression? Why did he not say anything before, tell me? I guess one night together doesn't really call for that sort of information*, she thought sadly.

"Mum, you doing okay?" Mitchell whispered into her ear.

"Fine, I'm fine," was all she could manage in reply as she sat, stunned into silence under the onslaught of emotions coursing through her body.

Chapter Fourteen

Trevor felt sick with nerves. It was too late for doubts now—the room was packed and he had a truckload of items for his silent auction. Everything appeared to be going well, but the moment Laura had walked into the room, Trevor had gone to pieces.

He had not seen her for weeks, had kept busy, occupied with organising the night. He'd tried not to think in too much depth about any of the ramifications of his big announcement. Not that he particularly cared what the general public thought or said—he was prepared for some negativity. It was what Laura Harris would think that had him in knots, had his stomach cramping so badly he wasn't sure he could keep standing.

When Laura had floated into the room, Trevor's world had lit up as if someone had hit the switch on a powerful spotlight. She looked breathtaking. Rookie had really come through for him, had managed to get his mother here.

That conversation with Rookie last week had been a touch-and-go thing. At first Rookie had been furious with him, protective of his mother just as Trevor had expected him to be. What had shocked Trevor had been Rookie's understanding, his complete forgiveness and unyielding support after Trevor had explained how he felt, what he thought had happened between Laura and him, and how much he wanted another chance with the boy's beautiful mother. Rookie had understood.

Mitchell 'Rookie' Harris was mature beyond his years. And Trevor had been enormously relieved when Rookie had confided that Laura was also miserable. Rookie had told Trevor that he believed his mum 'had it bad for him'. But he'd added that if Trevor ever hurt her again—intentionally—he would bury him in the ground so deeply that no one would ever find him. Trevor had believed the threat—the young man had sounded very serious. Trevor hadn't thought that Rookie had it in him to be threatening but hadn't doubted him for a second.

"Everything is good to go, Mr Hughes." A young, male voice drew him from his thoughts.

"Thanks, Riley. You have been an enormous help. Why don't you go take your seat and I'll get this show on the road? And hey, kid—call me Trevor or Trev. You make me feel old."

Trevor watched Riley bounce away. The kid was amazing—there was always a smile on his face and a skip in his step. Now there was a kid who'd had it rough, losing both parents while still so young. Thankfully, his sister and Brodie had his back. *And mine too*, he added to his thoughts quickly. "Okay, Trevor, here goes nothing."

Trevor strode to the stage, his gait loose-limbed. He wanted to portray strength and confidence even if he was shaking in his boots. He took hold of the microphone, took a settling breath, then changed his life forever.

"For those of you that don't know me — and maybe there are a few of you out there who have not met me — my name is Trevor Hughes." Trevor paused to let the room settle.

"I'd like to welcome you and sincerely thank you all for being here with me tonight. Tonight is an important moment for me. We are here to bring aid to a cause that is of personal significance to me. Tonight we are here not only to raise much-needed funds, but also to bring light to a subject that most people fear. A subject most are reluctant to speak of, or even acknowledge."

Trevor steadied his resolve and staring straight ahead forged on.

"Tonight is all about the issue of mental illness and how it affects those who are suffering from it. My hope is that by the end of tonight, depression will become less of a taboo subject. That the general population not affected by this debilitating disease will become more accepting of those of us who are struggling to cope. You see, I am well qualified to speak on this subject because I have suffered from depression for most of my life."

Trevor heard the murmurs from the crowd, knew that the gasps of shock from those seated in front of him were for different reasons. His friends would be surprised that he had never confided in them. His peers and the other members of the press would be thinking of the best headlines to sensationalise his story, and the others were the people he needed to convince that depression was not just being sad, something to just get over. He needed to show these people that depression was an illness. And, as Brodie had said, people didn't turn away from or judge diabetics, just as they shouldn't turn away from or judge people suffering from mental illness.

"When I was a teenager, I began to question my life. I didn't feel that anything I did was good enough. Nothing made me happy. My mates went on and on about how lucky I was, how great it must be to be so good at playing rugby league and to have all the girls after me. But for me it was just another thing to obsess about. What would happen if I didn't play well, if the team didn't win, if I let everyone down? At the time I didn't realise that this wasn't normal. There were days when just leaving my room was a struggle.

"I was so full of fear, so unhappy. I couldn't understand why people wanted to live my life. How everyone around me could be so happy, contented, carefree. I tried to talk about it but was told to cheer up, be happy. It wasn't that easy. This state of misery and fear carried on into my professional playing career. Before every game, I would be so afraid of not living up to other people's expectations of me that I would be physically sick.

"I was so sure I wasn't good enough. Every blemish, every mistake I made would haunt me, have me hiding away from friends and colleagues, deep in despair. I was sure that I was a fake and everything in my life was about to come crashing down. I can remember a sense of relief when I suffered my career-ending injury that at least I wouldn't have to face the gut-wrenching fear that had become part of my usual pre-game routine. This relief was short-lived, though, as I realised that without rugby league I had nothing."

Trevor tried not to think about the nearly silent group of people listening to him air his dirty laundry, and he focused on the memory of those dark days as he continued.

"The pain of my knee injury was nowhere near as bad as the pain in my mind, in my soul. I was worthless. It is hard to put into words my mindset at the time, but hopelessness, having no hope, figured prominently. All the fears that had consumed me over the last few years were becoming real. I had let everyone down by being injured. The team were short on players, my family and friends didn't get to go to the games, didn't get the good seats. I had nothing to look forward to, not that I could remember ever looking forward to anything in my life anyway. My thoughts went dark, desperate.

"I know I keep using that word — 'dark' — but for me it was like some clichéd, thunderous dark cloud hovered over my life. There was no light. I didn't see a reason to be part of a world that I could not contribute to, that I was unworthy of. And I felt unworthy — the darker my thoughts became, the more *desperate* I became. Sadness and misery consumed every breath I took, every minute of every day. I had convinced myself that there was only one way out, one way to make the pain go away, and I was ready to take that final step when a young Jets player intervened."

Trevor paused and looked to where Brodie was seated. He didn't think the man would be concerned about being named publicly, but Trevor just wanted to be sure. Of course, he needn't have worried. Brodie James was smiling back at him, nodding in a gesture of support as always.

So Trevor continued, "I hardly knew Brodie James — he hadn't been at the Jets long, and I wasn't the most sociable bloke around — but his kindness literally saved my life. He brought a glimmer of light, of hope.

How Brodie knew what was wrong, I don't know, but he helped me reach out to the right professionals, who in turn explained that what I was feeling was due to an illness. That it wasn't normal for people to be so fearful, so desperate, so despairing of life. The doctors explained that something in my brain had short-circuited, and more importantly that I could be helped. Through counselling and medication and with Brodie James' help, I managed to get past that dark time in my life. But for most people suffering depression and anxiety it is not an easy road, and being completely cured is unlikely. This is an illness that sufferers learn to live with, to manage.

"As you all know, I have moved on from my rugby league-playing days, I have been fortunate enough to be given a chance at a new career. A career I love. A career that I do find happiness in. A reason to get up every morning."

But the most important part of Trevor's monologue was about to come, when he spoke of his inability to connect in a relationship for the fear of a partner seeing his darker side.

"And as well as a new career, I have made some remarkable friendships. People that I can count on, people I trust and respect. For me to enjoy this — being around friends — is a new feeling. The only thing that I haven't been able to do is let a special someone into my life. Letting a woman get close to me still causes me fear. Is there someone out there that can cope with my darkness? Should I inflict that side of me on anyone permanently? Mates are one thing, but I can leave them at the end of the day, retire to my solitary place and sort through my emotions at my own pace. Retreat from the world if need be.

"I didn't feel I had the strength to share life's journey with anyone on a permanent basis, share the normal ups and downs. I believed that I didn't have the strength in me to help a partner who might need my emotional support. It was hard enough dealing with my own problems. So I kept an emotional distance to women I dated. Retained an emotional detachment. Kept anyone looking for a relationship with me at arm's length and only showed part of my personality, hiding the rest away."

Trevor was shaking, his chest tight, but he was determined to face this last fear. He hoped Laura was listening, wanting her—above all others—to understand why he had reacted so negatively to her words. He could not look at her for worry over what he might see in her eyes. But he would face her later. That was the promise he had made himself.

"But recently, that all changed. I met someone that has made me want to take that risk—someone full of light, of sunshine and happiness. I felt an instant connection to this remarkable, beautiful woman, really wanted to give it a shot at something permanent, something real and honest, but once again I let fear pull me away. Let fear stop me from taking control of my own life, of hoping for happiness. I told myself she deserved better, that I had no right to sully her bright light with my darkness, that I was unworthy of someone so wonderful, so special. And once again, my friendship with Brodie James helped me see the light."

Trevor took a steadying breath deep into his lungs. Took a minute to calm his riotous emotions, and took the even braver—or perhaps masochistic— opportunity to focus his sights on Laura. She was sitting ramrod straight, clasping her napkin tightly, and Trevor could see the train of tears cascading down her cheeks. He prayed that he was not too late in his explanation. His public apology. *This is it, buddy, your closing argument. Make it good.* The little voice in his head encouraged him on, for a change.

"This function tonight is my way of finally facing up to all of my fears. No more hiding. By speaking so openly and honestly with you all here tonight, and in front of the members of the press in attendance, about my struggles with depression, I'm hoping I can better educate those who may not understand this crippling mental illness. I also hope that the beautiful woman I pushed away might now understand me a little better, believe that I didn't mean to cause her any pain, that I really thought at the time I was doing the right thing by protecting her from my illness. And perhaps she might even forgive me. Might give me a second chance to prove to her how much she means to me."

Trevor spoke further of his hopes that by making this very public announcement—or confession, of sorts—that he would be able to help others. Others who might feel the same way he had. He had let fear rule his life for too long, had been ashamed to speak up and ask for help. Felt shame at not being man enough to cope with life. But there was no shame in admitting you were not perfect, or admitting you had fears or worries. It was not shameful to be sad, depressed. What *was* shameful, he went on to say, was ignoring that call from someone who needed help.

Trevor explained there was a support network out there, albeit struggling financially to provide the services needed. It was up to people like him, in the public arena, to speak out, to connect with others and to bring help to these groups and organise the financial aid they so desperately needed. And most importantly, to connect with anyone who felt they were alone. To help, or to carry out an act of kindness that could ultimately save someone, just as he had been saved.

Trevor stepped away from the microphone, his mouth dry from speaking for so long. He took a deep breath, took stock of how he was holding up, and realised that he felt good—lighter if that was at all possible. Then he heard the applause and as he looked out to the tables full of people who had sat through his speech, Trevor was moved beyond words. Not a single person that he could see was still seated— everyone was standing and clapping. Trevor felt acceptance flood the room.

He had made a difference. All his struggles, his personal fight with the black dog of depression had led him to this moment, this point where he could make a stand.

Chapter Fifteen

It all became clear to Laura, as the tears rolled down her cheeks at the words Trevor had spoken. The fight he had been battling. She now understood that what she had seen in Trevor that morning, that look he had given her, was due to his insecurities. She now understood what he had meant by 'baggage' and 'demons'. The words he'd spoken of disappointing those around him had just been a side-effect of the depression he fought. He was a good man, a man with a big heart, and brave. *God*, Laura thought, *he's brave beyond measure to put himself out in the spotlight as he has done.*

To put himself directly into the line of fire for the gossips to feed on.

She could never be that strong.

What did it mean for her? Why was she here? She believed it was her Trevor wanted to connect with. She certainly hoped that it *was* her. If one thing was clear in Laura's mind, it was the fact that she was still attracted to the man — his body, his soul, his bravery — and to hell with the baggage.

Now all she had to do was get a moment with him in private. But at the moment he was surrounded by reporters. They had microphones shoved in his face, were hurling questions at him. She had to do something to help.

"Brodie, JT, Mitchell—don't just sit there! Go save Trevor from the circling sharks. Caitlin, go sing or something, please? We need to give him a chance to catch his breath."

"Sure thing, Mum. C'mon, boys, let's circle the wagons around Trev."

"Yep, I'm all over it, Laura. I'll go hit the stage. Any requests?"

"Thank you, Caitlin. Just sing anything. Your angelic voice would distract the devil himself."

It was good to have friends, and it was good she didn't mind barking orders, Laura thought as she watched her plan take effect. The men ran interference with the reporters, then as Caitlin's melodic voice filled the room, everyone returned to their seats. The food was being delivered. And better still, Trevor was heading her way. She wanted to stand and throw herself into his arms, but she waited.

Now she was afraid. She was letting fear hold her back.

It was wrong—if Trevor could be brave, so could she.

So Laura let herself go. As Trevor reached their table, she stood and flung her arms around his neck. She stood on tiptoes to reach his lips and crushed them under her own. Not caring that they were in full view of the restaurant, that her son was probably watching in horror. Laura didn't care about anything but letting Trevor, who now had his arms wrapped around her, understand that she was proud of him. That she wanted him, no matter what.

That their connection was still alive.

"Trevor, I understand. I'm sorry for not giving you a chance to explain, I'm sorry for running off. I misunderstood, panicked. If only we had talked it over... All this time I thought you had just wanted a one-night stand, and you really *were* trying to protect me, not just let me down gently. I'm such a fool."

"Shh... Honey, let's sit down. I think we may even be upstaging Caitlin right now. Not that I care. I'm just so relieved to feel you in my arms again. Rookie was right—you do still have a thing for me!"

Laura did not understand what Trevor meant about her son. But she didn't care. She sat back in her seat, dragging Trevor down next to her. She clasped his hand, not willing to let go of him just yet as her heart flip-flopped in her chest. Laura heard Mitchell snicker next to her, and she smiled.

"Nice way to get your message across, Mum. By tomorrow every paper in Sydney will have a photo of you and Trevor lip-locked. And Mum, I couldn't be happier."

Laura grasped her son's hand in her free one. Eating any of the food in front of her was last on her to-do list. She was holding the hands of people special to her—men on either side of her chair that she was proud to be associated with. Her son, whom she loved with every ounce of her being, and a man she believed she could love very easily, if she didn't already.

Happier than she had ever felt, Laura sat back and enjoyed the moment, enjoyed the music. Caitlin's singing about love touched her deeply because Laura could relate to the meaning and sentiment of the song—love might bring pain but it also brought so much happiness.

"I have to go, Laura."

"What? Go where?" Laura stuttered, panicky, having been jolted from her romantic dreaming at the sound of Trevor's voice.

"I need to check the auctions, make some money. Get this night over so I can have you all to myself."

"Get to work, Trevor. Make money, loads of it. I'm so proud of you right now I may burst. I'm thinking of ways that I can show you how proud I am, but we will need privacy…a lot of privacy."

Laura loved the way Trevor squirmed in his seat as she whispered in his ear. The hunger in his demanding kiss left her in no doubt that he had understood her praise and promise.

Watching Trevor control the rest of the night's events—effortlessly and with humour, intelligent conversation and relevant anecdotes—made Laura hot. She was so hot for him it was a wonder no one had picked up on the heat emanating from her body. It was clear that she wasn't the only woman in the room who was interested in Trevor. But Laura had observed with interest and a huge amount of relief that he never encouraged or flirted with any of the very forward and tactile females.

"Comes with the territory," Mandy said. "These men attract women like honey attracts bears. All those mama bears want their honey, but don't worry—our honeys are very good at repelling bears." Mandy giggled. "Oh no, not again! If I don't stop with the giggling I'll wet myself—this baby is sitting right on my bladder. Gosh, Laura, I'm starting to worry that the bub is going to take after JT and be huge. I'm terrified. Just take a look at JT's big head. Imagine that squeezing out your womb!"

Laura looked to where Mandy was pointing—at her fiancé, JT—and couldn't stop the shudder as she imagined what Mandy had described.

"You can rest assured that your baby is going to be much smaller than that, Mandy. You'll do fine. Just remember, there are drugs now to help you cope with childbirth."

"Yeah, I know, Laura. Got them all ordered, just in case." Mandy winked. "Between you and me, I think JT will need every one of them! Looks like the men have finished. Thank goodness. I can't wait to put my feet up. Good luck with Trevor—I think you guys make a great couple."

"Thanks, Mandy. So do I. We just need to get to know each other before we jump to any more conclusions."

* * * *

Laura felt a tingle up her spine—an excitement of what was to come—as she watched Trevor wrap up the night's festivities. The auctions had been a huge success. She had bid on a few items, and been the top bidder for two—a jewellery piece donated by Mandy and a hamper full of champagne, strawberries and chocolates. Laura could think of a few ways to use those chocolates and strawberries, and Trevor starred in all of her ideas. Laura had also quickly made a donation to the night, when she'd realised what was happening, offering a spring clean of a house or office to the highest bidder.

Laura saw a woman approaching and knew immediately that it was Trevor's mother. The family resemblance was unmistakeable. Laura smiled in the woman's direction, hoping to get off on the right foot. She wasn't at all prepared for the attack.

"Do you think that was very appropriate behaviour, attacking my son like that? No wonder Trevor is acting so selfishly at the moment—talking all this rubbish about being sick and bringing such embarrassing attention to his family, upsetting his father. And you... Such a mature-looking woman, when my son is obviously so much younger. It's disgusting. Frank is fuming—gone straight to the car. But I just couldn't let you get away with it. It is obviously all your doing, this...this...horrid night."

Laura was astounded at the woman's nerve, the audacity to speak to her in such a way. This person had let Trevor down, and—to Laura's horror—was still doing it. How could Mrs Hughes not understand the monumental gesture Trevor had just made, all to help strangers, people he had not even met? Yet his own mother had still turned away from him. It was a shame, but Laura would not be intimidated.

"Think what you want, Mrs Hughes. I don't care what you or your husband may think, believe or feel. All I care about is that your son is the bravest, most thoughtful and caring man I've ever met. I nearly lost him once, but I don't intend to let that happen again. I will support him in his fight to overcome this illness that has affected him for so long. Unlike you—shame on you. I am a mother and I would never leave my son to battle any pain or illness alone. I am shocked that any mother could. So don't you go tainting this wonderful evening with your snide comments."

Laura was really on a roll—she was so angry that this woman, this sad excuse for a mother could even comment on what had been such a successful night.

She couldn't bear for Trevor to hear any of this negativity. Laura could understand, clearly, why Trevor felt he had disappointed his loved ones, but it was they who were the disappointments not Trevor.

"If you can't say anything in support of Trevor, Mrs Hughes, I really think you should just leave. Let him be. He doesn't need to hear your bitterness."

"Well, I never… What a rude woman, attacking me this way. A mother, you say? Pffft…probably left a tribe of unwanted kids with a stranger just so you can flirt with my son. I think he needs to hear how you've spoken to me…"

"Your son *has*. Hello, Mother."

Laura's heart nearly stopped when she heard Trevor's voice behind her. She worried over what he might have heard. Would he be disappointed with her that she had clearly distressed his mother? The way the woman was behaving, anyone would think Laura had physically attacked her. *Again, me and my big mouth – when will I learn to just keep it shut? But then again, why should I? The woman had it coming.*

If Trevor was really upset, Laura supposed she could apologise, but she would feel sick doing it. Trevor deserved to be loved and held in high regard. Not to be belittled by those who should be his greatest supporters.

Chapter Sixteen

Trevor had actually managed to forget his parents had insisted upon attending tonight. He hadn't warned them or told them what the fundraiser was for, and had been convinced that they would not be pleased. Hearing the way his mum had got stuck into Laura made him see red. The hide of her to blame Laura for what he was doing, what he had admitted to publicly! It certainly wasn't Laura who had let him down in life, and his little ray of sunshine had really had his back.

He could see where Rookie had got his protective streak—definitely from Laura. Trevor had felt a deep gratitude for the way Laura had taken his mother to task for her lack of support. His heart had filled with joy just knowing that Laura felt enough for him to speak up, and to compliment him, call him brave. Trevor could have exploded with the happiness she'd instilled in him with her outspoken words. But he was not going to sit by and let his mother threaten her, belittle her or make up lies to cause Laura pain. *No bloody way.*

"Mother, I had the misfortune to hear every word that was spoken…"

"Did you hear her rudeness, the way she spoke to your mother?"

"No, Mother. I heard you attack Laura, and I heard your disparaging remarks about my life and the decisions I've made. You have never been there for me, so let's not pretend it's any other way. Go to Dad, make sure he is okay. He needs you. Laura and I have places to be."

Mrs Hughes gave a gasp of shock as Trevor took Laura by the hand, turned and led her to the back of the restaurant, putting as much distance as he could between his mother and Laura.

"I'm so sorry you had to deal with that, Laura. My parents have their own problems. I'm leaning towards the idea that they both have some sort of mental instability themselves. Dad is always down, and Mum has to fret over him every minute. There was never really any time or energy left for me. In fact, the only way I got any praise from her was if I did something that made my father happy, and I didn't achieve that very often, I'm here to tell you."

"Oh Trevor, you have nothing to apologise for…and anyway, I'm quite capable of looking after myself when it comes to other women. You obviously have never been involved in a parent-school committee."

Laura's teasing had a calming effect on Trevor—she was fine, able to deal with his mother. He really needed to start giving her more credit. Laura was one in a million. Trevor felt as though maybe he had won the jackpot.

"Can I take you home, Laura? I know you came with your son, but would you let me do the honour of escorting you home?"

"That depends on which home you will take me to. I rather hoped it might be yours, Trevor."

"Honey, that would be more than I could wish for. We need to talk, though, so you have to promise not to ravish me until we've finished." Trevor could not believe that he was joking, making light of their budding relationship, but it felt good.

"I don't make promises I'm not sure I can keep. Maybe you'll have to tie my hands together or something."

Laura's cheeks flamed with colour as she realised the implications of what she had said, and Trevor loved that pink tinge. She was delightful in her embarrassment and he jumped at the chance to string it along.

"Hmm, bondage, Laura? Who would have thought you would be into that type of thing? But hey, I'm a modern guy — I'll give anything a go. Tying you up and having you at my mercy — now that sounds like a hardship I could endure."

"Modern and a comedian — who knew?" Laura laughed. "Trevor, you can tie me up as long as you remember I get reciprocal rights." A sexy wickedness was so clear in her voice that it sent Trevor's libido into overdrive. "I just have to find Mitchell and let him know I may not be home tonight."

"You tell that son of yours that you may not be home for *days*, honey. I have a feeling it will take a while for me to get through some of the plans I have dreamed up for you. The things that I need to do to you."

Trevor was delighted to see Laura blush deepen as she headed off to find her son and make her goodbyes. He knew he was grinning from ear to ear but couldn't begin to hide the happiness he was feeling.

"So tonight's been a huge success all round, then, judging by that smile on your dial." A familiar chuckle followed the accurate statement.

"Yep, Brodie. It has. And I feel all the better for it, and not just the Laura situation—which for the record is fucking gold—but the other stuff. The fact I feel like I'm making a contribution to society. Making a difference."

"Mate, you've been making a difference in people's lives forever. You help out with any and every fundraiser going, bring joy to lots of folks every week through your show. Don't sell yourself short, Trev. You're one of the good guys. I'm proud of you, buddy. Good job."

"Brodes, thanks mate. Fuck, our conversations are getting really, really weird these days. Being married has turned you into a marshmallow, my friend. Toughen up, fella." Trevor couldn't hide the emotion in his voice, though, even as he joked to lighten the mood. His mates were solid. Not afraid to let you know how they felt, and the fact they were known as hard, tough men didn't alter that fact.

Laura left Trevor and went in search of her son. She wanted to let Mitchell know that she would be going back to Trevor's and staying the night. And though the upcoming conversation made her feel a tiny bit embarrassed, Laura had no doubt that her son would take the information in his stride, and not cause her any anguish because of it. He had been a conspirator in the night after all, fully aware of Trevor's intentions to rekindle their short relationship. So if Mitchell had qualms, he could have not insisted she attend with him. *Bless his interfering heart*, she thought lovingly as she continued her search.

Laura found Mitchell sitting at a table, deep in conversation with a young woman. Laura had seen the woman—just a girl, really—around. She was the head coach's daughter, Phillipa Rodgers. The poor girl had been saddled with the unflattering nickname 'Pipsqueak'. Laura shuddered every time she heard the young girl called by the name, resigned to the fact that men could be so thoughtless when it came to the sensitivities of a young woman.

Mitchell had his back to Laura, but she could tell by her son's relaxed pose, by the way his arms rested on the table, shoulders loose, and by how he leaned in close to Phillipa, that he was in no need of rescue. In the past, Laura had been forced to intervene to save Mitchell from the grips of fanciful young groupies. Her son had always been relieved when she had. But this time, Laura felt no sense of entrapment or panic from her son. She could see the adoration in Phillipa's face, though—the girl was facing towards Laura as she approached. Eyes bright, cheeks flushed, Phillipa looked enchanted by whatever Mitchell was saying.

Laura had a brief moment when she thought that maybe she should intervene and remind Mitchell that Phillipa was very young, probably only seventeen— not that it was easy to tell these days, especially when girls dressed up. But Laura pushed the thought aside. Mitchell had proven himself able to act maturely, and he certainly didn't need advice from his mother on this. Laura was convinced her son would act in a gentlemanly fashion when it came to Phillipa. *The fact she's the coach's daughter will seal the deal anyway*, Laura mused. *Not a good career move to upset your coach.*

She cleared her throat behind Mitchell's head. Phillipa quickly looked away from Laura, her cheeks flaming red and a little sound of dismay coming from her lips, but Laura smiled in her direction, drawing back the girl's attention.

"Evening, Phillipa. Having a nice night?"

The poor girl nearly choked on her response. "Oh, yes, Mrs Harris. A lovely time, thank you."

"That's good, dear. Sorry to interrupt, but I'd just like to say goodbye to Mitchell." Laura turned to her son, who was now leaning back in his chair, his eyes not having left Phillipa's face throughout the exchange.

"Hey, Ma! What's up?"

"I'm heading off now, with Trevor," Laura said, lowering her voice as she mentioned Trevor's name. *No need to advertise any further*, she thought. "Will you be right to get home by yourself? Have you been drinking?"

"No, Mum, on the lemonade tonight. Wanted to keep my wits about me just in case." He winked. "It's all good, Mum. You head off, I'll catch you some time tomorrow, okay?" he added, taking the need for Laura to explain any further from her hands.

"Thanks, Mitchell." Laura started to walk away, but couldn't hold back a final comment, hoping that her son would understand her concerns.

"Hey, Rookie." Laura used her son's football nickname to gain his attention, saw him turn his head, a quizzical look on his face at her using the term. "Be good, and if you can't be good, be careful, son!"

Chapter Seventeen

After making the necessary goodbyes to their friends and Laura's son, then leaving said friends all smirking in their wake, Trevor finally had Laura to himself. They had made idle chit-chat on the journey back to his home. It wasn't until they were sitting side by side in his living room that Trevor turned the conversation in a more serious direction. He held Laura's hands in his as he told her in depth—being completely honest, leaving nothing unsaid—about his illness.

To her credit, Laura sat silently and listened to Trevor's story. She squeezed his hand on occasion, but mostly she just listened.

"I want us to be together, Laura. More than anything, but you have to understand this doesn't go away, and while I'm in control and haven't had a bout for years, it could happen. I'm scared of being a liability in your life. What if being with me turned you into someone like my mother? I shudder at the thought, honey."

"I understand you have fears about us, Trevor, but you have to remember, so do I. I am forty-two years old and you are thirty-four — that is a huge difference. I have done the family thing. Do you want children, Trevor? Because I'm almost past that stage of my life. Don't you see? Relationships have difficulties on both sides. We just have to work through them together. If we talk everything through then maybe it won't be so hard. You haven't lived through my PMS yet — just ask Mitchell, I can be pretty dark myself. And I'm not making light of your illness, I'm just pointing out that I have my problems too, that you will have to live with."

"We can do this, Laura, I'm positive. Stop worrying about the age thing — to me you are perfect, and to be honest I never thought about kids. Never really put too much thought into the future. I don't think I'm father material, anyway."

"Stop judging yourself so harshly, Trevor. You don't know what sort of father you would be."

'It's not really something I see myself doing, Laura. I think fatherhood is too much responsibility."

"Being a parent is that, I can attest to it. It feels so different now, knowing that I don't have Mitchell to worry about every day. Sometimes when he's travelling with the Jets, the house seems so empty. It is time I resumed my life — Laura's life — and I kinda hope you will become a part of that, Trevor."

"So do I, honey, so do I. Come here, let me kiss you."

Laura crawled into his lap and Trevor did not waste another moment. He took her mouth with his. Lips on lips, tongue to tongue, they were finally connected again.

Their kiss was all-consuming, hot yet tender at the same time. Their tongues explored and danced as Trevor changed the angle of his mouth to achieve an even greater, deeper access to Laura's mouth. Their teeth clashed as their passion intensified. Sighs, moans, the slurp of a kiss made up the background serenade to their passion. Trevor could have kissed Laura all night. He loved the taste of her, and the mewling sounds she made drove him wild with need. He stroked the softness of her blonde hair, drifted his hands down the slope of her neck, her shoulders, to rest at her slim waist.

Trevor moved his lips from Laura's to travel down her neck, nipping and kissing her delicate skin on his journey. She moved her head to the side, granting him easier access. Laura's eyes were closed, her lashes fanned over her high cheekbones as she arched her back, pressed her body into his. Chest to breast, Trevor could feel her nipples, the hard buds pushing against his skin. He drifted his hands lower to clasp the round globes of her backside—he pumped and kneaded the softness, enjoying the feminine feel of her body. Laura was now kissing his neck, nipping at his ear, her bites sharp and the sting sending even more heat to his already swollen groin. His cock was so hard it was painful, pressed against the zipper of his pants. He needed relief before he caused himself a permanent injury.

"Lift up a little, honey. If I don't loosen my pants I may be ruined for all time. I'm so fucking hard for you, I feel like my cock will break if I don't allow it some freedom."

"Quick, unzip." Laura chuckled. "I certainly don't want you disfigured or impaired in any way. I want you hard and raring to go. Make love to me, Trevor. Now."

"Bossy much, Laura? I was enjoying myself just touching and kissing you. What's the hurry? We have all night."

"All I can say is that you obviously aren't as hot or horny as me. I think I will die if I don't get some relief…and soon. Please, Trevor."

Laura was wrong—Trevor was in blissful agony as well. He could not ignore her plea, though. Trevor wanted to ease her need, wanted to give her an orgasm, then he could take his time to slowly build her up to climax again. Trevor figured he could probably last at least three of her orgasms before he would give up the fight and bury himself in Laura's hot folds.

"Lose the dress, Laura. It's so pretty—I don't want to damage it. Plus I need to see you naked in my lap—bare, ready for me."

Laura removed her dress without argument. She also unhooked her bra, but because she sat straddling him, she had not yet removed her panties.

"This pretty little thing looks so sexy on you. But I would prefer them off. Are they particular favourites?" he asked.

When Laura looked at him in a confused way, Trevor decided that he didn't care if they were her favourites—he would buy her more, bagsful if need be. Trevor grabbed the side of the fabric sitting high on Laura's hip and ripped the seams apart, before doing the same to the fabric on the other hip. Laura gasped, then a little giggling sound escaped her lips. The sound was so melodic it reminded Trevor of the sound of wind-chimes in a summer breeze.

"Oh, that was incredibly hot, you getting all caveman-like and ripping my clothes. I could have stood up, you know."

"Naw… I liked my way better, honey." Trevor ended the conversation by attaching his lips to Laura's left nipple. He gently bit down on the pebbled bud before sucking it into his mouth.

"Yes. Oh, yes, Trevor…"

Trevor continued the attention he was paying Laura's breasts, while moving his fingers gently up and down the outsides of her slit. He could feel the heat, the moisture that had built in that heavenly place. With his finger, he probed her entry, then pushed in to her, then pulled back out. His finger was wet from her juices—he contemplated, for just a moment, spreading that juice around her clit, but thought better of it. A taste of her—that was what he needed.

He sucked at his own digit, licked all her sweet essence into his mouth. Then he repeated the gesture, this time plunging two fingers deep into and out of her moist cavern before licking them clean. Again and again he plunged, withdrew and sucked. Laura squirmed on his lap. His rod pressed hard against her, the pressure only slightly relieved by the opening of his pants. He needed to get naked as well, but he wanted to make Laura fall apart, scream his name as he brought her to release. But he also wanted to suck her sweet pussy dry, quench the never-ending thirst he had for her juices.

"Decisions, decisions," he moaned.

"Mmm… Did you say something?" Laura hummed in his ear.

"Just deciding what I want to do to you first— whether to get naked with you, or just eat your pussy first. I can't make up my mind. It all seems so good."

"Get naked, Trevor. Let me feel the warmth of your skin against mine."

"Are you cold, honey? I didn't even think…"

"No, not cold—burning, melting for you. Definitely not cold, but I still want to feel your skin against mine. Flesh to flesh, no barrier between us."

Trevor decided that Laura was right—no barriers between them sounded good—but he had to move her so he could achieve that goal. As he gently lifted her smaller frame from his lap, ready to place her next to him on the couch Laura began to struggle. Worried that he was hurting her, Trevor let her go, let her move herself, only to discover that she had a plan of her own. Laura slid between his thighs kneeling on the carpet. The grin she gave him sent lightning bolts of pleasure through his system. Trevor remembered that look—that wicked, wonderful look. And so did his cock.

"Here, let me help you undress. I promise I'll be extra careful!" Laura giggled as she teased Trevor, purposely brushing her hand over the hardness in the front of his pants, then cupping him gently. "Hmmm, you feel kinda worked up again. Isn't that how you described it last time? When you cautioned me on the zipper thing."

"Oh, hon, I'm past worked up—I'm about to explode." Trevor gritted out.

"Maybe I can do something to help, then," Laura purred.

She leant forward so as to reach the opening of his pants. With one hand, she carefully lowered the zipper completely—it had already been at half mast from when he had unbuttoned earlier to give himself more room, but now he was completely open. Laura grasped the waistband of Trevor's pants.

"Lift."

As he did, she pulled them down past his hips, repeating the motion with his boxers. Once freed, Trevor's shaft stood tall, rigid. As if it were beckoning her, she could not refuse its call. She ran her tongue around the circumference of his erect penis, the mushroom-like head, the joining of his skin. She laved and licked, explored every bulbous vein, every satiny bit of skin that covered his impressive form. Laura loved the taste of him, the slightly salty, musky maleness. She lapped at the pre-cum that formed at the eye before swallowing his erection down into her throat, loving the moans and grunts Trevor was making.

When he took hold of the sides of her head and drew her away, she didn't fight him. It was time he buried that hard cock — that part of him that differentiated his maleness from her femininity — inside her dripping wet and throbbing pussy, where it belonged. "I need you, Laura, need to bury myself in you, want to come inside you."

"I need that too, Trevor."

Laura lay back on the carpet and spread her legs for him in an invitation for him to take her. She watched as he extracted a condom from the wallet he took from his now discarded pants' pocket. He rolled the latex on and her mouth watered. Her folds wept with cream as the moment drew close — the moment she'd thought she would never feel again, that fullness she had craved for weeks and had been unable to attain at her own hands.

Trevor knelt over her, nudging his cock at the opening of her wet, eager, molten heat. Then he thrust into her. The movement and the feeling were all she had been waiting for. His rock-hard cock rubbed against her sensitive clit as he entered, and the sensation it evoked was pure bliss. Her orgasm built, soaring to a peak, unstoppable. The pleasure was so intense, so pure that she screamed with delight.

"Trevor!" she yelled as she dug her nails into his shoulders, her heels pressed into his backside as she strove to ride the wave to completion. The rhythm of his thrusts grew frantic, desperate, as she felt him tense over her.

"Fuck…"

It was the only word to escape his mouth that she understood, as once again she imagined she could feel his heat, the pressure of his seed as it filled the condom.

They were both spent, sated. Trevor's body crushed hers, but the feeling was so wondrous, so comforting that she did not care if he smothered her. Laura did not move, hoping that the moment would never end.

"I'm too heavy for you. I'm sorry, I just can't move, give me a second." Trevor's muffled voice disturbed the silence.

"No, I'm fine — enjoying the fact that if you smother me, I will die feeling this good. This happy."

Trevor lifted from her, his limp cock slipping from her. She sighed over the loss.

"Oh, I miss you already," she whimpered.

"Don't fret, hon. I intend to be back inside you very soon, but I need a minute. And I think maybe next time the bed might be a more comfortable surface."

"What's the matter, old man, floor a bit hard for you?"

"Not for me — I had your softness between the floor and my body. I was thinking for you, but hey, if you're okay with it, hell, I'm not about to complain. In fact, I vote we try every surface there is."

Before Laura had a chance to say a word, Trevor flipped her so she lay belly down on the floor. He lifted her hips in the air, and she knew her butt was now sticking up in his face, giving him a unfettered view of her pussy lips. She could feel the moisture that still leaked from between those lips, but didn't have the energy or desire to fight against the new position, or be self-conscious over it.

Laura felt Trevor's cock, already hard again, breach her opening. The mushroom-shaped head pushed past her tingling folds, folds tender from all the attention her pussy was now receiving, but she didn't care about any discomfort—she wanted more. She wanted Trevor buried so deep inside her that he became part of her. She thrust her hips back towards him.

"I told you before I wanted to take you from behind. I've imagined this, and it feels as good—no, better than I could have believed. I love the shape of your arse. One day I'd like to take you here, if you'll let me."

Laura dropped her head to the floor as Trevor softly touched the puckered opening to her back passage, gently massaged that tight ring of nerve endings. It was a part of her that she'd never dreamed could feel sexual, sensual. Never in her wildest fantasies had she thought she would want anyone to touch her there, but she came alive. The sensation or the image— whatever it was it was—was enough to send shivers of anticipation rocketing through her. She had never had sex that way, and the slightly shocking idea sent her reeling with desire. And again, with little effort, little direct stimulation to her clit, Laura climaxed, the orgasm shattering her system. She thought that she might die from the pleasure.

Trevor bit his tongue the moment after he'd voiced his erotic thought. The image of his cock riding her tight butt as his fingers stroked her pussy was so hot he'd forgotten to censor his words. But judging by the way her body responded, her pussy tightening and throbbing around his buried cock, Trevor realised that Laura was not opposed to the idea. *At a later date, though*, he thought. *No hurry*. For now, he was content to explore every other sexual position, every way to make Laura moan with pleasure. And he wanted to know her mind as well.

He would not blow this second chance—this time, he would take the time to understand her, to get inside her head. He would find out how to make Laura happy, how to make her fall in love with him. Because Trevor was more than halfway there already, he decided as he held her, thrust into her tight pussy, slammed his balls against the globes of her delectable arse. As he felt his ejaculate ready to explode from his dick, he remembered he had not used a condom, so reluctantly he pulled out of her wetness. He let his cum spurt over her lower back, drip down between her cheeks, as he fell forward and covered her body, the feel of his cum sticky between their skin.

"Close call—sorry, honey, sorry about the stickiness, but I had to pull out. Didn't know if you were protected and I forgot the condom, only just remembered at the last second."

"Mmm…feels good between our bodies, our skin… Another connection." Her voice sounded dreamy, tired.

Trevor stood and scooped Laura up in his arms, ignoring her squeal at the sudden movement. He tenderly kissed her cheek as he rested her head against his chest and carried them towards his bathroom.

He would bathe Laura first, clean his seed from her skin—although the thought of it there, his cum marking her as his, did strange things to his mind. Possessive instincts bubbled close to the surface, reminding Trevor how much he wanted this connection to her.

He examined his mind, his feelings, and found no fear disturbed his inner thoughts—there was no niggling voice that heralded doom. After they were both cleansed of the sweat and passion from their lovemaking, more comfortable, Trevor would take her to his bed so they could get some sleep.

He would hold her in his arms and dream of future happiness, safe in the knowledge that he had Laura's light in his life to help combat his darkness.

PIPPA'S
FANTASY

Dedication

To Amy — thank you so much for your continued support and hard work in helping me become a better author.

Chapter One

"Pip, if you could have anything you wanted just for one night, what would it be?"

Phillipa Rodgers — Pip or Pippa to her friends — sent Cassie a bewildered look, wondering what had brought about the odd question from her best friend.

"Well, Pip, it's your twenty-second birthday and you are now a professional sports physio, about to begin the grown-up phase of your life — you know, responsibility and all that." Cassie giggled. "If you could have or do anything, just for one night, what would it be?"

Cassie was looking at Pippa as if she knew some big secret and couldn't wait to tell it.

Phillipa Rodgers and Cassandra Davies had been best friends since they'd met on their very first day of school, eighteen years ago. Since that day, they had shared everything — the ups and downs of life, good or bad. Tears, fears and successes. They had always been confidantes, whether it was for a first kiss or the loss of virginity, each girl had been there to support the other. They had cried over broken hearts and celebrated the good times, but always together. Pip and Cassie were inseparable.

Pip—once blonde, like her friend—had recently dramatically changed her hairstyle. Her formerly curly, waist-length hair was now cut short and coloured blue-black in a style that feathered around her face. Pip's eyes were a darker shade of blue than Cassie's cornflower ones, her face slightly more pointed compared with Cassie's more cherubic features.

The girls were out partying to celebrate completing their university degrees, dressed in the latest fashionable, chic clothes. Pip, having finished a physiotherapy degree and a year at a teaching hospital, was about to begin her career in earnest, specialising in sports physiotherapy. Cassie, with a Diploma of Education combined with her bachelor's degree in physical education, was starting her teaching role as a sports teacher at the local high school.

Now finally back on home turf, the girls had been enjoying the scene at a new club when Cassie had spotted Pippa's fantasy man.

"Well, if you really have to ask that question, Cass, you're not the best friend I thought you were. You know full well my one fantasy is, and has always been, to have long, hot monkey sex with Mitchell Harris."

"Hmm, yep, I knew that, Pip. Just thought I'd double-check before I told you the man of your seven-year fantasy walked into the club a few minutes ago. Take a look. He's standing at the bar," Cassie said as she pointed.

Pippa's gaze followed in the direction her friend pointed. Sure enough, leaning majestically against the bar and looking as if he owned the place was Mitch 'Rook' Harris, and he was as gorgeous as ever. The mere sight of him caused Pip to catch her breath.

Pippa hadn't seen Mitch in the flesh for over five years, but she noticed the changes in her first crush's looks immediately. The young, brash man destined for superstardom had completely filled out into one hunky piece of prime male. Rook's face was now slightly fuller, more mature. His nose — not as straight as it used to be — gave him an overall tougher, more masculine appearance. Once the 'pretty boy' of rugby league, he was now all grown up — and he was the complete package.

As Pippa sat staring, Rook turned from his conversation with the barman, and as if sensing he was being watched, looked towards her. Their eyes locked, and Rook's face broke into a sexy, broad smile.

"Oh, my God, he saw me, Cass!" Pippa exclaimed as she hastily broke eye contact with Rook.

"Well, Pip, now's your chance. What did you say? 'Hot monkey sex', wasn't it?" Cassie laughed at Pippa.

Pip had first met Mitch 'the Rookie' Harris when he'd joined the rugby league team her father had coached. Rookie had been a cocky twenty-year-old, full of potential. Quick and with a natural footy brain, he had been instrumental in the Jets' winning the premiership that year. Pippa had been a fifteen-year-old girl coming into womanhood, and Rookie had stolen her heart. He had been her first love.

"Not likely, after the disgrace of five years ago," Pippa answered with a hint of sadness in her tone. She'd thought fulfilling her fantasies with Rook before heading off to uni would be a good idea, but the humiliation when he'd calmly removed her hands from his body and told her 'no' was one she was unlikely to forget. "My God, I bared my breasts to him and he turned me down. I'm not his type. Rook will just have to stay a fantasy."

"Yeah, well, let's just see about that, Pip. Fantasy man is heading this way—and it's not me he's undressing with those sinful eyes. Stay calm and see what happens. This will be your last chance at him. You told me Coach James has a strict no-fraternisation rule, and as of next Monday, you will be part of the Jets staff. I don't think you will ever find a man that lives up to your fantasy of Rook—now is your chance to get him out of your system and then maybe you can move on."

Pip understood what Cassie was saying. Up to this point in Pippa's life, no man had been able to measure up to the fantasy she'd created around the Sydney Jets halfback, and Pippa was not sure if even the man himself could. Feeling a bit like a startled deer, she watched this more mature Rook saunter confidently towards their table. His blond hair, which he had once worn long and flowing around his face as he ran, was now short and flicked back from his high cheekbones.

"Hello, ladies, are you having a good time tonight? You certainly have brightened up the club with your beauty." Rook's voice was smooth and sexy as he spoke, and he didn't once take his eyes off her, Pippa Rodgers—the same woman he had once refused.

Pippa couldn't speak, worried that if she tried her mouth might just gape open unflatteringly.

Finally, to her relief, Cassie saved the day by making small talk, explaining to Rook that they were out celebrating, adding that it seemed like a great club. All the while, Pippa just stared at Rook, probably doe-eyed, and trying unsuccessfully to stop her body from reacting to the sight and smell of the man who had starred in so many of her fantasies. Her nipples tightened—she felt them pushing through the soft fabric of her dress as her channel clenched and grew moist in hopeful anticipation of being pleasured. She wasn't sure, but she thought she might have even moaned out loud.

Rook asked the girls if he could buy them a bottle of champagne in honour of their celebration and waited for a response, his silver-grey eyes twinkling.

Under the weight of that stare, Pippa felt she would just melt. She imagined herself as a piece of satin material sliding from the stool and pooling on the floor at his feet.

Finally, with every ounce of concentration possible and her tongue feeling as if it was stuck to the top of her mouth, she managed to squeak out a single word. "Yes."

"Okay, then, that's great. I'll be right back with the bubbly, and princess, don't you dare go anywhere." Rook touched his finger ever so lightly to Pippa's chin before he turned and backtracked to the bar, leaving her shaking in response to his touch.

"Oh…*Lordy*! I think I'm going to die. My body is on fire and all he did was touch my chin. What am I going to do, Cass? Do you think he knows who I am?" Pippa whispered anxiously.

"Pip, I don't reckon he recognises you. Why should he? You look so different now to when he last saw you. But, my girl, he certainly is interested. That's as plain as the nose on his gorgeous face. I'm feeling a bit like the ugly stepsister, here," Cassie joked, trying to lighten her friend's mood.

She continued, "Pip, go for it. Finally get Rookie out of your system once and for all. Don't even tell him who you are, just enjoy tonight for what it is—your fantasy. Then maybe you can move on and find a nice, rich man to make you happy! I'll stick around for a glass and then make up some excuse. Wake me as soon as you get home. I want all the down-and-dirty details, girl." Cassie winked at Pip just before Rook returned to their table, with a bottle in an ice bucket and three fluted glasses.

The loud *pop* as Rook effortlessly uncorked the bottle made Pippa jump, even though she had been expecting the sound. Rook expertly filled the three elegant glasses.

Rook handed the first flute to Cassie. He picked up the second and held it out to Pippa. As she lifted her hand to take the offered glass, he took it in his free hand. After brushing his lips over her palm he formally introduced himself.

"Hi, I'm Rook. What's your name, princess?"

Pippa froze. What should she say? Trying to stifle the sudden rise of hysteria overtaking her and knowing she had to think fast, she blurted out the first name that came into her head.

"Nice to meet you, Rook. My name is Cassandra," she said, ignoring the sputtering sound of her friend choking on a mouthful of champagne at hearing her own name coming from Pippa's mouth.

Finding her hidden seductress, even if it was for the first time, Pippa leaned towards Rook and, using the hand he still held, pulled him closer to her.

"Rook? That's a very unusual name. I don't think I've heard that before," she purred, taking the flute of champagne from him and sampling a small sip.

Pippa watched the movement in Rook's thick neck as he swallowed, mesmerised. She noticed his eyes glaze over, his tongue twitch over his lips. *Has it got incredibly hot in here or what?* she thought as the sound of her friend's voice broke into her reverie.

"Umm, guys? Hate to interrupt, but *Cassandra*, I have to leave," Cassie said.

Pippa had to stop herself from giggling, pleased at the sight of Rook's face filling with disappointment — he was probably thinking she would leave as well. He'd snapped his neck around so quickly in response to Cassie's comments that his head could have fallen off.

"It's okay. Rook, wasn't it? I'm sure you'll keep my friend here good company and send her home at midnight, before she turns into a pumpkin." Cassie grinned at Rook, winking as she made reference to his earlier 'princess' comment.

Rook, looking decidedly more comfortable with the new arrangement, went to great lengths to assure the real Cassie that he would indeed protect her friend with his life, ending with one of his best trademark heart-breaking smiles. The wattage of that smile had been known to send women swooning, as Pippa knew only too well.

Watching as the real Cassie grabbed her bag and walked away, Pippa couldn't help but wonder what she had just got herself into.

Looking for some Dutch courage to get her through the night ahead, Pippa up-ended her champagne glass and swallowed the bubbly liquid down in one gulp. Her mouth was so dry from nerves that the fluid hardly touched the sides. Trying to act calmer than she felt, the tornado whirling around in her stomach making it hard to breathe, Pippa — or was that Cassandra? — leaned in even closer to Rook and repeated her question about his unusual name. All the while, she searched his eyes for any sign that he recognised her as the coach's daughter who had all but undressed herself in front of him five years ago, only to be rejected and humiliated in return.

She pushed the moral dilemma of her contractual obligations to not get intimate with her co-workers firmly pushed to the back of her mind. Having decided to continue with the charade and see what happened, for better or for worse, Pippa was now determined to give herself this night and be damned with the consequences. All she had to do was make sure she didn't say or do anything that might clue Rook in to the fact that she was the girl from so long ago who used to follow him around making goo-goo eyes at him. "No problem!" she whispered into her empty glass.

Chapter Two

This was a first for Rook—he normally steered clear of the women that frequented his bar. It wasn't a clever idea to mix business with pleasure at the best of times, but add in the whole footballer thing and it was a headline waiting to happen. The media loved nothing better than a 'footballer behaving badly' story, but the woman was a stunner. Rook could not believe his luck. She looked familiar but Rook couldn't place why. She reminded him of some fairytale elfin creature with her shiny black hair that wisped around her pretty face.

Maybe she's in one of those TV soapies or something and that's why she looks familiar, he'd thought to himself as he'd headed towards the table she was sitting at.

Though at first she had seemed distant—her blonde friend had done most of the talking—the dark-haired beauty was now holding onto his hand and looking at him with a set of big, blue eyes the colour of the Pacific Ocean, and nearly as deep. It was all he could do not to smother those pert, pink lips with his.

She wanted to know about his name, so obviously she didn't recognise him. *This princess must be from out of town*, he thought. It wasn't very often that he didn't get recognised straight away, especially in his own club. The high public profile of his successful sporting career was something Rook had become used to over the last seven years. It could be annoying at times, but it was rewarding when he could use his profile in a positive way to help a charity raise much-needed funds or bring a smile to a sick kid's face.

"Well, Cassandra, Rook is actually a nickname. When I was younger it was 'the Rookie', but now it's just Rook. My birth name is Mitchell, but you can call me whatever you want. So, princess, do you live around here?"

Rook stared at her pretty mouth as her lips moved in answer to his question, imagining the feel of those soft, supple lips under his.

"Yes, I've just moved back to the area. I've been away finishing my studies. I love the inner west, but this is the first time I've been to this club. It's not bad. I don't mean to sound clichéd, but do you…*come*…here often?"

He nearly swallowed his tongue when she smiled seductively back at him as she emphasised the word *come* quite suggestively.

Rook loved the sound of her voice. It wasn't shrill or cute—it was deep and sexy, the sound of it caressing over him, making his cock twitch with awareness.

"I'm glad you like the club—I own it," Rook admitted proudly as he refilled Pippa's champagne flute. "I've tried hard to keep the club drug- and trouble-free, safe for all patrons… What did you study?"

"Oooh! I love this song," Pippa purred. "Do you dance, Rook? I just love dancing to this song."

Rook quickly took the hint. How could any red-blooded male refuse the purring of her voice? At that moment, with her looking so eagerly at him, the flutter of her lashes over those baby blues adding to her questioning plea, Rook was definitely not only red-blooded, but also very hot-blooded. The chance to put his hands on the gorgeous woman was not one he was about to miss. So, forgetting the conversation, Rook took her by the hand and led her to the dance-floor.

He could not believe the intensity of the attraction he was feeling for this stranger. As he pulled her into his arms, his whole body went up in flames. Where their bodies rubbed together, his skin felt as if it had been licked by a firestorm. He had been with plenty of women over the years, his league career making him even more appealing to some women, yet he had felt this initial electricity only once before. But that had been so long ago — years ago, when he'd been but a youngster.

Rook was a little shaken up over the sexual tension he was feeling. It was not like he had even been looking to hook up tonight. He had just popped down to speak to his bar manager about some shift changes when he had felt her eyes on him. Rook didn't understand why he had cared that she was looking at him — lots of people stared at the Sydney Jets halfback, and he was used to it.

But this had been different. He had felt her eyes on him, had been instantly drawn to her from where he'd stood half a room away at the bar. Rook was glad he hadn't wasted any time in introducing himself, especially now that she was wrapped in his arms. He could feel the hard nubs of her nipples pressing into his chest and he was sure she could feel his hard length pressed up against her flat abdomen. Not overly tall, she seemed to fit nicely against him. She tucked her head under his chin and he rubbed it against her soft hair. Wisps of it caught in his stubble. Rook had known that her shiny black hair would feel silky to touch.

God, he had to taste her, couldn't wait any longer. He knew he was moving fast but she seemed to be just as eager, if the way she was rubbing her hot, lithe body against his was any indication. The fact that she didn't seem to know of him was an added bonus, in Rook's opinion. There was just good, old-fashioned lust and want raging between them.

It had been a long time since Rook had wanted a woman this much, and he was enjoying the feeling, he had to admit. It felt good to be just regular Mitch Harris for a change, and he was going to see where the attraction led. Perhaps relocating to a more private arena, that of his apartment above the bar, would be on the cards.

Not keen on answering any questions regarding her studies—mentioning her physiotherapy degree was certain to raise red flags—Pippa had distracted Rook by requesting he dance with her. He had seemed only too happy to oblige her, quickly pulling her to her feet and leading the way to the dance floor.

Pippa had noticed they'd seemed to be the centre of attention. Obviously, the club's patrons had been keen to know who had caught famous Rook Harris' eye. She'd just hoped no one would recognise her as the daughter of the retired Jets coach.

As Rook had pulled her into his arms, his body pressing hard against her own, Pippa had forgotten all about the interested onlookers. Her body was sparking with desire. She could almost hear the electricity snap and crackle between them.

She was in heaven.

All her dreams were coming true. Rook's strong arms were wrapped around her, she could feel his erection pressed up against her stomach and her pussy ached for it. She was just wondering if she should grab hold of that hard form when Rook whispered in her ear.

"Oh, Cassie, you're so hot."

Pippa lifted her face to look up at him, confused for a moment by Rook whispering the wrong name. His lips came down on hers. Shocked, not expecting the movement, Pippa opened her mouth in a little gasp. Rook took full advantage and thrust his tongue in past her lips, caressing both sides of her mouth, exploring every inch before his tongue began to mate with hers. A dance of seduction.

Pippa was melting. She wondered if she could orgasm from just kissing, as this man she had longed for totally consumed her.

When Rook's mouth finally released hers, Pippa felt the loss. She wanted his tongue back inside her and moaned in complaint. Rook smiled down at her and ran his fingertip along the length of her bottom lip.

"Hell, princess, you have me so hot and horny I just want to rip the clothes from your sexy body and have you right here on the dance floor. Luckily, my apartment is upstairs. I promise you so much pleasure that the people down here will hear your moans over the music."

Pippa's mouth went totally dry, her tongue sticking to its roof yet again. All she could manage was a slight nod of her head in consent. The things Rook had said caused an overflow of sexual hunger. She could feel her folds weeping, cream coating her panties as images of him and how he would go about fulfilling his promise swamped her mind.

Rook led Pippa back towards the bar. He leaned over and said something she couldn't quite hear to the burly-looking barman. The man looked over at her as if he knew what was happening and smiled, before handing Rook another bottle of wine and two fresh glasses.

Pippa felt uncomfortable under the barman's gaze. *He's probably used to seeing women throw themselves at Rook*, she thought, feeling a bit sleazy. She was acting as bad as one of those groupies she'd had to watch fawn over the Jets players back when she'd been just a kid, hanging around the team because of her dad. To distract herself from the unsettling train of thought flitting through her mind, Pippa focused on Rook's very shapely back. She could see the rippling of his deltoids and lat muscles as he lifted the bottle and glasses in one hand.

Turning to face her, he graced her with another breathtaking smile as he spoke. "You ready to head upstairs? I want to make sure you know the score. What you're getting into. I'm about to spend a good few hours devouring your body, tasting every inch of it before I impale your pussy on my cock and fuck you long and hard. Are you okay with that, princess?"

The wicked grin that had appeared on Rook's face and the words he'd spoken made Pippa pull him along impatiently. Unfortunately, she didn't know exactly which way to go, so it was of course in the wrong direction. Her mistake was quickly rectified, though, by her silver-eyed fantasy man as he led her back towards the club's entrance, through a door marked *Private* and up the stairwell to a narrow landing and another door.

After pulling a set of keys from his jeans' pocket, Rook unlocked the door. It took Pippa a minute before she could get her bearings, her eyes adjusting to the soft lighting eventually. She was moving down a hallway. On the walls to either side of her, she glimpsed framed memorabilia spanning Rook's career, but didn't get the chance to study any intently as Rook continued farther into his apartment, finally coming to a halt in a large room.

Pippa found herself standing in what was obviously the living room. A kitchen was connected to the far side of the room by a breakfast bar. Rook's apartment was all male. A black leather sofa with two matching recliners sat in front of the largest television screen she had ever seen. A chrome and glass coffee table sat on a silver and black patterned rug. Black wall units containing DVDs, CDs and books ran the length of one wall, while the opposite wall was covered in dark vertical blinds.

The open blinds allowed enough glow from the streetlights and moonlit sky to fill the room, also revealing a spectacular view of the Sydney city skyline.

Pippa was drawn to the large glass windows and the view of the city. She could clearly see the lights of Sydney's Centrepoint Tower, the restaurant level sitting above the other buildings in the city. She could also make out the top of the grey metal arch that was the Harbour Bridge.

Behind her the soft strains of music filled the room, followed by the abrupt sound of another champagne bottle cork popping.

"Oh, that's cold," she whispered as Rook stroked a flute containing pink champagne down her cheek and across her lips.

Wrapping her hand around his fingers, which were still holding the glass, Pippa turned to face Rook. She brought the pink, bubbly liquid level to her lips and took a sip, running her wet tongue around the rim of the glass, then over her top lip. All the while, she looked up into Rook's silver eyes. *My God, I could drown in those eyes*, she thought.

Her desire, her need to feel Rook's hands all over her body made her impatient, giving her a surge of wanton courage. Pippa reached behind her back and undid the zipper that held her clingy dress together, then swayed slightly so the fabric fluttered from her body to pool around her feet.

She stood still, watching him.

Her lacy, sheer black bra and matching thong, thigh-high stay-up hosiery and six-inch stilettos were all that were between her and her fantasy.

Chapter Three

Rook loved her sexy underwear and her self-confidence, the way she had casually unzipped her dress and let it float to the floor. He had been trying to control his body's reaction to her lips rimming the lucky champagne glass—imagining that the glass was the head of his throbbing cock had sent shivers up and down his spine. When her dress had hit the floor, the only coherent thought in Rook's head had been, *I'm in lust!* Finishing the sweet, pink liquid in one mouthful and placing the glass on the table, Rook took a few moments to admire the view before him.

He could see her nipples pressing against the flimsy material of her bra and his mouth watered—he wanted to taste those ripe berries. Dragging his eyes away from her pert breasts, Rook let his gaze drop lower over her small waist, flat stomach and womanly shaped hips. He lingered for a few seconds to admire the tiny scrap of material that just managed to cover her pussy before moving on to relish the sight of the bare tops of her creamy thighs. His gaze roamed all the way down her long, shapely, stocking-covered legs to her feet, arched high in the sexiest 'fuck me' stilettos he had ever seen.

It was one awesome picture. A wet dream come true.

"Fuck, you're beautiful, Cassandra." It was all he could manage, before he dropped to his knees and nuzzled the soft mound between her legs. Worshipping all that beauty.

Rook ran his hands up and down the length of her silken legs as he rubbed his face against her covered pussy. He loved the way she arched her hips closer to his face, and as a reward he slipped a finger under the wisp of fabric that covered her soft curls and ran it down one side of her labia and up the other, giving the hard little nub of her clit a quick flick.

She moaned and shivered as his finger slowly entered her tight pussy — he felt the slight quake run down her whole body. Finding it hard to control himself, Rook stood and took her mouth with his, thrusting his tongue in and out, matching the rhythm of his ministrations down below. He could feel her inner muscles clench hungrily at him.

Ignoring her moans of protest, Rook pulled his cream-coated digit away from her wetness and licked it clean. She tasted exotic and sweet. Intoxicating.

He moved his attention to her tightly puckered nipples, first blowing lightly on one before tugging at it with his teeth as he rolled and pinched at the other. Rook, inspired by her crooning sounds and the never-ending rub of her body against him, flicked open the front clasp of her bra, catching the tender soft mounds into his palms as the bra released the glorious gifts from its hold. He smiled inwardly, the knowledge he was turning her on pleasing him, as she threw her arms around his head and dragged him closer, pulling his mouth hard against one of her protruding nipples.

"Rook!" She cried out his name in a desperate plea.

After suckling for a few moments on each nipple, Rook returned to his knees and slid her panties down her legs, lifting one of her feet at a time to release the frilly lace completely.

"Princess, lean back against the chair and put one leg over my shoulder. I want to drink you dry."

Rook was happy when she complied with his request, and he parted her folds with his thumbs, thrusting his tongue into that warm channel. The woman was so wet and tasty. Rook could have eaten her pussy for hours, but the pain of his rock-hard length pushing against the front of his jeans was distracting him. He needed to fulfil her needs first, make her come apart against his mouth, so he could ram his cock into her warm, inviting pussy. He added two fingers to her moist channel, devouring and thrusting in and around as he flattened his tongue over her clit and applied a steady pressure. He heard her whimper and felt her nails score his scalp. She was close. Rook picked up the pace and the pressure.

The clenching of her inner muscles and release of warm, sweet juices over his chin, combined with her long, low groan, were enough to confirm her orgasm. He continued to lick and suck until she pushed frantically at his head.

"Stop! It's too much." She moaned the words softly.

Releasing her leg from his shoulder and steadying her against the back of the chair, Rook moved a little away from her enticing scent and rose from his knees. He quickly shucked off his shirt, boots and jeans, finally allowing his cock to pop free, and covered the hard length with a condom he'd retrieved from his wallet. Rook lay down on the rug, on his back and reached for her hand.

"Come ride me, princess."

Chapter Four

Pippa had never, in all her dreams, come close to imagining the feeling of Rook's mouth on her pussy. She was lost in the moment. Her fantasies had been nowhere near as good as the real deal. When he'd brought her up and over the abyss, her body had shuddered uncontrollably in pure delight.

The sensations engulfing her were new to Pippa. She had never experienced anything like them before. In her few previous sexual encounters, she had never been brought to orgasm by a man's mouth. In fact, she had very rarely orgasmed at all.

Was it just because it was *Rook's* mouth? Pippa didn't know and didn't waste time thinking about it. She was going to make the most of this one night and ride Rook's shaft for all she was worth.

Pippa straddled Rook's body and slowly impaled herself on his hard length, her wet pussy swallowing him greedily as her muscles clenched around him. The sight of him lying beneath her was almost enough to bring her to climax again. Rook's broad chest was covered in a thatch of blond curls. His pectoral muscles contracted under her palms. She stroked and counted off the distinct raised outlines of the six-pack of muscles that made up his abdomen—the man was truly cut.

She was trying to take mental photographs of the scene in front of her, wanting to remember, in detail, every moment of this night and this man—to freeze the moment in her memory bank forever. Something to remember, to savour, to bring out on those lonely nights when all she had to quench her sexual desires was the vibrator she kept hidden in her bedside drawer.

Lifting her body up and then thrusting down on his shaft, using her strong thighs, she rubbed and caressed Rook's chest, enjoying the look of pleasure on his face. Reaching one hand behind her hips, she found the sac bouncing underneath Rook's cock and cupped it, gently rolling the soft flesh in her fingers. Rook's silver eyes became larger, looked hungrier as he grabbed her hips, pressing his fingers almost painfully into her skin, and started to pound into her, his rhythm becoming more forceful. One minute she was sitting astride his hips, the next she was sprawled out beneath him. He had taken control, rolling her over, and was now pumping into her, his pelvis grinding up against her clit with every thrust.

Pippa could feel the pressure building in her body again as his cock continually bumped against her G-spot. Every touch and thrust brought her closer to that edge, towards the high of yet another exquisitely pleasurable climax. Heat and pleasure consumed her and as Pippa's body finally shuddered in completion, she heard Rook moan. He thrust his hips one last time, straining, before collapsing down on her.

Aware that Rook would need to dispose of the condom soon, Pippa lay still under his weight, enjoying the feel of it on her, the warmth of his body on hers, making the most of every second she had with her fantasy man. Willing it to never end. For time to stand still so she could remain in this moment of pure joy. Her dreams, her desires, had finally become reality. *And oh, what a reality.* But, just as she had anticipated, Rook all too quickly extracted himself from her body.

"Wow, that was… Are you okay? I didn't hurt you, did I?" Rook spoke softly as he stroked her cheek, and rained kisses over her throat and shoulder. He lifted his head and propped himself up on his elbows.

Pippa was caught up in the beauty of his eyes, his face. Those high cheekbones, that mouth. Everything she had ever dreamed of, staring down at her.

"I need to bin this rubber—why don't you come and have a spa bath with me? I've got a beauty installed in the bathroom. We could have a relaxing soak together."

Pippa smiled at Rook's tender attitude. It could have been awkward, the whole post-coital thing, but it wasn't. As he stood and held out his hand to help her to her feet, she felt completely at ease, even though they were both completely naked.

They walked hand in hand down another hallway, past what appeared to be Rook's bedroom, and into a large bathroom.

Pippa was fascinated at the way Rook casually removed the used rubber and tossed it into the waste bin, not at all embarrassed or uncomfortable with his actions in front of her. All the while, he was chatting away about the benefits of a long soak in the spa to ease stiff or sore muscles after a game, or strenuous exercise—the latter comment was followed by a cheeky grin. Pippa realised it was the first time Rook had mentioned playing rugby league. It was almost surreal, standing nude in Rook's bathroom, watching him clean his manhood in front of her as if it was the most natural thing in the world.

Pippa couldn't help the sour thought that invaded her mind—she wondered how often Rook must have sex with strangers to get that nonchalant about what seemed to her such a personal cleansing ritual. But as disturbing as the thought was, she quickly banished it again. There was no time to dwell, no reason to taint her fantasy night.

Pippa loved being in the spa, wrapped in Rook's arms. Being able to stroke his legs and feel all that masculine power beneath her fingertips made her pussy clench in neediness again. When Rook began nibbling on her ear and neck, she couldn't contain the moan that spilled from her. She lifted her mouth to his and licked at his bottom lip, begging for entry. Rook quickly granted her leave to explore his mouth, doing the same to hers in return.

Rook's kisses were intoxicating. Pippa had been kissed but never so thoroughly that she lost her grip on reality. She let her mind drift and just enjoyed the feel of his tongue as it plundered and consumed her mouth. She was in heaven. She didn't know how long they had been kissing for—it could have been minutes, hours or days—but she felt the loss when Rook pulled away.

"Kneel up and lean over the edge of the spa, princess. I need you again. Oh, babe, I need to feel my cock buried deep inside you. Are you wet for me, as ready for me as I am for you? I can't get enough of you."

Rook's words were rough, almost a demand, but the look in his eyes was so desperate that Pippa felt cream coat her inner folds. She could not deny him. She wanted him, had always wanted him.

He entered her in one movement. His length filled her so completely as he thrust into her again and again. His body surrounded her, his hands on either side of her, gripping the side of the spa to give him support as he took her, ramming himself into her over and over. She clenched, pushing back on him, feeling his balls slap against her. It was lustful. Powerful. Primitive. It did not take long before another tidal wave of pleasure began to build, an uncontrollable peak her body careened helplessly towards. She did not want it to stop.

Crying out—"More!" and "Harder!"—Pippa was finding it difficult to hold her body up under the onslaught of his passion. She clung to the side of the spa as her breasts bounced over the edge, the sensitive undersides of her bosom dropping onto the coldness of the bath's tiles, the shock of that chilly sensation in complete contrast to the rest of her body's fierce heat, causing her nipples to tighten even more. Sensations surrounded her, owning her.

Finally, as Pippa forced her body down and Rook thrust his up, her orgasm exploded. It felt as if the Sydney Harbour's New Year's fireworks display had been released inside her head. Pippa shuddered and screamed Rook's name as she trembled. Tremors of pure pleasure arced and raced throughout every nerve ending of her sated being, immersing her in a sensation so sweet, so delicious that she wanted to prolong the sensation—maybe forever.

Rook tugged her back down onto him, immersed them back into the warmth of the water. The bubble of the jets, as they came to life once again, massaged her limp body. Heaven could only wish to be this wonderful.

The spa was a great idea, Rook thought. The whole awkward issue of what to do after sex had been quickly sorted. He'd never cleaned his dick in front of a woman before, but somehow it didn't seem unnatural in front of Cassie. As Rook sat in the warm spa with his arms around her middle, hugging her to his chest, stroking the undersides of her floating breasts, he felt complete. He just wished he had turned on the main light so he could see her more clearly. Her little moans and sighs as he stroked her leg filled him with emotions he could not comprehend. He could not remember sex ever being so intense.

Holding this woman in his arms felt so right. Rook really didn't understand his emotions or what was happening, but he knew that Cassandra was definitely becoming part of his life, no matter what it took to convince her. The thought made him smile.

Decision made, Rook began to nibble on the sexy earlobe that had been resting so temptingly against his lips. He had just experienced the most satisfying, erotic moment of his life. Just remembering the image of her draped over the edge of his spa, her delicate back arched as he took her from behind, had his dick growing hard again. The fact that she hadn't hesitated to comply with his demands of her had added more to the fulfilment. She was a dream come true — the way she had submitted to his needs so easily, the sight of her body stretched over his spa bath, spread for him, those round globes of her arse beckoning invitingly… Rook had not been able to resist thrusting his throbbing shaft into her pussy forcefully, filling her. She'd been so responsive to him, slamming herself back onto him. He'd thrust up, and their mating had been almost animalistic in its intensity.

The temptation to roar like a wild beast, mark her as his, had been hard for Rook to deny. He had almost shouted, "Mine!"

When she'd screamed his name, Rook had exploded into her body, shooting his wad high and hard, filling her with his warm seed. He'd felt the orgasm start from the tip of his toes and race up his body as his balls had grown tight and the blood had rushed from all other parts to centre on his dick. Rook had thought he would pass out, but had had just enough energy left to pull them back into the water, to drag her against his chest.

As they lay panting, trying to recover to catch their breath, Rook finally realised his mistake—his lack of protection. What had he been thinking? Well, that was easy to answer—his brain had not been thinking, but, by God, his cock had.

"Cassandra, that was fucking amazing. You are amazing, *this* is amazing… Lying here with you in my arms. We have to see each other again. I also owe you a huge apology. I forgot to use a condom. Shit, babe, I'm so sorry. I never forget. But I can assure you I'm clean. Don't suppose you are on the pill?"

Rook waited for Cassandra to answer his question or make some comment about the fact they had just shared unprotected sex. He was starting to think she hadn't heard him, maybe had drifted off to sleep as they lay in the warm, soothing waters of the spa. That was, until he heard her quick gasp of breath and felt her whole body go tense. He relaxed his grip around her waist as she struggled free of his embrace and scrambled away from him, moving as far from him as she could in the small confines of the tub. The spa water, which had seemed so relaxing, was now churning and splashing up between them.

"Oh, shit. Umm, yes, I am on the pill... I didn't realise..."

"I'm so sorry, princess. I really have never forgotten a condom before. It was very careless, but you're so goddamn hot I wasn't thinking straight. I know that's no excuse, and I want you to know that if anything might happen..."

Rook was desperately trying to put into words that he felt a connection to Cassandra and wanted to see her again, but before he could make his thoughts clear, she interrupted.

"Look, we made a mistake—both of us—but I'm sure it will be fine." Cassie had her hands over her breasts, obscuring them from his view, and Rook thought that his princess' voice sounded a bit shaky.

It didn't surprise him that she would be worried—truth was, he was worried as well. But not as worried over the lack of protection as he was about her attempts to hide her body from him, or the way she was clearly distancing herself. Rook wanted Cassandra back in his arms so he could reassure her that it would all be okay.

"I'm sure everything will be fine, princess. I really mean it when I say I want to see you again. I don't know anything about you, not even your last name—which is totally wrong, and I'm sorry about that too. Move back over here with me and let me put my arms around you while we talk for a while. Get to know each other, maybe sort out where and when I can take you out for dinner."

God, he sounded like he was begging, but for a reason he couldn't explain there was something about this woman—apart from the mind-blowing sex they had just shared—that intrigued him. Made him want to see her again, which was totally out of character for him. Usually, he just wanted to get away from the willing groupie or one-night stand as soon as he could.

"Look, I don't think that's such a good idea. I'm sorry, Rook, but I really need to get out of here, go home. Do you have a towel I can use to get dried off?"

Chapter Five

Pippa had been revelling in the knowledge of how mind-blowing the sex with her fantasy man had been, so it had taken her a few moments for the realisation to sink in that Rook had been speaking to her. The fact that he'd called her Cassandra had brought her crashing back to reality quickly. It had reminded her of her deception. She had put both of their careers in jeopardy—well, only his, really. Hers had hardly begun. And he was being so sweet. So caring, not the way she had expected him to be, given that she had so eagerly spread her legs for him, like some kind of slut. Her fantasy was starting to feel a little tarnished.

She had to go now. She was just about to fall apart and tell him the truth. And that couldn't happen. Pippa had tricked Rook into breaking one of the Jets' golden rules—*no fraternisation between staff*. She had lied to him about who she really was and their past. She had to get away now, as much as that broke her heart. At least she had some breathtaking memories, ones that would keep her warm at night. No one could take those away from her.

Trying to act cool and collected, Pippa rose from the spa and grabbed the towel off the rack Rook had pointed to. She wrapped it around her naked body. "Hey, Rook? Thanks. I'm sure there is nothing to worry about, it's been great. *You've* been great, but I do need to get home. While I get dressed, can you call me a cab?"

"Bloody hell, what's going on?" When Rook stood up, Pippa had to tamp down her desire to take one last look at his amazingly sexy form. He was raking his fingers through his hair and he sounded agitated. "I don't want to put you in a cab. I want to drive you home. I promised your friend I would look after you."

"Look, it's all good. I'm a big girl and can get home all by myself. I'd rather take a cab," she said as she finally worked up the courage to look at Rook's face. "Let's not make this more than it is. It's been wonderful, you're a fantastic lover, but the night is over."

She was just holding it together. The confused, hurt look Rook was giving her almost had her throwing her arms around him and begging him for forgiveness. But she knew there would be no hope once the truth was out there. They both had careers to think about. Being together at the Jets was not an option, given the club's views on this sort of thing.

* * * *

It was a relief to Pippa to not have to exit back out through the club. That walk of shame she could do without. Rook reluctantly led her through another entrance, this door leading to a different street frontage altogether. All the while, he tried to convince her to let him drive her home.

"At least give me your number. Maybe we can hook up again sometime."

As the taxicab pulled in, Rook leaned towards her to catch her mouth, obviously intending a farewell kiss. At the last second, Pippa turned her face so that his lips only landed on her cheek. She threw herself into the cab without a backwards glance, not answering his plea for her phone number. *He'll know how to contact me soon enough, unfortunately for him,* she thought sadly as the tears began to flow, now unstoppable, down her cheeks. She mumbled her home address tearfully, so that only the cabbie would hear, and slammed the door closed quickly behind her. The loud noise of the door closing, ending her fantasy night, sounded as loud to Pippa's ears as the crack of her heart splitting in two.

The moving car now took Pippa away from the night she had so longed for and the man she had always wanted. Even the frequent, worried glances from the driver were not enough to stem the overflow of her emotions.

The whole night had been a huge, wonderful mistake, Pippa was now realising. A fantasy no longer, the reality was set in stone.

No other man could ever take the place of Rook in her heart.

After assuring the taxi driver that she would be fine, that she was just emotional, Pippa stumbled up the path and into the house she shared with Cassie. Not bothering to turn on any lights, Pippa just rushed straight to her room, threw herself across her bed and cried. Cried until she was worn out, cried until there were no tears left in her. She was unable even to voice any words to let a worried Cassie know what was wrong. Those words eluded her as Pippa's heart broke into a million sharp splinters.

* * * *

Rook was still shaking his head over the demise of such an amazing night. One minute, he had been planning on taking this complete stranger out on a date, and the next she was running away without so much as a backward glance.

Sometimes his life felt so out of control. He knew he should be happy—he was playing the game he loved and he owned his own nightclub—but something was still missing in his life. He had this reputation for being some kind of womaniser, had helped build it by being less than selective when it came to bedding a woman, but the truth was he was tired of it.

That younger Rookie, so excited to be signed by a professional team, had just wanted to play rugby league. The fact that he made a good living from it was a bonus. He had been able to help his hard-working mother start up a business that put her more behind a desk and less behind a mop and bucket. He was forever grateful for that. But the public scrutiny? Well, he hadn't signed on for that. Hadn't even thought about it. No, notoriety had come without him choosing it, and with it had come the fans. He had been swept along, believing in his own hype. Taking advantage of it. But it had all started to wear thin quickly.

Rook really appreciated the traditional footy fans and their love and loyalty for the team he played for. They cheered at the games, paid their hard-earned cash to see the Jets team week after week. He could even understand their disappointment when the Jets lost. He loved the Jets and winning as well, but the women who just wanted to be able to say they had slept with him and made themselves available to him for a quick fuck had lost any sort of appeal lately. His fame and his high-profile life was not his reality. In his world it was all about hard work. Training all the time and travelling from game to game.

Did he not deserve to find someone special to share his life with? His gut was telling him that this woman, this Cassandra, was somehow different, someone worth getting to know. But apparently the feeling wasn't mutual. Perhaps this was some sort of karmic payback for his less than stellar lifestyle in the past.

"Fuck me," he said for the umpteenth time, no closer to understanding what had gone wrong. He had gone over every aspect of the night, remembering every inch of her body, every touch of her skin. There was something that made him uneasy, but he couldn't quite put his finger on it.

Sitting in one of his black leather recliners, Rook finished the remains of the now sickly sweet-tasting, bubbly liquid and stared off into the pre-dawn sky.

"I've got to find her again."

Chapter Six

Pain was the first thing Pippa felt as she opened her eyes.

They were swollen and, she had no doubt, red from the amount of tears she had shed. There was so much pain in her heart as she relived the memory of fleeing Rook's apartment, not once looking back. The pain was made sharper by the knowledge that Rook had not recognised her. She had meant so little to him, been so inconsequential in his life that he'd had no memory of her at all. And after all the hours she had spent trying to survive her humiliation at his rejection of her, the infatuated teen willing to offer herself up completely to him. That night, so many years ago, still haunted Pippa. What on earth had she been thinking, throwing herself at him like that?

She had been an innocent young girl heading away from home for the very first time, to begin a university degree at an institution many miles away. She had been infatuated with the young star of her father's rugby league team for the past few years, and Pippa had decided that it was time to let Rookie know her true feelings towards him—to seduce him before she left town. If she gave him her virginity, he would obviously give her his undying love and promise to wait for her to return to the big city so they could marry, buy a white picket-fenced house and live happily ever after.

Unfortunately, Pippa had not envisioned Rookie's reaction to her little fantasy, had not let him read the script she had so often dreamed of. The poor guy had looked nothing but embarrassed for her as he'd pushed her bare-breasted body away from him, and fled.

Looking back at her younger self, Pippa was horrified at her own naïvety. She couldn't even fathom how she had worked up the courage to seduce Rookie, let alone to strip off her shirt and thrust her breasts at the poor boy—and in her own family's backyard, at an event the whole Jets team had been attending. But still the humiliation of his rejection tore deep. Especially now, with the knowledge that he had slept with her tonight, albeit as a relative stranger, confirming beyond doubt that he just hadn't been into her back then. Yes, she had made a complete fool of herself thinking that Rookie would have been even slightly interested in her—a young innocent—that way, when he had women throwing themselves at him.

But now she'd lived her fantasy and the night had been magical. She needed to focus on that. *You got exactly what you wanted, Pippa,* she told herself angrily. *Now you just have to learn to live with it.*

Pippa dragged herself up from the bed, hoping that a shower and fresh clothing would make her feel better. *Yeah, right, like that's going to mend my shattered heart.*

Clean, but still emotionally empty, Pippa headed towards the smell of coffee drifting from the kitchen, knowing her friend deserved an explanation for the hysterical behaviour of the previous night.

Cassie was understanding and supportive, as usual. Pippa knew she was lucky to have such a good friend.

After many coffees and rounds of toast smothered in Vegemite, a few more bouts of tears and outpourings of grief, Pippa was starting to feel slightly better. She had a lot to be happy about—the night with Rook and the memory of it had been everything she had dreamed of since she was fifteen, and more. She should focus on those memories. Then, all she would have to do was act strong as she faced up to him at the Jets' training session tomorrow, all without becoming a blubbering basket case. *No worries!*

Her first session as her father's beloved Jets team's new physiotherapist and injury recovery specialist could, in fact, be her last. Pippa only hoped Rook didn't tell her new boss—his ex-teammate and now coach, Brodie James—what she had done. Technically, Pippa tried to convince herself, she had not been part of the team last night, so the team rules had not applied to her, and wouldn't until contracts were signed tomorrow.

"Hope Coach James is not too pedantic about his rules," Pippa whispered to the room with a long sigh.

* * * *

Rook would be glad when the season began. He hated all the pre-season training, especially the sand hills. Running up and down the soft sand hills at Kurnell made his legs quiver with exhaustion. The pain from muscles grown soft over the off season, as they were worked back into shape ready for the brutal aspects of the total-body contact sport that was rugby league, was not pleasurable.

The pre-season training seemed to get harder each year. Probably as Rook got older — or that was what his once idol, teammate and now coach liked to joke. Rook had been a cheeky know-it-all teen when he first met Brodie James. Brodie had been captain of the Sydney Jets and the Australian team. One of the best forwards in the game, he had been partnered in the front row with the fiercest, toughest prop forward ever — Jonathon 'JT' Thomson. Cap and JT had helped Rook become the man he was.

Brodie had been the strongest male mentor in Rook's life. Rook had often wondered how his life would have been if he'd had a father of Brodie James' calibre — not that his mother hadn't given him everything. She had, at personal cost to herself. But still, Rook often just speculated on what it would have been like to have a male around the house. Someone to teach him stuff that only men knew, someone who would have taken some of the burden off his mother as she'd raised him. Brodie James would not have let her work so hard. Rook was sure of that. Then again, Rook had sorted out that problem, invested in his mother's cleaning company, so she didn't have to do the menial tasks anymore.

Coach had called a team meeting before today's training run, to meet the rest of this year's coaching and medical team. Rumour had it JT was going to take up a role as assistant coach, and one of the younger players had overheard Coach James talking about someone called Rodgers joining the staff. Dave Rodgers had been Rook's coach way back in that first premiership-winning season, and Rook was interested to see if that was the person Brodie had been overheard speaking about.

Enjoying the banter around the meeting room, listening to the young, up-and-coming players regaling stories of recent conquests or the older players marvelling at the latest technologies used in the modern games to enhance performance, Rook didn't notice the training staff enter. But hearing his coach calling out for everyone's attention, Rook, as the newly appointed captain, also tried to hush the rowdy group of men.

"C'mon, fellas, settle down. You can gossip about your recent sexual exploits later. Coach wants your attention."

After a few hoots and hollers from his teammates, the room quieted down and everyone's attention focused on Brodie. Rook took in the faces of the staff standing behind his coach, most familiar from last year. There was the conditioning coach, Bob, the sprint coach, Flash—who was another former player— and as rumoured, taking up an enormous amount of space, stood JT.

JT's position as a specialised coach for the forward pack and assistant coach to Brodie was not surprising to Rook, not with JT's pedigree. It was the last—but certainly not least—member of the Jets staff that left Rook absolutely shell-shocked. He recognised her straight away. Unbelievably, it was his princess from the other night.

He was still coming to grips with that discovery when it only got worse for Rook. He all but swallowed his tongue while he listened to his coach, Brodie James, introduce her.

"Some of you may remember this young lady. She certainly has been around the Jets for a long time. I'd like to introduce you all to our new physiotherapist in charge of injury prevention and recovery, specialising in some new and innovative areas in this field that will be invaluable to our team's success. Miss Phillipa Rodgers or Pippa, as she likes to be called these days, is the daughter of my good friend and mentor, the Jets' previous premiership-winning coach, Dave Rodgers. I'd like you all to welcome her aboard."

As the mumbling sounds of approval filled the room, Rook could not tear his eyes away from the woman standing in front of him. The woman Brodie was introducing. Everyone else was clapping and enthusiastically welcoming the staff and coaches, but Rook was too shocked to move. He couldn't seem to fathom all the information that was whirling through his brain. Her name wasn't Cassandra. It was Pipsqueak Rodgers. Phillipa Rodgers. Pippa.

"What the fuck is going on?" The words came from Rook's mouth a little louder than he had hoped. A few people looked over in his direction, startled by his outburst. One of them was JT.

"Hey, Rook, what was that? Did you say somethin'?" JT said as he headed Rook's way. "You okay, buddy? You're looking a bit pale. Not coming down with that bloody flu that's doing the rounds, are you? Mandy insisted I invite you over for a bit of a get-together on Wednesday. She and the kids will be disappointed if you're too sick to come," JT continued without really giving Rook a chance to answer. "Elaina is such a beauty and little Jay is starting to really enjoy kicking a footy around. Caitlin reckons Riley will be home from uni as well. So, are you in? Food is on about noon."

Rook was in such a state of shock, he didn't think he would be able to speak. He had really fucked up.

Sleeping with Pipsqueak could cost him his career. She knew that. What sort of game was she playing with him? He couldn't quell the waves of anger that started to swell inside him. He needed to get away— from her, the room, everyone—and think.

"Hey, Rook, you gonna answer me, mate?" JT asked, confusion and concern now showing openly on his face at Rook's inability to speak.

"Yeah, JT. Tell Mandy I'll be there at noon. Wednesday… Right. Gotta go. Tell Brodie I'll catch him later," Rook managed to rasp out to JT before turning and escaping from the room.

Chapter Seven

Pippa had been antsy all morning, waiting for this moment—the moment Rook realised her deception. Meeting Brodie James and the rest of the staff had been a bittersweet moment. Pippa had finally achieved her goals and become a part of the team that had meant so much to her as she was growing up. It had been so much a part of her father. Now she was employed and would be working next to such great ex-players as JT, Flash and Brodie. Pippa couldn't help but wonder, though, if it was to be a very short career. Would Rook tell Brodie about their tryst, or would he keep mum? Would he refuse to work with her? It would not be a good start to her career to have the captain against her appointment.

Expecting the worst—maybe anger or confusion—Pippa was shocked at the look of hurt that appeared in Rook's eyes. Those dazzling silver eyes that had been so full of hunger and passion the other night were now just staring at her, boring a hole straight through her heart and soul. Pippa did not hear Brodie's total endorsement of her. She missed seeing the looks of acceptance and approval of her pedigree and training that came from the other Jets players. All Pippa could focus on was the look of betrayal on Rook's face.

Pull yourself together! Finally, the mantra she had been repeating over and over in her head started to sink in. Pippa tore her gaze away from Rook and listened to the conversations taking place around her.

"Yes, Pippa is going to be an asset to the club. The work she has been doing to enable a speedier rehabilitation of injury, utilising some of the latest techniques, will be of great value to us. Quick recovery and the ability to get our best players back on the field are crucial in today's game. Isn't that right, Pippa?"

Luckily, Pippa heard Brodie's words and was able to answer him coherently.

If there was one thing Pippa knew, it was her job. Letting her brain take control over her cold, stony, broken heart, Pippa met and answered questions from the interested group surrounding her. She couldn't see Rook anyway now, and didn't know whether that was a good thing or a bad one.

The longer he stays away from me the better. It will give him a chance to get over his anger and maybe we will be able to work together, she thought, trying to find a positive angle in the face of such an impending disaster.

It was a good feeling, though, to be so easily accepted by the group of male athletes who could have reacted indifferently or been wary of the fact she was a woman. League had done a lot of growing up in the last decade—women were now treated with respect, their knowledge of the game accepted by most. Pippa was finding out firsthand that her views and speciality were going to be appreciated. It made her feel even worse, guiltier, that she had blatantly broken one of the cardinal rules by having a sexual encounter with one of her fellow Jets team members. *Maybe I should tell Brodie,* she thought miserably, *before this all gets too far along.*

"Well, I think that went well, don't you?"

Pippa's remorseful thoughts were interrupted by her new boss' question, and she gave him her full attention as he continued speaking.

"When JT and I were discussing your appointment, he was joking about when you were just a kid. All the time you spent hanging around, waiting for your dad. He also reminded me about the almighty crush you, and every other young girl, had on Rook. Do you remember?" Brodie seemed amused at the reminiscing.

Pippa froze, trying to ascertain whether Brodie was fishing or just innocently reflecting. In a voice calmer than she had anticipated, Pippa answered, "You mean back when I used to be so jealous that you took Riley into the sheds with you, but Dad would never let me in? Must have been my subconscious wanting to win one over on Dad, 'cause here I am, finally in those sheds after all." She gave a half-hearted laugh, trying to deflect the fact she hadn't mentioned her crush.

"You sure have, Pippa, but between you and me, your dad's as proud as punch that the Rodgers name is back linked to the Jets again. So am I. Anything you need, don't hesitate to ask. Oh, yeah, JT and Mandy are having a get-together on Wednesday and you're not only invited, but *expected* to be there. Okay?"

The conversation was obviously finished. Before Pippa could reply, Brodie's attention was called elsewhere. Left with her own thoughts, Pippa decided that she would just leave well enough alone—she really did want this job, and just hoped Rook would get over her little charade. After all, she had survived his rejection before.

Chapter Eight

Rook was still shaking when he got home. He threw his keys at the wall as he entered his apartment, in a futile attempt to dissipate some of the anger that was overwhelming him. Even though it was still early afternoon, Rook grabbed a beer from the fridge, cracked the top, and took a long pull of the bitter-tasting amber liquid. He didn't usually drink during the week, and never when the sun was still up.

"But desperate times call for desperate measures. Cheers to you, Rook!" he said to himself as he tipped the bottle up again, draining the remaining fluid. He grabbed another bottle, opening it and flicking the lid at the closed waste bin before heading over to flop down on a black leather chair, still trying to work it all out in his head.

"Is this some sort of ploy to get back at me for knocking her back five years ago?" he wondered aloud. "That's why she seemed so familiar, that electric feeling… Yep, it was always her." Rook remembered how hard it had been to push those hands away from his body all those years ago.

"What choice did I have?" he groaned. He had been told by both Coach Rodgers and his then assistant, Brodie James, that Pipsqueak was totally off limits to him. They had threatened him, saying his contract would be ripped up if he took advantage of her attraction to him, calling it just a crush! A young girl's fantasy!

No one had ever asked him what his feelings were towards the attractive, fun-loving girl.

"No, that's right. Bloody footy player not good enough for the coach's daughter," Rook grumbled, his anger not diminishing any as he recalled the night she had attempted to seduce him.

Pipsqueak—he'd never liked that nickname. It belittled her. Rook had never understood how others had not seen that she'd hated the title. She had been Phillipa to him, at least in his mind, and he had thought of her often, but she had been far too young for him. She had probably been just shy of eighteen the night she had followed him outside.

Rook had been at a party for the team thrown by the coach, her father. He had spent the night watching Phillipa, watching the dutiful daughter as she'd helped her mother play host to the rowdy group of burly men. She had carried trays of food back and forth and refilled drink glasses, all the while laughing and smiling at Rook's fellow teammates. He had been screaming inside, not wanting her to look that way at anyone else but him. Annoyed that she had intentionally not come near him at all.

Rook had wondered if maybe she had lost interest in him, her 'crush', as Brodie had called it, just a childish memory for her. She was, in Rook's eyes, certainly not a child anymore. He had gone outside into the backyard to get some fresh air, to get away from her smiling face — smiling at everyone but him.

He hadn't heard her follow him, had been surprised when she'd appeared almost out of thin air. The memory of her, so nervous, yet bold in her attempt at seducing him, was one Rook could not forget, right alongside the guilt and regret he still felt for the way he had treated her that night. She had removed her top and stood bare-breasted in front of him. It had been the most beautiful sight he had ever seen. When her hands had connected with his skin, the jolts of desire had seemed to burn a path over his body and straight to his heart. He'd truly liked the girl, had for a long time, and it wasn't the threats to his career that had made Rook walk away. No — it was that he'd known that he was unworthy of her.

She'd deserved more.

Rook had tried to avoid being alone in her company, more to protect her from him really — not that he had always achieved that goal. He remembered one night in particular, the night of Trevor Hughes' fundraiser. He had sat with her long into the night, chatting about life, about movies she liked, the music she listened too, mesmerised by her natural beauty. Her aura had been that of a sweet, likeable young lady, a girl he'd really felt very attracted to, but he had also realised that she was too naïve and inexperienced for him.

Given the clear threats to keep his distance from her, Rookie had come to the conclusion that he would have been taking advantage. Phillipa had a life ahead of her, and from what her father had bragged, a life that was going to be very successful. Rook didn't want to be the uneducated football player from a single-parent home who was holding her back. So, trying not to waver in his resolve, he had used every ounce of self-discipline he could muster while ignoring the look of pain on her beautiful face. As her eyes had filled with tears at his rejection, Rook had just fled from Phillipa, that night she had come to him with her heart on her sleeve in the darkness of her family's garden.

It was amazing to Rook that he had felt the exact same reaction to her touch again, so many years later.

"How could I have not recognised her? So she changed her hair, cut those blonde locks and coloured them black. Hadn't I secretly looked into those incredible blue eyes enough to remember them? What a fuck-up! Does she hate me that much, after all this time?" he chastised his stupidity aloud.

"Well, Princess Phillipa certainly isn't innocent anymore." Rook lifted his beer in salute at his own words as he remembered the things they had done the previous Saturday night.

He decided wisely, after finishing the sixth beer, that he would just get over it, but that she sure as hell wouldn't be touching him with her hot, deceitful little hands. He wasn't planning on getting injured. He drunkenly told himself that he would just steer clear of her sexy self and let her look after the other guys.

An image of her hands massaging the masculine bodies of his teammates flashed like a sword through Rook's mind. The image did not make him feel any better. No, not any better at all.

So after Rook had drunk the last beer from his fridge, as he contemplated the idea of going down to his club and raiding the well-stocked bar, he fell into a drunken slumber. He dreamt of the life he had imagined when he had discovered he had not used a condom—the life that contained Phillipa with a blonde-haired toddler nestled on her hip. Her blue eyes twinkled and the smile on her face showed the love he assumed was for him. But then the dream changed and another man appeared as the recipient of Phillipa's love, while Rook faded away into oblivion.

Chapter Nine

When Pippa arrived home Cassie was sitting on the couch reading, looking relaxed and contained, dressed in her usual attire of jeans and long-sleeved T-shirt with her blonde hair pulled back in a ponytail. Pippa couldn't help but note the differences between them now. At one time, they had commonly been mistaken for sisters. It wasn't just the change in Pippa's hair colour—it was more. Cassie had this air of calm surrounding her these days, an aura of confidence, probably honed to perfection due to her role as a teacher. The thought of standing in front of a roomful of angsty teens was enough to make Pippa break out in a sweat. Cassie had once confided in her that teenagers were like sharks—one sniff of blood in the water, or more literally fear or indecision, and they attacked unmercifully.

Pippa, in contrast to Cassie's calm demeanour, thought she probably looked like she had been through the washer twice. She collapsed down next to her friend, exhausted from her emotional day, and let out a long, drawn-out sigh. Cassie, taking one look at her, shook her head.

"Day didn't go so well then, I'm guessing by the look of you, Pip."

"It was horrible, Cass," Pippa replied mournfully, kicking off her shoes and tucking her legs up underneath her body. She wrapped her arms around herself, trying to hold the emotions and hurt at bay, to keep them from tearing her in two.

"How 'bout I make a pot of chamomile tea? I think we could both use a cup. Then you can tell me all about your day. In the meantime, Pip, sit back and take a few moments, try and relax. I'll be right back," Cassie soothed. Then she headed off into the kitchen, leaving Pippa to her own thoughts—thoughts she didn't really want to deal with, especially not on her own.

Shutting her eyes and letting her head fall against the back of the couch, Pippa listened to the sounds Cassie was making in the kitchen, familiar sounds. She heard the rumble of the kettle boiling and the chink of crockery as Cassie made the tea. Pippa hoped that if she concentrated on those sounds around her, her thoughts would refrain from making her relive the drama of the day.

"Here you go, Pip." Cassie handed Pippa a steaming cup of the aromatic tea and sat down beside her.

Pippa sipped at her tea for a few moments, but it did little to help her mood. Finally, she spoke.

"You should have seen the confusion in Rook's eyes when he recognised me and then realised who I really was. His whole expression changed. He looked hurt, Cassie. I nearly blurted out the whole sordid truth to Brodie James right there and then."

"You didn't though, honey, did you?" Cassie's serious tone momentarily distracted Pippa from her tale of woe.

"No, I didn't, but I don't feel good about it. You should have heard the glowing endorsement Brodie gave me. I feel like such a fraud. I've let everyone down. "

Pippa was fighting back tears as she spoke and trying to ignore the ache in her chest. Occasionally, she rubbed absentmindedly at that painful spot over her heart with her closed fist.

"Did Rook say anything?" Cassie quietly asked. "Did he talk to Brodie, give you up?"

"Before I could talk to him, maybe apologise or something, he was gone. One minute he was there and then the next..." Tears started to roll down Pippa's cheeks.

Cassie wrapped a comforting arm around her shoulders.

"Don't do this to yourself, Pip, regret and 'what ifs' aren't going to change what happened. Move on. Eating yourself up won't help. What's done is done, sweetie. You really need to concentrate on your career now... Your future," Cassie said.

"I just feel so guilty, Cassie, and then to top it all off I had this weird conversation with Brodie about Rook being my teenage crush. It was so humiliating."

"Let it go... You have wanted to work for the Jets for a long time, and now you have that chance. Grab it— whatever happens with Rook will happen. Just let him have some time to get over the shock. Look, sweetie, he's a man. His ego took a bit of a hit. But he got his end in. He will get over it, probably just as soon as he finds another conquest."

"Do you really think so, Cass?" Pippa asked, trying to garner strength from her best friend's words.

"Yeah, hon, I do. Just give it some time."

But just as quickly as the hope began to surface that Rook might forgive her, the idea of him with another woman broke Pippa's heart all over again.

"Maybe…" Pippa sounded less than confident even to her own ears as she sipped at the cooling tea. "I'll try, Cass. In fact, I have to start pretty soon. JT invited me to a get-together at his place. He said it would be a good chance for me to mingle with some of the team, let them get used to having me around. And on the positive, it will be great to catch up with Caitlin and Mandy again."

Pippa remembered how the two senior members of the Jets squad her father had coached had fallen hard for their respective wives. Both men had met their other halves a matter of weeks apart from one another, and to top it off, both women had lived in the same apartment building.

Pippa, only fifteen at the time, had loved the romantic—but quite public—wedding proposal JT had made to Mandy. Most people had thought that JT was too tough or macho to make such a romantic gesture. He had proven to be very much in love with his woman, and had retired at the end of that season so as not to be away from his new family.

Pippa had spent a lot of time hanging out with Caitlin's brother, Riley. Caitlin had been the sole carer for Riley back then, as their parents had been tragically killed in a car accident. Riley had been quite a lot of fun, for an eleven-year-old boy. The fact that Rookie had seemed to have a soft spot for Riley and had spent time with him had also worked well for

Pippa. It would be great to see the now grown-up Riley again.

Maybe Cassie was right—she should just move on, make the most of her opportunities, get on with her life. Forget Mitch Harris.

Easier said than done. Like I haven't already tried that one!

"Hey, can I be your plus-one to the party? Wouldn't mind getting up close and personal with some prime Aussie beefcake, and I don't work for the Jets," Cassie said, wiggling her eyebrows at Pippa.

Pippa was very thankful to have such a supportive friend. Everything Cassie had said made sense.

"Sure you can, Cass. Hey, I need all the moral support I can get. And thanks for the pep talk."

"Don't even mention it, Pip, that's what we do for each other. I've got your back, partner." Cassie spoke the last words in a deeper voice, trying to imitate a Western gunslinger. It was such a bad impersonation that Pippa could not deny the smile that forced its way to her lips.

* * * *

After the day she'd had and the emotional replay of it to Cassie, Pippa was wiped out. She could not face the thought of food and so—after making excuses to Cassie about being tired and needing a good night's sleep to face the next day, and after a quick shower—she took herself off to bed.

She tried to not obsess over Rook, but every time Pip closed her eyes it was his face she saw. First the face that had hovered over her during their mating, those silver eyes hungry for her, which was quickly replaced by today's Rook—the look of horror on his face and in those eyes as she had been introduced to the team and he'd realised her deceit. So it was not surprising that he filled her dreams.

As was the usual case, Pippa's dreams began back in the garden of her childhood home, the place where she'd discovered what true humiliation felt like. Although in Pip's dreams, the story sometimes changed.

"Rookie, it's me, Phillipa. Where are you?" she whispered in the darkness, until Rookie's form stepped out from the shadows.

"I'm over here, beautiful. I've been waiting for you all night."

Pippa raced to him and threw her arms around his neck, and Rookie lifted her up and swung her around, like in some cheesy movie scene. "Kiss me," he said. His lips closed in on hers and the feeling was so good, so unbelievably sweet that Pippa melted in his arms.

The dreams always started this way…

Rookie's hands roamed over Pippa's body, warmth radiating from his touch, leaving her skin burning with desire. She always wanted more. He cradled her breast, rubbed his palm over her now distended, sensitive nipple. "My God, I want you so much…every time I see you, I just want to have you," he whispered in her ear. The words she longed for him to say, the words that made her want to give him everything.

"Take me, Rookie. I'm yours…always," she replied breathlessly, panting.

Rookie laid her gently down on a blanket that seemed to miraculously appear from nowhere. "Take your top off for me, beautiful. Let me see those lush breasts of yours."

And Pippa did. She bared her breasts for him to see – only him.

"They are the most beautiful breasts I've ever seen, and the feel of them is so fucking amazing," he said.

Rookie touching her was heavenly as an arc of pleasure raced from her nipple down past her clenching tummy, making her pulsating labia feel moist and swollen, evoking sensations throughout her body that up until now she had only reached from her own hand. She moaned, made little noises that made Rookie squeeze harder, pinch and caress more frantically.

"Let me touch you too. Take off your shirt, Rookie," Pippa whispered self-consciously, almost begging, pleading. She was not sure of what she should be doing, what she needed to do to satisfy Rookie. To make him hers.

He did as she asked, and she stroked her hands over his chest. It was firm, muscled, not an inch of fat to mar his perfect form. She played with the few curls of hair that adorned his chest, feeling the softness of them. She tentatively touched the small buds of his nipples with her fingertips, marvelling at the feel of him. Her sigh was loud as she enjoyed touching him, finally, after having spent so long wanting him to notice her.

"Can I touch your pussy?" he asked politely, and although Pippa felt nervous, her mouth drying in anticipation, she nodded in assent.

Rookie's touch was light at first, exploring her, testing, but before long she was riding his hand. "That's right, beautiful, take what you need. Let me make you fly. Let me show you pleasure that you never imagined was possible," he said as she slid back and forth on his fingers – two now – trying to find what she was striving for, what her body signalled that it needed.

She felt the moisture build where Rookie's fingers explored. She was about to reach that glorious peak as her body tensed and arched towards him, the final goal that would ease the ache, the longing. But just as it seemed attainable, he removed his fingers, leaving her adrift and feeling as if she might die from the unattained release.

"I need to be inside you now," he said, his voice sounding so desperate.

Rookie slowly slid her underwear from her. Still dazed from what his talented fingers had nearly done for her, the summit she had nearly reached, she submitted, unsure of the emotions that rode her. Not sure if the tears that she felt building were from frustration or happiness.

Rookie crouched over her, his silver eyes – the ones that made her heart skip and her breath catch – gleaming with some emotion she did not understand. A hunger, a fierceness that was almost enough to frighten her but also thrill her. This was Rookie, and she loved him – had loved him for almost three years, from the time she'd first seen him at the age of fifteen. So she lay still as he spread her thighs and adjusted himself. Pippa couldn't see between them, but she could feel the hardness against her. Felt herself parting, allowing him entry. It was a strange sensation as her virginal muscles fought his entry. She tried to relax, inhaled a big breath to calm her fear. She wanted him to see her as a woman – his woman…

Pippa awoke with a start, her body saturated in sweat, her chest heaving, her pussy wet, throbbing with need. Her frequent dreams of Rook Harris took many turns – some where he rejected her, the way he had when she was seventeen. Other dreams were fantasies where he made love to her tenderly, bringing her to orgasm in crashing waves of pure bliss, drawing out every ounce of passion as he whispered sweet nothings in her ear, manipulating her body to evoke such pleasure in her it was almost unbearable.

Then there were the dreams that left her wanting, when something would disturb her sleep and awaken her too early.

Of course, it would be this kind of fantasy tonight. Pippa cried into her pillow, refusing to sate her own needs – the needs of her unsatisfied body – as she might have done in the past, believing that she deserved this kind of torment for what she had become. Her torrent of tears finally ebbed enough that emotional exhaustion claimed her.

Chapter Ten

Pippa was nervous as she and Cassie arrived at JT and Mandy's Cabarita home. Cabarita was a lovely inner-western suburb of Sydney, situated along the Parramatta River, a waterway that fed into Sydney Harbour. The old federation-style home, typical of the area, was large and spacious, perfect for entertaining. The backyard was shaded by enormous gum trees and landscaped with many native Australian plants — kangaroo paw, red waratah and grevillea. Lavender shrubs and yellow wattle scented the air, as well as the pretty white sweet-smelling flowers of the flourishing frangipani trees.

Pippa couldn't believe how much JT's children had grown. When she had left Sydney nearly five years ago for university, Elaina had been a shy three-year-old and Mandy had still been expecting their second child. Now Elaina was a smiling, confident seven-year-old with curly black hair and big, brown, owlish eyes. JT's son, Jay, was a little tank just like his father, and was happily kicking a footy around the yard.

Mandy and Caitlin looked different as well—both women were absolutely radiant. Married life obviously agreed with them, Pippa concluded. She was amazed at the radical changes in Mandy's appearance. When they had first met, Mandy had been a little scary-looking, dressed in all black, a bit like a goth. It was hard to believe this was the same woman, now wearing a pretty yellow sundress, her long, curly hair adorned with frangipanis.

Caitlin, who had always been a natural beauty, was still stunning, but now quite rounded. Pippa guessed that the beautiful redhead was probably at least seven months pregnant. And as they came rushing up to hug her, her nerves disappeared. Pippa was quite overwhelmed by the genuine warmth of the welcome she received, but finally remembered to introduce Cassie to the women.

"Mandy, Caitlin, I hope you don't mind but I bought a friend along. I was a bit nervous and Cassie is good backup." She laughed. It wasn't long before the women were all chuckling and reminiscing, regaling an enthralled Cassie with stories about the old days.

Caitlin also filled Pippa in on the latest gossip. Pippa found out that Caitlin and Brodie already had a son.

"Luke Patrick is two, and just between you and me, Pip, be glad he is inside taking a nap. He is quite the handful. And as you can probably imagine, Brodie spoils him rotten."

Pippa loved the melodic sound of Caitlin James' voice. No wonder she had made a living singing.

"What a load of rubbish, Cate," Mandy said with a laugh. "Don't you believe a word of it, Pippa—Luke is an angel compared to Jay. If Jay isn't destroying something, then he is thinking about ways to destroy something. My boy is just like his daddy, steamrolling over everything in his path!"

Pippa was having fun catching up with Mandy and Caitlin. She and Cassie had fit in easily and all four women were clearly enjoying each other's company and their conversation. Pippa was pleased to have some familiar female company around the Jets club to help settle her in.

Distracted, she nearly jumped out of her skin when a large hand fell on her shoulder and a very deep, husky, but unfamiliar voice said her name.

"Pipsqueak, what the hell did you do to your hair?" the male voice growled.

"Riley Walters, you watch your mouth. That is no proper way to greet Pippa. You might be big, but not too big for me to clip around the ear, especially if Brodie or JT are around to give me backup," Caitlin lovingly chastised her now very grown-up brother.

Pippa nearly fell out of her chair as she gazed up— then up some more—at the giant of a man who had once been her gangly-limbed, red-headed young friend.

"Riley Walters! What happened to you? Did you take illegal growth hormones, or is just being around Brodie and JT enough to make you become enormous too?" Pippa said as she jumped up and threw her arms around Riley's neck.

Riley took advantage of the situation by picking Pippa up and swinging her around a few times before setting her back down to her feet gently.

"So, it's Pippa now, is it?" he said with a broad grin. "Yeah, you don't look much like a pipsqueak any more... You look mighty fine actually, if you don't mind me saying. And by the way, who is this gorgeous babe with you?" Riley added cheekily, and he took Cassie's hand, bringing it to his mouth to give it a quick kiss.

"Oh, my God, Riley, you have definitely changed." Pippa chuckled. "This is my best friend, Cassandra Davies. Cassie, this is Riley—remember the little kid I used to talk to you about?"

"Ouch, that hurt, Pipsqueak!" Riley turned his smile in Cassie's direction as he spoke. "Nice to meet you, best friend Cassandra. And I would just like to point out that nothing is little about me anymore!"

"Riley!" Mandy and Caitlin both chanted in unison, trying to curb any future risqué comments from the very forward young man.

"I'm honoured to meet you, Riley. Pippa has spoken of you often. And yes, I can see that you are all grown up, big and strong." Cassie seemed to be enjoying the conversation immensely.

Riley was indeed all grown up—in fact, he was gorgeous. Pippa guessed him to be about a hundred and ninety centimetres tall. His swimming had helped produce a set of incredibly wide shoulders and a broad chest that tapered down to what appeared to be a flat stomach and slim waist. His legs seemed to go on forever, and while not as thick with muscle as a rugby player's, they certainly looked fine in the tight-fitting jeans he was wearing. She couldn't see his butt, but guessed it would be fine as well! But what really gave Riley his sex appeal were his eyes and that sinful curve of his mouth.

Pippa could not believe she could even think such a thing. Riley was only eighteen, but he oozed sex appeal, possibly generated by his confidence, but also helped by those big, emerald-coloured eyes—they made Pippa melt, and it seemed to Pippa that they had the same effect on Cassie. To top it off, his lips just seemed to beg to be kissed — they were quite full, and the sort of lips a woman could really nibble on. Riley's strong jaw was covered in just a hint of ginger stubble. He wore his hair cropped very close to his scalp and it made him look all the more masculine.

Pippa was very impressed with how her friend had grown into such a hunk.

"Well, Riley, I bet you're just breaking hearts all over the place," she said teasingly.

"Of course he is, princess. I taught him everything he knows."

The sound of Rook's voice caught Pippa off guard. She hadn't seen Rook arrive or realised he had been watching her reunion. She now felt uncomfortable, wondering if he had noticed her appraisal of Riley's grown-up look, watched as she'd ogled her old friend.

"Rook, my man! How are you going, buddy?" Riley grabbed Rook in a big bear hug, obviously excited to see the man who had once been an idol to him.

"But what's with the *princess* tag? Don't you remember Pipsqueak? Hey, the two of us almost stalked you back in the day." He laughed good-naturedly, not realising the awkwardness of the situation.

Pippa heard Mandy and Caitlin groan at Riley's tactless remark as she turned bright red.

Rook ignored Riley's comments and turned his attention to a now speechless and suddenly uncomfortable-looking Cassie.

"Well, hello there. I don't believe we have met — or have we? I'm Mitch Harris, but everyone calls me Rook. What's your name?"

Riley, not understanding the game Rook was playing, jumped in to introduce Cassie. "Hey, Rook, meet Cassandra Davies, Pipsqueak's best friend."

"Cassandra, you say?" Rook drawled as he also favoured her friend's hand with a kiss. "What a lovely name."

Pippa could see the look of embarrassment on Cassie's face—her features were flushed, her eyes downcast, averted from Rook's piercing stare. Luckily, for all concerned, Brodie arrived at that moment and hijacked the conversation before it could get any more uncomfortable.

"Glad to see everyone is finally here," Brodie said as he gave his wife, Caitlin, a quick kiss on the lips. "Hey, Cassandra, nice to meet you. Any friend of Phillipa's is always welcome—after all, Pippa is just like a daughter to me and JT."

Pippa couldn't help but catch the icy look that suddenly flickered in Rook's eyes. He muttered something under his breath that she couldn't quite catch.

Brodie had come seeking help to set up the tables so everyone could sit and eat. So as Rook and Riley went off with Brodie, Pippa collapsed back into her chair, any happiness she had felt totally sucked from her body by Rook's cold behaviour.

"I should go in and check on Luke. I'm sorry, Pippa—Riley might look all grown up, but he's still a bit immature when it comes to knowing what not to say," an apologetic Caitlin said as she struggled to get her pregnant form out of her chair. "He just wouldn't get that you might be embarrassed over the memory of your teenage crush."

Mandy also left to oversee the food preparations, refusing any offers of assistance from Pippa and Cassie, ordering them to just sit back and enjoy the hospitality as she hurried away.

"Well, that was awkward." Cassie sighed when she and Pippa were alone again. "I think it's safe to say that Rook is still a bit pissed at you, Pip. But boy, that Riley's one hot dish…mmm… Shame he's so young, though—I could just eat him right up, especially those incredibly yummy lips of his," Cassie mused, and made 'nom-nom-nom' sound effects to accompany her observations.

Pippa couldn't speak, so just nodded her head dismally at her friend's accurate descriptions of both Riley and Rook. Her heart was shattered, and she felt dirty. The night that she'd so often fantasised about had quickly turned into a memory that would torment her forever.

Chapter Eleven

Rook made it through the rest of the gathering, but only just. With a conscious effort he managed to stop looking at Pippa, stop searching for her at every moment, stop seeing red when she spoke to any of his younger teammates. He had almost turned around and left again, when the first thing he'd seen was Pippa in the arms of another man. It had taken a moment for him to realise that it had just been Riley holding her.

But the relief had been short-lived when Rook realised that Pippa was practically undressing Riley, those beautiful blue eyes of hers roving up and down young Riley's body. It had made Rook feel sick to his stomach.

He had not been able to stop himself from going over to the group. He had been like a moth to a flame. Making that stupid comment and putting the real Cassandra on the spot had been juvenile, but Brodie's 'daughter' comment had just about done him in. Was he always going to be reminded that Phillipa Rodgers was too good for him?

Or so people thought. But he knew the truth. The fact was, Pippa was the type of woman to lie and have sex just to get even with someone. Not to mention that she had quite publicly checked out a younger man. She was also the type of woman who could break your heart—Rook could attest to that firsthand. She was a danger to men everywhere.

He was just biding his time until he could leave without drawing too much attention. So after spending some time playing with Luke and Jay—the little blokes falling all over him as they all rolled around on the lawn, tumbling and fighting over the footy—Rook made his excuses to leave, explaining that he was expecting a big night at his club, and needed to set up. Rook noticed the real Cassie choked on her drink as he made a comment about his club, Jetstream.

Riley had been murmuring, all afternoon, about how much he wanted to go to Jetstream – much to Caitlin's disapproval. She thought her brother too young to go to clubs and gave Rook an imploring look, trying to gain his support, he guessed. But Rook found he was unable to dissuade the young man from making his arrangements to meet up at the club later that night, no matter what his overprotective sister might believe. Not that Rook could blame the woman—Caitlin had been looking after Riley for a very long time.

Rook was seriously not happy, though, when he stumbled onto the conversation Riley was having with Pippa and Cassie.

"C'mon, Pip, Cass! What will it take to convince you both to come with us, accompany a bunch of good-looking blokes to Jetstream?" Riley was trying hard to sell his idea. "We can have a few drinks and dance—it'll be great. Rook will be there so it's not like we can get into any trouble. Hey, he can organise a VIP area just for us. I'm sure Rook would be okay with that."

"Leave it, Riley. If the women don't want to go to Jetstream, that's their business," Rook finally growled at Riley through gritted teeth.

He wasn't sure what to be most upset about, the fact that Riley was inviting Pippa to Jetstream, or the amount of effort it was taking Riley to get her to agree to join him there. Did the idea of being at Jetstream seem that unappealing to Pippa, or was it just that it was his place, and *ipso facto* she might have to spend time with him, be reminded of the things they had done together?

Rook was so confused — confused about his own feelings when it came to Pippa, about why he was making such a big deal about the whole thing, about her deception. And more disturbingly, why his gut had burned with jealousy when he had seen Pippa in Riley's arms earlier. For the life of him, Rook couldn't understand why he was spending so much time dissecting his reactions. He was not normally an emotional wuss. It was driving him insane.

"Well, guys, don't forget the season is just around the corner. The last thing this coach wants is bad press about his players being drunk and disorderly." Brodie's commanding voice cut into Rook's thoughts.

"Aww, c'mon, Brodes — you're getting so old and boring these days. I hope it's not my sister that's turning you into an old prude," Riley teased Brodie. "Ouch!"

Riley cried out as JT, always one to have Brodie's back in a fight, clipped him over the ear good-naturedly.

"Now see here, young fella, don't go disrespecting your elders. Brodie James was renowned for his sensibility and lack of fun way before your gorgeous sister came into his life."

JT's comment and actions resulted in Caitlin and Mandy giggling uncontrollably, obviously in on some private joke. Rook was feeling anything but happy at the idea of having to be sociable with Pippa again. His life was becoming one giant fuck-up, he thought as he finally managed to escape, with the sounds of laughter and merriment echoing behind him.

* * * *

Pippa didn't think it was a good idea to go to Jetstream with the group, but not going would raise even more questions and Riley, it seemed, was not going to take no for an answer. Going would give her the further opportunity to bond with the Jets players, though. The day had been good in that respect — if she ignored the disaster over Rook, she had to admit that the rest of the team had been nothing but polite and friendly. So finally she surrendered to Riley's persistence. She and Cassie made plans to meet everyone at around eight o'clock, giving themselves plenty of time to go home and change first.

Always the gentleman, Brodie walked Pippa and Cassie out to Pippa's car, thanking them both for coming and extending an open invitation for Cassie to attend some of the Jets home games to see the boys in action.

"Look after my boys, Pippa. I am expecting you, as a member of my staff, to watch their backs. If you think things are getting out of hand, ring me. I'm hoping being at Rook's bar will help keep everyone well-behaved and under control."

Pippa sat erect in her car seat, focusing straight ahead, trying to stay strong. Brodie's parting comments had rushed all those guilty feelings straight back to the surface—it took all of Pippa's resolve not to break down and confess. He thought of her as a responsible person. He didn't know that she had already let him down. The thought of disappointing Brodie was like a knife piercing Pippa's already broken soul.

* * * *

As promised, Riley was waiting out front when Pippa and Cassie arrived at Jetstream. As their cab pulled up to the kerb, he opened the car door and helped them both out. Pippa once again had to admire his good looks—Riley Walters was a hunk. Eighteen or not, he was sexy as sin. Pippa could tell that Cassie was really enjoying his attention.

Bypassing the queue, Riley led Cassie and Pippa straight to the club's entrance. The very large and burly doorman smiled as he opened the door for them. Pippa could hear the groans of complaint from the people in the queue as they headed inside.

"Rook introduced me to me to Jerome, earlier. He didn't want us having to wait in the queue. Apparently Rook's place is the 'in place' at the moment," Riley shouted above the music, two fingers in each hand making imaginary speech marks in the air as they headed towards the back of the club.

Rook had reserved a large seating area for the group. Six Jets players were already seated, drinks in their hands. The men smiled and nodded a welcome to Pippa and Cassie.

Pippa glanced at the ice-bucket sitting on the table. A bottle of champagne—the same brand that Rook had supplied the other night—sat chilling inside, and two empty champagne flutes sat ready to be filled. Raising an eyebrow in query, she looked at Riley.

"Rook thought you girls might like some bubbly," Riley said, shrugging his broad shoulders. "Would you rather have something else?"

"No, Riley, champagne is great. Want to pour me a glass, handsome?" Cassie said as she held up a glass to him and smiled.

* * * *

Pippa shouldn't have come—she was miserable. Everyone else was having a great time, enjoying the music and dancing. A couple of the guys had asked her to dance, but being on the dance-floor just reminded her of her night with Rook. Cassie, on the other hand, was having a wonderful time, or so it seemed to Pippa.

Pippa spent most of her time talking to country boy Gareth. The Jets player seemed ill at ease with the amount of attention he was receiving from the women in the club, which was lucky for Pippa, because Cassie's night had been monopolised by Riley—they had danced and talked exclusively. Some of the other guys had moaned about this fact to Pippa, but when Riley had overheard the grumbling sports stars, he'd just given them a big smile and dragged Cassie away for another dance. It didn't seem as if the age gap between her two friends made any difference to their attraction for each other. But it was making Pippa feel lonely not to have her best friend beside her when she needed the support.

She had only spotted Rook a few times — not that she was looking, she told herself. Once he had come over and spent a few minutes talking to Gareth and the guys, flirting with the gaggle of women who had closed in on the group of footy players. He had filled her champagne glass without a word, then left again. The other times she had spotted Rook, he had been at the bar, talking to the barman or customers. But for most of the night he was nowhere to be found. Pippa assumed Rook was upstairs in his apartment, and she was trying as hard as she could not to let the image that Rook might not be up there alone enter her head.

Just remembering his apartment was enough to bring a whole new world of hurt crashing down on Pippa. Luckily, before she went down that road again, Gareth continued their ongoing conversation.

"It's been really great chatting with you, Pippa. I've found it hard to have a reasonable conversation with a woman since I moved to Sydney," Gareth confessed to Pippa. "I'm not looking for a relationship, or a quick tumble in the sack, and that seems to be all the women around here want." He added with a sad shrug, "Don't suppose you'd take pity on an ol' country bumpkin and take a few spins around the dance-floor with me? I don't mind the odd dance, but I'm hesitant to ask any of the unattached females... It just isn't worth the hassle — they're all so forward, it scares the hell outta me!"

Pippa could tell Gareth was genuine. He had acted so politely towards her all night, checking her drink and chatting with her. Gareth had spoken at length to her of his hometown, mentioning one girl's name more than once in the conversation. Pippa knew there was a story there but didn't want to pry. The country-bred man seemed to have a sadness around him, and

Pippa understood that emotion well, so she agreed to his request for a dance.

"Sure thing, Gareth, it would be my pleasure. I think both of us could use a friend right now — I know I can at least. I don't mind protecting your virtue from the hordes of hungry city womenfolk," Pippa added with a grin as she took his offered hand.

* * * *

The DJ had made the announcement for last drinks, telling the crowd that he was only playing a few more songs and that if they had put off dancing, it was now or never. Pippa was still on the dance-floor with Gareth.

When the DJ changed to a slower mix, Pippa grimaced and looked up at Gareth, unsure whether she should make an excuse to end their dance. He just smiled and took her in his embrace, but held her at a respectable distance from his body. Pippa was relieved that Gareth had understood her uncertainty. As they moved around the floor, Pippa could see Cassie and Riley swaying to the music, snuggled up against each other. A couple of the other guys were also up close and personal with women that they had only just met tonight.

Pippa was caught by complete surprise when Rook appeared next to Gareth, and whispered something to him.

Chapter Twelve

Rook had reached his breaking point. Seeing Pippa dancing and having a good time was too much. He had tried to keep himself occupied and it had been a busy night, but his gaze seemed to be drawn back to her time and time again. When Gareth headed to the dance-floor with her in tow, her hand in his, after spending a good chunk of the night with his head bent towards hers in deep conversation, Rook nearly crushed the glass he was holding.

"Would you just go and dance with her, and stop mooning about like a love-sick puppy?" Rook was taken aback by the comment from his barman—he hadn't realised he was acting so obvious.

"It's not that easy, Mick."

"Yeah, boss, it really is. Walk out on the dance floor and cut in. If the guy doesn't go, get Jerome to kick his butt to the kerb. That's why you pay him the big bucks, boss-man—to clear out the unwanted." Mick the barman laughed.

So Rook had done exactly that, convincing himself all the way out to the dance-floor that he was just looking out for Gareth. He was a shy country boy—who knew what the likes of Pippa could do to crush the guy's heart? Gareth needed his captain to look out for him.

"Yeah, right, 'cause I'm the type of shmuck who *does* know," Rook mumbled to himself, then tapped Gareth on the shoulder.

Gareth relinquished the floor to him without argument. Rook held his hands out to Pippa to take up where Gareth had just been standing.

"Sorry to spoil your fun, princess, but I just thought I should remind you that Brodie does not think much of staff dalliances, and Gareth is important to the team." Rook had only spoken to her so he could explain that his actions were purely for the team—trying hard to convince himself as well.

Unfortunately, the moment Rook took Pippa into his arms and felt her softness against him, all sanity was lost to him. His body heated and his cock hardened in recognition of her, remembering the pleasure she had bought him. But he did not—could not—miss the look of shock that appeared in her eyes, and he was angered by it. In response, Rook pulled her closer to him, roughly dragging her body up against his. *Hell, is dancing with me that horrible, after all the ways she let me touch her the other night?* The bitter thought caught in his mind.

Rook didn't care what she was saying—watching her lips and mouth move as she spoke just made him want to kiss her. He had to taste her. If he could just feel those lips against his, maybe he would regain some coherent thought. She was bewitching him, filling him with need. Nothing else in the world was of concern to him. Just the feel of this woman, her warmth, her smell, invaded his very soul. It was all too much. He could not control his cravings for her need. Rook knew he was gripping her too roughly, but he was fighting for control.

Chapter Thirteen

Rook's hurtful words tore at Pippa's already damaged heart. *Not only does he hate me, but he thinks I'm some sort of slut.* The thought, as it raced through her mind, nearly caused her knees to buckle as agony tore through her chest. Rook's slightly painful grip on her was the only reason Pippa managed to not crumple to the floor.

To top off the whole painful interlude, the moment Rook had laid his hands on her, her traitorous body had gone into lust overdrive. There was no way he could not feel her hard nipples poke at him, not with the way he had her pressed hard to his chest. She could feel the beat of his heart against her breast, could feel her body soften, moisten in readiness for him. She was mortified. She had to get away from him, now. Gain some distance from him before she made a fool of herself…again.

So Pippa focused on his accusation and how best to reply.

"Rookie, I am well aware of Brodie's expectations, now that I am officially a member of the Jets staff. You have no reason to fret over Gareth's virtue. I have no intention of doing anything that would jeopardise either of our careers. So you can go back to whomever it was you were chatting up." Pippa was relieved that she sounded much calmer than she was actually feeling, even referring to Rook by the nickname from his youth.

Although she did notice that she hadn't struggled to break away from his grip yet, even though she knew she should.

She watched, horrified, but excited when, as if in slow motion, Rook lowered his head towards her.

Was he about to kiss her?

Would she just let him take her that way in front of everyone?

Giving in to the lust about to claim her, she let herself draw nearer to him, their lips all but touching. Pippa could feel the heat from Rook's breath. His mouth was so close she could almost taste him, feel his tongue against her own.

"Hey, guys, are you okay? Funny, Rook, but it looked to me as though you were either about to hit Pipsqueak or kiss her," Riley said, not even a trace of humour apparent in his voice. He physically stepped in between Pippa and Rook, pushing their bodies apart, breaking Rook's hold on her.

Rook glared at Riley. Riley, holding his ground, glared back. Pippa held her breath — she wasn't sure if the men were about to come to blows or not, but she could almost feel the testosterone surging around her.

"What have I done?" Her words were lost in the surrounding noise of the club as she watched on in sheer horror at just the thought that she could be the reason that these two friends — Riley and his teenage hero — were about to come to blows, knowing she only had herself to blame for this drama unfolding in front of her, in such a public arena.

The moment seemed to last forever, but finally Rook abruptly turned and walked away, without saying a word.

Pippa burst into tears.

* * * *

Riley had insisted on escorting Pippa and Cassie home. "So, you going to tell me what that was all about, what's going on with you and Rook?" he asked, the minute he set foot in Pippa and Cassie's home.

"I've made a huge mistake, Riley." Pippa sobbed as she found herself once again explaining her deception and subsequent night with Rook.

Pippa was reluctant to meet her childhood friend's eye as she confessed her sins, didn't want to see the condemnation on his face at her actions. But when she did finally find the courage to lift her head and face his wrath, all she found was a look of concern in Riley's eyes.

"I'm sorry, Pippa, I'm struggling with this. How did Rook not recognise you? Even with the change to your hair colour and length, I knew it was you straight away, and I didn't get all up close and personal." He added, still shaking his head in apparent disbelief, "Did it ever cross your mind that maybe Rook knew all along and was just going with it...playing along?"

Pippa knew that hadn't been the case. She had seen the look on Rook's face as Brodie had introduced her at that initial meet-and-greet session.

Rook had been dismayed at her deception. It was the only thing that could explain his continued animosity towards her.

"You know, you could be right, gorgeous. Sexy and smart—it's my lucky night," Cassie chimed in. "I've been telling Pip to just let it go, but even I felt the tension between them tonight, Riley. I think Rook needs to get over himself. He's not a saint, or at least his reputation doesn't hold up to that idea. So they had a night—big deal."

Pippa was exhausted. She was sick of talking, sick of thinking, and it seemed that her two friends had struck up their own personal friendship. To be honest, Pippa did not even want to think about what was going on there. But it certainly looked cosy, what with Riley settling in, looking as if he was in no hurry to leave.

After excusing herself, Pippa went to her room and crawled into bed, leaving Cassie and Riley alone in the kitchen to finish their tea, and more than likely dissect the night and its drama some more. *And goodness knows what else,* she thought, trying hard not to accidentally picture her two friends together, sexually.

As she lay staring up at the ceiling, Pippa wondered if her heart would ever mend or the pain lessen. She had actually deluded herself, for just a moment, into thinking Rook was about to kiss her, as he'd held her on the dance-floor just before Riley had intervened. But that possibility had been quickly squashed by Rook's silent, angry exit. She was thankful for small mercies that Rook and Riley had not fought—that would have been an uncomfortable conversation to have with Brodie and Caitlin, trying to explain why Brodie's team captain and his brother-in-law had come to blows.

Chapter Fourteen

A month passed quickly.

Pippa had managed to tread carefully around Rook, making sure she was never alone with him. He had not requested any pre-training strapping or massage, so it had been relatively easy to keep a distance between them. The rest of the team had made her feel welcome, and had listened attentively to her advice with regards to the treatment of any injuries. The players had all become comfortable enough for her to massage and work on them.

All except Rook.

Gareth had proven to be quite an ally, and very easy to be around. Pippa found herself spending more and more time in his company. Gareth was interested in her Kinesio strapping methods and was trying them on his hamstrings, having torn tendons in both hamstrings at different times in past seasons.

Country-born Gareth was finding life in the city difficult, complaining to Pippa that city girls were too forward for him, the streets too busy, and the life too fast. He loved playing rugby league—it was the only thing that was keeping him away from the open spaces of his hometown, Gunnedah, a rural town situated in the far north-west of New South Wales.

Pippa felt sorry for Gareth, but could understand how the city women found it hard to resist him. The shy country boy was easy on the eye. Tall and muscular like most rugby forwards, he had broad shoulders and bulging biceps. Pippa could picture him in R.M. Williams boots, hat pulled low over his blond hair, shading his blue eyes from the sun, and his arm muscles bulging from lifting bales of hay back on the farm, instead of the metal weights he was now lifting in the gym.

Pippa also learned more about Gareth's apparent sadness. He had left a woman back home, which she had guessed. The tale was difficult to hear and her heart broke for him as he told her of *his* Emily.

"It's a lost cause, Em and me. I just need to move on and forget about her," Gareth admitted to Pippa one night as they sat together amicably, feigning interest in the television, but really both just needing to connect with another soul.

It was clear to Pippa that 'moving on' had not happened for poor Gareth yet. The city seemed not to have lessened his loss at all. Gareth was not just a very talented footballer—he was also an all-around nice guy. He gave one hundred per cent on and off the field, and was always one of the first to volunteer for any good cause.

"Is it really that bad? You don't think there is any chance of her waking up and realising how much she is missing out on? Gareth, you're a great guy. I can't believe anyone would let you go... She's crazy, in my opinion. Any woman would be lucky to have you."

"Thanks for the endorsement, Pippa, but I have to learn to live with it, 'cause being miserable is getting mighty tiresome."

"Here's to misery, then, and friendship." Pippa raised her teacup and tapped it gently against Gareth's sports drink.

Pippa understood misery and being apart from the love of your life, and especially the feeling of being rejected by that love.

* * * *

Pippa had been relieved to find that she liked most of the team—the men, ranging in ages from late teens to late twenties, were good-natured and polite. Some of the guys were a bit cocky and sure of themselves. But then, that was to be expected with the way the fans treated them like royalty one minute and the devil incarnate the next, depending on the team's successes.

Life had settled into a routine. Cassie had started her teaching position and was enjoying her role at the local high school. She had made an immediate impression on her students by talking about spending time with the Jets players and coaching staff, and admitting her best friend was the team's physio. She told Pippa that she would use any advantage to get the kids to take an interest in what she had to teach them, but was sick of spending half of every lesson fielding questions on what Rook was really like and how Gareth's hamstrings were, and would he be fit for the first round?

Cassie and Riley were spending a great deal of time together. Riley was back at university, studying sports management. He also worked at the local pool—the same pool at Leichhardt that he had trained and competed in as a youngster — teaching learn-to-swim classes and coaching the more talented swimmers. Most nights, though, Riley spent with Pippa and Cassie.

Pippa could see that the pair were growing very close, which just made her feel even more heartbroken and lonely. Gareth had joined them on a few occasions, as he seemed to enjoy the family feel of their home — especially the home cooking, he had commented on that fact more than once — but Pippa just felt he was as lonely in life as her and was reaching out for companionship. Cassie and Pippa both enjoyed cooking, and it was always more satisfying to cook for an appreciative guest or two, so it was no hardship. And of course, Cassie could get another snippet of team-talk to tell her students the next day.

Gareth had even organised with Brodie for a few of the players to go along to the school and give the students some tips on participating in sports and staying healthy. Cassie had scored some brownie points with the school principal over that coup.

All in all, life was rolling on productively for both Pippa and Cassie, but Pippa still felt hollow inside. Every time she saw Rook her body went into overdrive — her heart would race, her mouth would go dry, and the gnawing ache in her chest would start.

Nothing had changed.

Since the time she'd been fifteen, seeing Rook had always affected Pippa the same way, but now it was worse. Now she knew exactly what she was missing.

* * * *

Finally, it was the first game of the season. The pre-match preparations were in full swing when Pippa arrived at the ground. Caterers were setting up the food stalls, cleaning staff and ground staff were racing around, and everyone was seemingly panicked. Pippa made her way to the medical and treatment rooms to begin her own preparations. She laid out massage liniment, cut strapping and black Kinesio tape, filled ice bags, made sure all was in readiness. She was nervous, and tried to put it down to first-game nerves...but she knew it was more than that.

It wasn't long before Pippa didn't have time for nerves, as the treatment room was filled with masculine bodies. The smell of liniment was strong in the air as the players were rubbed and strapped in readiness for the battle ahead. Pippa had a team of student physios to assist her as well as the usual strappers, and was busy giving advice and supervising proceedings, not really paying attention to the half-naked bodies that lay on the massage tables around the room, just the individual muscles and tendons that needed attention.

Pippa noticed one of her trainees was a little overawed and was not massaging professionally enough. She quickly moved the girl aside, and got to work warming and loosening up the player's tight muscles — time was limited and all the players needed to be seen. The minute her hands made contact with skin, she realised her mistake. The electric charge that sped up her arm left no doubt as to who was face down on the table and her body's reaction to him was instantaneous.

Rook.

Pippa hesitated slightly and looked up, only to be scorched to her core by Rook's silver eyes, as he lifted his head from the table and turned towards her.

Pippa hurried to finish Rook's massage. Her body was on fire. She tried to ignore the feel of his muscles beneath her fingers as she massaged up his well-toned calf over his hamstrings, then his lower back, fighting the ever-present urge to grab hold of his gorgeous behind.

"Sit up, Rook, and I'll strap your ankles," a flustered Pippa managed to croak out.

Rook slowly rolled over onto his back. It was impossible to not notice the bulge in his Speedos, as his erection strained hard against the tight material of the swimwear he wore under his playing shorts.

Pippa's mouth went dry at the sight of his arousal. She casually dropped the towel that she had been drying her hands on over his lap, hoping to prevent any further embarrassment for Rook, and set to work strapping tape around his ankles. Strapping would give extra support and stability to the joints throughout the punishing game. When she had finished, the tape securely fastened, she finally looked up. Rook was staring at her, the hunger showing in his eyes so apparent it made her heart skip a beat.

The room was full of people, the noise levels high, and yet for Pippa, there was no one else but Rook.

Just Rook…and desire.

It was as if they had been sucked into a different dimension. The room's sounds and smells were muted, distant. They must have held eye contact for an eternity. Just as Pippa was about to confess to Rook her reason for deceiving him—that he was her fantasy man and always would be, but that she had worried that he would again refuse her advances if he had known her true identity — Brodie summoned the team to come together for warm-up.

Pippa watched Rook drag his gaze from her. She put her hand on his arm, trying to stop him from leaving before she could make her confession, but he just shook off her touch.

Rook walked away.

Rejected her again.

Would she never learn? Pippa slumped back to her knees, trying to pull her emotions back under control.

"Hey, Pip, you okay?"

Gareth's voice was full of genuine concern and maybe something else — Pippa couldn't quite make it out.

"Come on, I'll help you up," he said, and he gently lifted her to her feet. "You and Rook need to talk. It's obvious, the attraction between you two. I don't mind admitting I'm as jealous as hell, and I hate to see you hurting like this over him. I wish I could make you forget him." Gareth, looking saddened by his inability to fix the situation, just shook his head before leaving her to join the rest of the team.

Pippa was confused at Gareth's words. Her mind was reeling. How on earth was she going to get through the season? She was having enough trouble getting through the first game. Perhaps she should take up her father's offer and relocate to the UK. Her father, now coach of a rugby league team situated in the north of England, had more than once offered her a position with him. That way, she could be reunited with her mother as well. And at this moment in Pippa's life, a hug and some sympathy from her mum was definitely required.

But Pippa still had a job to do today, so she pulled herself together, at least for the moment. While the players and coaching staff went through their last-minute game plans, Pippa busied herself tidying up her equipment, checking supplies and wiping down the massage tables as her team of workers buzzed with excitement over their recent hands-on experience around her.

During the game, Pippa stayed behind in the now empty Jets treatment room underneath the grandstand, waiting for half-time, when the players would return for a brief respite from their action-packed game. She would need to work quickly then, to treat any injuries and re-tape as need be, so the team could return to the field for the second half and finish the game. There would be no time to worry about Rook or Gareth.

After the game would be equally as hectic. Pippa and her team would apply ice-packs to injuries and record those injuries that would need extra attention during the week. She was hoping that all the activity would keep her from thinking about Rook, and how good he had felt beneath her fingers again. The errant thought caused images of their one night together to flood her mind. Tears pooled behind her eyes, and Pippa bunched her hands into fists and pressed them into her eye sockets to keep the emotional flood that threatened from spilling free.

A commotion coming from the tunnel drew Pippa's attention from her gloom. She heard Flash Mannering, the team runner, shout for her. Flash was one of the former players—his role at the Jets was to run onto the field during the games and give players water or instructions from the coach, or to assist injured players. By the sound of the agitation in his voice, Pippa knew something was terribly wrong. She hurried out of the treatment room and into the medical room.

Chapter Fifteen

Rook knew the minute he heard the crack that his knee was gone, probably for the season. He knew enough about cruciate ligaments to know that if he had torn his, he was going to need surgery and a long rehabilitation. As he lay on the medicab, being transported off the field, he was not only devastated but also in a shitload of pain.

Right from the get-go, his day had been fucked up, starting with when he'd been getting strapped and warmed up. It didn't matter that he had been lying face down on the massage table—he had instantly felt the change when a strapper's hands had been replaced by the electrifying sensations of Pippa's fingers, setting fire to him. He had only with incredible fortitude been able to resist the urge to drag her into his arms. The second she had touched him, his body had gone haywire—sensory overload. His cock, rising into a full, rigid erection, had tried to burst free from the confines of his tight underwear.

He had managed to keep out of her clutches for a month, but of course it had to be on game day that she finally caught him. It was the last thing he'd needed, to be distracted by her—he'd needed to be fully focused on the game. God knew where it would have led if not for Brodie calling everyone together for a last-minute strategy talk, breaking him from her hypnotising hold. It had taken a mammoth strength of will to force his gaze from her and walk away, but he had.

Then there was the unmistakable animosity he'd been feeling from Gareth. Rook had noticed the change in his teammate's demeanour just before they'd taken to the field, but there had been no time to find out what had been bothering the country boy. God, his life was really going down the toilet fast.

And now this! He was well and truly fucked.

Rook was feeling very sorry for himself as he threw his arm over his eyes and tried to block out the sensations that were beginning to overwhelm him—not just the pain from his leg, though that was excruciating, but the thoughts that niggled away at him that this could be the end of his football career. The only thing, apart from supervising the running of his bar, that Rook knew how to do. The one thing he was good at. The kid from a broken home had made good with his ability to play rugby league at the top level—what would happen if he couldn't take the field again?

What would he do with his life?

"Pip, it's Rook's knee—looks bad. What should we do first, Doc?" Flash shouted out over the engine sounds of the medicab as it stopped outside medical room door.

* * * *

The club doctor was bent over Rook, trying to keep the leg immobile. He shouted at Pippa to get plenty of ice and compression bandages ready. The first priority was to keep the swelling and fluid under control. Pippa didn't have time to react to the fact that the injured player was Rook—she just went into action and readied the supplies the doctor had requested.

Pippa could hear Rook moaning from the pain as they moved him from the transport medicab to one of the treatment beds. Her heart broke for him—she knew that if he was in this much pain then the injury was a bad one, most likely something to do with the ligaments and tendons of his knee. She could only hope that it was just a strain, and not a tear that would ultimately need surgery.

As the doctor carefully examined Rook's knee, trying to flex it and check the stability of the patella when bent, Pippa watched the pain register in Rook's eyes, saw the strain make his jaw tense and his lips disappear into just a thin line. His face paled, going a sickly shade of grey. She felt helpless, could not take the pain away from him until the doctor gave her the go-ahead to administer something. *Why hasn't Doc given Rook the green whistle?* she wondered, angered that the painkiller had not been administered already. *Why must he suffer?*

Pippa was desperate to help Rook. To soothe that pain etched over his handsome face. She curled her hand to her side, digging her nails into her palm just to stop the temptation to stroke his clenched jaw line.

As soon as the doctor was finished with his investigation, they strapped Rook's swelling knee with a compression bandage, elevated the injury and packed it in ice.

"Rook, I can't be sure until we get an MRI, but I think you might be lucky. It feels like a strain or grade one tear of the medial collateral ligament. I noticed that when bent, your knee—while painful—is still quite stable, not loose and floating around. If I'm right it's a good prognosis. With the proper care and rehab we'll have you back on the field before the end of the season. Any tear over a grade one—that is more than ten per cent of the tendon's fibres torn—and you would need surgery and be looking at a very long recovery and rehabilitation period."

Pippa listened intently to what the doctor was saying to Rook, but wondered if Rook was taking any of the information in. He looked distraught, and it was more than just the pain, she knew. All players worried about forced retirement due to injury, but Pippa was convinced Rook would be able to make a full recovery. She just had to convince him of that. Unfortunately, the half-time siren sounded and Pippa had to leave Rook in Doc's care, and to his own demons, while she tended to any running repairs needed on the Jets players who would be returning for the second half of the game.

The atmosphere in the team room was thick with tension. Everyone seemed to be trying to deal with the knowledge that Rook, their playmaker and captain, would not be returning to the field. Brodie, as a coach should, tried to inspire and fill the nervous players with the confidence that as a team, they could bounce back from the obvious setback. He was changing some of the game plan to make allowances for Rook's absence—Gareth was to take over the captaincy role. The half and playmaker role would be covered by a youngster from the substitution bench, Josh McQuade.

Although a young man full of potential, the new rookie would probably be slightly out of his league.

Pippa was amazed at how calm Brodie and JT remained under the circumstances—really able to inspire the players. The Jets team was full of self-confidence and hyped up as they headed down the tunnel and back to the field for the final period of the game.

Pippa hurried back to Rook the moment she was free. He was still lying, unmoving, flat on his back with his arm thrown over his eyes. But he did have that magical green tube clenched between his teeth. Sucking on the methoxyflurane's powerful analgesic would ease his pain—or at least make him not care about it. He was still wearing the game-day strip, down to the footy sock and studded boot on his uninjured leg. He looked as if he had been abandoned. The ice-pack on his injured knee had begun to melt and water was dripping onto the floor. Pippa filled another bag with ice and replaced the melted bag. She mopped up the spilt water with a towel before she finally took a tentative peek at Rook's face.

His silver eyes pierced her heart, the forlorn image he portrayed more than she could bear.

"Oh, Rook, don't look so sad. It'll be okay, you can bounce back from this setback. I will do everything possible to get you back on the field quickly," Pippa whispered, emotion choking her voice as the man she loved—had always loved—lay before her, looking so defeated. "C'mon, Rookie, where's that cocky, spirited footballer I've loved since I was fifteen gone?"

Pippa could not believe she had actually let those words spill from her lips. All she could hope was that Rook would not take her confession seriously—she was so rattled, and acting anything but professionally at the moment.

As Pippa busied herself fussing with the already perfectly positioned ice-packs, trying as best she could to act nonchalant over her words, she felt Rook's hand on her arm. Too nervous to face him and deal with the words she had blurted out, her heart pounding inside her chest — the noise, Pippa believed, loud enough for Rook to hear — she waited for him to acknowledge her slip-up. She did not notice the doctor had entered the room until she heard him speak to Rook.

"Okay then, Rook, I've made an appointment for you at the hospital for your MRI scan. It will give us a clear idea of what we are dealing with here." The doctor continued his one-sided conversation with Rook, unaware of the emotional tension between the two original occupants of the room. "For the time being, we will put you in a knee brace and fit you out with crutches. Stay off the leg completely, keep it elevated and iced. Under no circumstances add heat. I've heard you like to recover in a spa, Rook. Don't go anywhere near it. Clean yourself up in the showers — Pip can help you with that. Go home and rest until the scan. I'll let you know what comes next once I get a look at the results."

Pippa choked back a gasp as the doctor mentioned Rook's spa, the memories of her time with Rook still very fresh in her mind. Her eyes, which only moments ago had been reluctant to meet Rook's, were now drawn as if by some magnetic pull to his. She was once again trapped under the weight of his stare, mesmerised by him.

It was clear to her that the memory of their tryst was still just as prominent for him, as well.

Pippa had to focus on the doctor's instructions, but it was not an easy accomplishment when her body was on fire, needy from the memories of Rook and what he had done to her in his spa. Images flashed through her mind, reminding her of the way she had sensually exploded. Her nipples tingled as she remembered the feel of the cold tiles as her breasts had bounced on the side of the spa, while Rook had slammed into her body from behind. Pippa felt the red flush flow up her neck onto her cheekbones as she fought to regain control over her traitorous body, could see that Rook understood what she was feeling, as if he had somehow tapped into her memories and thoughts.

"Phillipa, did you hear me? Do you understand my instructions? Can I leave Rook in your capable hands?" the doctor repeated sternly.

"Yes, Doc — get Rook cleaned up, fit the knee brace and send him home on crutches to rest up for tomorrow's MRI."

Pippa was starting to believe she had a future on the stage at the way she'd been able to act so in control when she'd finally answered. Even her voice had sounded quite normal, when on the inside she was in turmoil. Her emotions were building, raging throughout her body like a tornado looking for its most destructive path. How on earth was she going to help Rook, the man who shook her to the core, shower and dress without becoming a blubbery mess of female hormones? *Surely one of the male members of the Jets staff should take over from here?*

Chapter Sixteen

Pippa was so caught up in her own thoughts that she did not seem to realise her face was projecting her emotions, or that Rook was watching her with a morbid intensity.

He thought he'd heard her say she loved him, but the look of distaste was clear for him to see—it was written all over her, obviously put there at the thought of helping him shower. He must have heard wrong. The way she was looking now was not the expression of a woman in love, he was certain—it was that of a woman shocked at what she was about to endure.

Rook had also thought he'd witnessed a flicker of desire flash in her ocean blue eyes as the doctor had mentioned his spa, but he must have misread the situation there as well. He assumed it must be the pain medication clouding his mind, and making him see things he wanted to see as opposed to the truth. He really needed to get over Pippa Rodgers. Move on. She just wasn't interested.

"Shit, what a cock-up this year is turning into. The whole fuckin' year is shot. All that training, and what for? I didn't even last through the first game." Rook couldn't help his angry tone or his raised voice as his frustrations grew in proportion to the receding pain. "And now I'm going to be forced to endure your presence and good intentions twenty-four fucking seven, not to mention the pitying looks from every other goddamn person I know, and that's all before Mum gets wind of it…"

The unexpected sound of Pippa's mobile phone ringing made them both jump, and interrupted his tirade.

"My God! What now?" Pippa exclaimed as she grabbed her phone from her pocket and read the screen to see who was calling.

She was in shock at Rook's outburst, wondered if anyone else had heard him rant at her. She just wanted to crawl away and find some hole in the ground to hide in. She had not realised how much Rook hated her until now. How could she possibly stay on at the club now, knowing how he felt about her, knowing for a fact he didn't want anything to do with her and with her heart breaking every time she saw him? Distracted again by the sound of her phone, she finally registered the caller ID.

"It's Caitlin James. Why would she be calling me?" Confused, still looking at the screen, Pippa had a thought. "She probably wants an update on you, Rook. She'd be one of those terrible 'goddamn people' who care about you," Pippa said harshly as she connected the call. "What do you want me to tell her, Rook? Should I tell her you hate the fact that she cares? Perhaps I should just tell her to give up on you. You seem to have already given up on yourself."

Chapter Seventeen

Pippa gasped into the phone as she listened to Mandy, desperately trying to comprehend what she was being told. Caitlin had gone into early labour!

What…? Caitlin had been in labour most of the day but had decided not to mention that piece of information to her husband, not wanting to disturb his coaching preparations. *Great idea…* Caitlin was crazy — what on earth had the woman been thinking, keeping such a whopping big secret? She was in labour…about to give birth… And to top it all off — *hooray* — it seemed Pippa had been voted to be the one to go and break the news to an unsuspecting Brodie — but not until after the game, and with instructions to not let him panic. *Yeah, right!* The man was going to go through the roof, Pippa thought.

"Oh, shit, Mandy, how am I going to stop him from panicking? He'll have the shits Caitlin didn't tell him before he left for the game as it is," Pippa squeaked back into the mouthpiece of her phone. "Yeah… Okay, I'll try. You just tell Caitlin to hang on till Brodie gets there or it will be a slow, painful death for us all if he misses out on the birth."

Pippa closed her phone and stared off into space, wondering if it wouldn't be better to just go and break the news to Brodie now. She felt the warmth of Rook's hand the minute it touched her skin. Why was it that Rook's touch could make her body flame? Even when she was so distracted?

"Pip, honey, what's wrong, baby? You've gone so pale — are you okay?" Rook asked. He reached out and took her arm. "Caitlin and the baby will be fine."

Pippa was confused at the turnaround in Rook's manner. One minute he'd been full of anger and animosity towards her, and now it felt as though he was sincerely worried about her. Her head was spinning.

"Oh, it's nothing, really. I just have to wait until after the game to tell Brodie that Caitlin is at the hospital, giving birth to their child. He should take *that* information calmly. What do you think, Rookie? Will I survive his fury at my waiting until after the game, or should I go tell him now, and risk Caitlin and Mandy's wrath later? Choices! Lucky me!" Pippa explained, beginning to sound a little on the hysterical side.

"Shit, that is quite a dilemma." Rook seemed to think about what Pippa had said for a few moments, his own injury temporarily forgotten.

"If it was my kid, I would want to know, even if I was on the field still playing. I think you should go tell him, Pip. Brodie deserves to make up his own mind where he wants to be."

"Why are you so worried, Rook? You should be pleased. After Brodie kills me you won't have to put up with me at all," Pippa snapped back at Rook, but was unable to hide the hitch in her voice as a sob broke free.

"He won't have time to kill you, baby. He'll be too focused on getting to the hospital, becoming a dad again."

Rook talking about being a father had nearly made Pippa pass out—she could visualise him holding a little bundle with a head covered in thatch of blonde curls in his arms and making cute cooing sounds. It took her a few moments to clear the disturbing and heartbreaking thoughts from her head so she could concentrate on his recommendations.

"Yeah, I think I will go and tell Brodie the news. Will you be okay being alone for a while, or should I go get Flash to stay with you?"

"Go, Pip, I'm good—not like I can go anywhere just yet. I'm sorry for my outburst before, just feelin' a bit sorry for myself. I'll wait right here for you to come back, but if you would prefer someone else to help me shower, I'm good with that too," Rook replied. "I don't want to make you uncomfortable, Pip. Just do what you need to do."

Rook had appeared almost reluctant to pull his hand from Pippa's arm so she could leave him, and Pippa felt the loss of the warmth from his touch the moment he did. She didn't want to leave either. His hand on her arm had been enough to warm her insides and curl her toes—but she did have to go.

As Pippa raced up the stairs towards the coach's box high in the top of the stand, she wondered why Rook had said he didn't want her to feel uncomfortable. He was the one acting so uptight and tense around her—why should he care how she felt?

And what was with the endearments? One minute he was complaining about being near her and the next he was calling her 'baby' and stroking her arm in comfort. Being all caring and sharing, talking about babies and things.

"Aaargh, *men!*" she groaned as she climbed the stairs, deftly sidestepping the fans as she went hurtling by.

Now sure is not the time to worry about my problems with Rook, she policed her thoughts. *Now is the time to try and break the news to Brodie about his impending fatherhood without him going ballistic.* What was that saying about not shooting the messenger? Pippa sure hoped Brodie James was aware of it as she stopped in front of the door marked with the sign that read 'Home Team Coach'. Taking a deep breath to steady her nerves, Pippa knocked on the door between her and Brodie.

It was JT's voice that shouted out for her to enter, and she crept inside.

"Pip, what the hell are you doing up here?" JT asked. He seemed annoyed at her intrusion as he turned his focus back to the game, almost dismissing her presence at once.

"Um, yeah. Ah, I've got some important news for Brodie," she stammered nervously.

"Look, Phillipa, I'm a bit busy right now—can't it wait? The boys are just managing to hang on to this lead and I need to concentrate on the game," Brodie grumbled, never taking his eyes from the view through the glass window of the coaches' box.

"I know that, Brodie! But I think you will want me to tell you about the phone call I just took from Mandy Thomson."

At the sound of his wife's name JT stood up and whirled around to face Pippa. His stance was frightening, and it took all Pippa's efforts not to shrink back from his glare. "What the fuck is going on, Pip? What's happened to Mandy?"

"No, n-n-not Mandy, JT… Caitlin…it's Caitlin. Mandy has taken Caitlin to the hospital — the baby is coming early. They didn't want me to tell you till after the game, but I thought you needed to know now, Brodie… I'm sorry for disturbing everyone."

"Shit…shit…shit! Pip, I need to get to Caitlin." Brodie dragged JT out of the way so he could speak directly to her.

"What exactly did Mandy tell you? And thanks for coming straight away. I really would have been pissed if you had waited. What's with that woman of mine, anyway, wanting you to wait?" Brodie, agitated but still in control, stood patiently while Pippa repeated Mandy's telephone conversation and the plan — already put into action — for Riley to look after all the youngsters. Pippa did not even try to answer Brodie's last question, though she didn't think he was at all interested in her view of Caitlin's reasoning.

Brodie made hurried arrangements so he could join his wife at the hospital. He left JT to look after the team. There were only ten minutes of the game to go and the Jets were just in front on the scoreboard — it would go down to the wire.

Pippa was left with the instructions to make sure the guys warmed down correctly and to take stock of any injuries, so she could give Brodie an accurate account later. Brodie promised he would call as soon as he had any news on Caitlin and the baby. JT would have to go to the after-match functions on Brodie's behalf and make his apologies. Then, with a grin that resembled the iconic smiling face of Luna Park, Brodie bolted out of the door.

"Well, that went well." Pippa giggled as she left a slightly green-looking JT, obviously worried about his upcoming responsibilities — or was it the thought of childbirth? Pippa couldn't be sure — and headed back to Rook and the busy after-game schedule ahead. She shivered at the thought of the shower she was still to help Rook have, in between all her other responsibilities.

"Yep, I'm in way over my head this time. Well, no use putting it off, Pip. Take a mouthful of cement and harden up, princess. This is what you get paid the big bucks for," she mumbled to herself as she jogged back down the stairs to the treatment rooms, trying to bring out the professional physiotherapist in her, the one she had spent years training to become.

* * * *

He'd missed the connection immediately — his body, which had been sparking at even the slightest contact with hers, had felt cold and empty the minute she'd left. It had reminded him that he was still lying broken and useless on a table under a grandstand, not sure of what his future held. Unlike Brodie and Caitlin, who would soon be happily welcoming the newest addition to their perfect life.

A perfect life that Rook could not ever imagine attaining for himself — especially without Pippa. It seemed highly unlikely they would be together, given that she could hardly stand being in his presence. He wished he hadn't blurted out all that stuff about her being around, but he had been so hurt at her look of distaste at the thought of helping him shower that he had wanted some revenge.

"Wish Mum was here. I could do with some advice about now, not to mention some TLC. Fuck, I'm such a wuss."

And now he was even talking to himself. Rook groaned as he lay back and threw his arm over his eyes once again in frustration. "How the hell am I going to survive the rest of today, let alone the rest of my life?" he whimpered.

Chapter Eighteen

Rook sat, leg propped up on a chair at Jetstream, feeling sorry for himself. *Again!* It seemed to be his regular mood these days. He had not yet figured out which was worse, the injury he was dealing with or being forced to spend so much time with, and in such close proximity to, Pippa. He was frustrated at having to use crutches to get around, frustrated at the slow progress his knee was making, frustrated that no matter how hard he tried, he could not keep his body from reacting whenever Pippa touched him, but mostly frustrated that she never acted anything but professional when she had her hands all over him.

She had helped him shower, holding him up like some invalid as he'd quickly cleaned the mud and grass from his body—not that there had been much, hell, he'd only been on the field for less than a quarter of the game. Never once had she seemed interested or even slightly moved by his near naked body. In fact, distracted was more the vibe she had given off. Meanwhile, it had taken all of his control—and the occasional jolt of pain from his knee when he'd purposely moved it—to stop himself from getting a hard-on. It had been a mortifying enough experience without him sporting a woody and Pippa thinking it was because of her... *But it was because of her, stupid*, a voice in his head corrected.

Pippa had then efficiently organised Gareth to drive him and his car back home. Gareth had hardly said two words to him during the whole drive home. Rook had been expecting some show of pity or sympathy about his injury, but the cowboy hadn't said a thing. And that had pissed him off—yeah, he'd whinged about not wanting anyone to make a fuss, but shit, a consoling comment or two might have been nice from his teammate. But no—Gareth had sat stony-faced, eyes on the road the whole way home, only breaking his silence to ask Rook where he wanted the car parked.

Then, to add insult to injury—literally—he'd had to watch, peering out from his living-room window like some kind of stalker, as Pippa had picked Gareth up and headed, Rook guessed, back to the club for the after-match function. While he had been left alone with his misery and a noisy nightclub downstairs full of strangers who had, in conjunction with the pain from his knee, kept him awake all night.

The results from the scans taken the day after the game had been favourable. Rook had been relieved that as there was only a slight tear to the tendon, he was not going to need surgery, just time and rehabilitation. That was the part that was killing him—he hated all the time he was spending doing nothing but thinking. He was driving himself, and those around him, insane. Rook knew he had to do something about his attraction to Pippa, but what? That was the question.

Rook was thankful that he had such good friends. Brodie, JT and the boys had eventually all shown their support, offering assistance and advice for both his injury and running his nightclub. There had been more Jets players frequenting his bar than ever before, all ready to lend a hand. *Yeah, all but Gareth, that is.* Rook still hadn't found out what was wrong with him, what was getting under Gareth's usually happy-go-lucky persona.

Rook had also discovered that Mick didn't really need his help. He was a hell of a bar manager and barman. Rook thought that most of the time he was just in Mick's way, propped up like he was. And that was another cause of his dark moods. His bar ran without him, the team was still managing a few wins without him, and the new rookie was getting better and better.

His mum, Laura, had also been underfoot constantly, fussing and generally getting under his skin. Finally Trevor, Laura's new husband, had come to Rook's aid and taken her back home, giving Rook some breathing space. Trevor was one of the good guys. Forced to retire early from the game, he had turned to a career as a sports commentator, and had been a constant in Rook's life for a while. But the reminder that Trevor had retired early due to a leg injury had only managed to darken Rook's mood further.

Rook had been overjoyed when his mum and Trev had got together, even if it had seemed a little weird at first that his mum had been dating. Rook had just tried not to think about the details too deeply. Of course, when you had nothing to do but think, those deeper, darker thoughts came crashing to the fore.

Rook had never met his father. His mum had raised him single-handedly. When he was younger he'd hated the stigma of being from a single-parent family — not that Rook had really missed out on much. His mum had put his needs before hers every time. Rook knew she had made many sacrifices on his behalf. Laura Harris had worked hard cleaning other people's homes to feed and clothe him. The work had also meant she had not needed childcare or babysitting expenses. As a youngster, Mitch — as he had been known before his footy nickname had taken hold — had accompanied her to work.

As a teen, he had been embarrassed by the fact that his mum had cleaned the homes of some of his fellow students. He had been forced to weather the storm of teasing comments about her, but he had really hated being taunted by the words from the song *Sadie the Cleaning Lady*, which had come from the mouths of the more vicious students when his mum had been around.

It had been playing rugby league that had changed all that for Mitchell Harris — he had quickly risen from the ranks of the bullied to those of the most popular when he'd been signed, while still in high school, to the Jets team. He had become 'the Rookie' and everyone had wanted to be his mate or his girl. Everyone had, all of a sudden, loved him. Best of all, Rook had been able to help his Mum set up a cleaning business — she now only took the bookings, did the bookwork and organised her small staff to do the physical aspects that were involved in cleaning a house, and she had blossomed in her new career as a small business owner.

The fact that the Jets team was once again, en masse, at Jetstream celebrating another team win was grating on Rook's nerves, as well. If one more person came over and commiserated on his injury and mentioned the fact that the Jets were still winning, despite his absence, he would rip their head off and shove it up their backside. The imagery of doing just that soothed Rook's dark mood for a few glorious moments.

Of course, watching Gareth dancing with Pippa to just about every song put an end to any fleeting glimpse of happiness Rook might be able to conjure.

He hated that feeling of jealousy when he saw the couple together. It wasn't as if they looked all that romantic—more comfortable in each other's arms—but just the fact that Gareth could touch Pippa was enough to make Rook see red. He wanted to drag her away from the man, carry her upstairs to his bed and fuck her till Pippa screamed his name and promised to be his. Which, considering he was still half a cripple, would be hard to achieve.

Having done nothing but think over the last few weeks, Rook had come to the sad conclusion that he had spent his whole adult life searching for Pippa. All the blondes that he had thought he was attracted to had been just poor imitations of the young girl of his dreams. How ironic that she now had dark hair, and he was now more attracted to her than ever. He was still lamenting the fact to himself when a familiar voice broke into his thoughts.

"Why don't you just tell her how you feel, Rookie?"

Brodie and JT stood at the bar next to Rook. Both men patiently waited for him to answer the question.

"I don't understand what you're talking about, JT. Tell who how I feel?" Rook finally answered, shocked that his coach was aware of his feelings towards the team's physio—the same girl Brodie had warned him away from back in the early days of his professional footy career. Rook had understood the threat and the fact it would have been the end of his contract if he went near her.

"Take it from men who have worn that same expression on their faces—there is no point in trying to fight it. Once a woman has gotten under your skin, it's fatal. There is no cure." JT laughed, punching Rook in the arm so hard he nearly fell off his stool.

"C'mon, Rookie, you've had the hots for Pip Rodgers for years. You don't think I know, all those years ago when you were warned off her, how much it took for you to walk away? You were a hell of a man back then, and you still are. Take it from me, Rookie, finding Caitlin was the best thing to ever happen to me. After all the shit with my ex, I had given up on the idea of marriage and kids. Now I have a beautiful new baby girl, a feisty little son and a gorgeous wife. That's what it's really all about!"

Rook was trying to comprehend what Brodie was saying to him. They knew how he felt about Pippa, and had for some time. What was more, they were giving him the go-ahead to try to start something with her.

"What about your 'no fraternisation' rule?" Rook asked his coach.

"I think this relationship was well on its way before Pippa started working for the Jets team, so it doesn't really count. What do you reckon, JT?"

"Yep, don't think it has any bearing in this instance. These two have been destined to be together since way back. I remember my Mandy telling me just that, years ago," JT answered.

"So what are you waiting for, Rook? You're not a *Rookie* anymore—step up, stop wasting time and go get your woman, before Gareth cowboys up and drags her back to some outback country town and turns her into his cowgirl. Actually, they make a nice couple, don't you think, JT?" It was Brodie's turn to give Rook a good-natured slap on the shoulder as he finished his teasing pep-talk with a laugh. Again, the slap—this time from Brodie—nearly knocked Rook right off his stool.

"I really wish you apes would stop whacking me. I just about fall off this stool every time. If I'm to fall on my face, it might as well be trying to woo my woman, rather than my coaches beating me up," Rook said, his spirits lifting at the thought of him and Pippa together, finally.

Chapter Nineteen

Pippa was glad that Gareth was acting normally around her again. They had not discussed his admission, that first game day, of wanting more than just her friendship. She had worried later, as she had reviewed her eventful day, that he might pull away from her, embarrassed by his admission. Pippa valued Gareth's friendship a great deal, and she really held great affection for him. She couldn't help but think of how much easier her life would be if it was Gareth's body she desired.

As they danced, Pippa tried to imagine Gareth's lips on hers or his hands cupping her breasts, tugging at her nipples or teasing her clit, but to no avail. She could not feel any sexual heat at all towards her friend. As much as it frustrated her—she knew that the man holding her in his arms was one of the good guys in life, someone a girl could really lose her heart to and depend on—it was Rook who sent her pulse rate racing and stole her breath from her lungs with just a glance.

"Stop thinking, Pip." Gareth gave her a little shake as he held her in his arms while they danced. "I guess it's time we talked about my big mouth."

Pippa shook her head.

"No, Gareth, let's not. I'd just as soon forget about that whole day. I really love having you around—you're becoming one of my dearest friends."

"It's okay, Pip, I understand. Really, I do. I don't know what got into me, blurting out my feelings like that. I think it was watching Rook leave you looking hurt again that did me in. I'm not blind—I can see I'm not the cowboy for you. But it doesn't hurt a guy to imagine what it could be like. I'll always be here for ya, Pip, and if it is as just friends than I can deal. I'd rather have you as part of my life in the big city than not at all. Who else would protect me from all those bold city girls, eh?"

"Oh, Gareth, it would be so easy for me if I could feel more for you, you know, in that way, but I can't. You're one of the good guys, Cowboy, and I'll tell you a little secret—I've tried to imagine you and me like that, have even thought about kissing you just to see if I could spark up some attraction, but it just doesn't work. I love you, Gareth, I really do…"

Pippa dropped her head on Gareth's chest as she whispered to him the words she knew he didn't want to hear.

"Just not in that way."

"C'mon now, Pip, don't get all weepy on me. We'll be right. I'll live—hey, I've taken a few hits in my time, on the footy field and in the paddock. I'll survive. But let's make a deal, you and me. If we don't get our love lives sorted by the time we are old and grey we'll marry each other. We can rock away in wicker chairs on my front porch back at the farm and reminisce over chances missed. Whaddaya say, Pip? Will you marry me then, 'cause I already know there will always be a place in my heart for you. Love you too, Pip."

"Yep, sounds like a good idea to me, Cowboy. It's a deal. It'll be our secret."

Rook could not believe his ears. He had hobbled out onto the dance-floor — sans crutches — to cut in on Gareth. He had rehearsed what he was going to say to her. It was time Pippa knew how long he had cared for her, perhaps even loved her. He could finally come clean and tell her how weak he had been, letting her think he wasn't interested in her.

God, if she only knew how hard it had been to turn away from her back then — how many frustrating times he had imagined that the younger Rookie hadn't fled. Hell, he still had dreams about her and that night. He'd always imagined the feel of touching her youthful, inexperienced body, caressing and kissing those pale breasts, making her writhe and moan beneath him as he took her innocence. Rookie was convinced she had still been a virgin when she had approached him that night, so long ago.

But then he had overheard them, out there on the dance-floor, as they'd whispered their words of love while wrapped in each other's arms. He'd managed to catch snippets of their conversation as they'd moved around him, unaware of his presence.

Could Rook trust his hearing over the loud music? It sounded pretty much like Gareth had proposed to Pippa. Not all that eloquently, in Rook's opinion, but he couldn't dismiss the fact that Pippa had said yes — or more precisely, "It's a deal," adding her personal endearment, 'Cowboy', to the acceptance.

But it was a secret for the moment, apparently.

"Bit late to be worried about breaking the rules now, princess—you're making a habit of it," Rook mumbled bitterly as he backtracked quickly to the bar—as quickly as he could manage, anyway, given the brace on his injured knee.

"What happened, Rook?" JT laughed. "Did ya get cold feet? Thought you were going out to claim your woman?"

"Fuck off, JT. Just 'cause you're happy with your picture-perfect life—wife 'n' kids and picket fuckin' fences—doesn't mean I have to want it. Came to my senses. See you later, Brodes… I've got a business to run here."

Rook grabbed his crutches, leaving his long-term friends, now his coaches, behind. He could almost feel the burn from their eyes on his back as he stormed off towards his office—well, hobbled with angry purpose, that was, as he was too angry to make use of the walking aids that were tucked under one arm. On the way, he noticed a busty blonde giving him the eye.

"Why the hell shouldn't I have some fun? It's not like I've got to get up for training in the morning. A hot, willing babe is just what I need to cheer me up." It sounded, even to his own ears, as if he was trying too hard to convince himself.

Rook changed his path and headed in the direction of the blonde, catching a waitress on the way past.

"Hey, Jem, bring us a couple of beers, honey. I'm just heading over to that blonde over there."

Rook nodded his head in the direction he was going as Jemima, the waitress, scooted towards the bar.

Chapter Twenty

She really was becoming quite the actress, what with having to pretend, day after day, as she manhandled Rook's tempting body, that he did not make her quiver with desire. But Pippa could not hide her despair as she watched Rook chatting up his latest blonde bombshell.

She'd managed to perform her duties as a professional member of the Jets medical team, never letting her hunger for Rook show through. Being careful not to broadcast her unrelenting desire for Rook to once again touch her, make her nerves sing and pleasure her body like no other man ever had. And it had been the most torturous of tasks. After having worked so hard to become a sports physio, thinking that that was what she wanted to do more than anything else with her life, Pippa was now having major second thoughts.

It wasn't that everyone she came into contact with wasn't pleasant. On the contrary, Pippa had been surprised that she had found absolutely no resistance to her working with the team of rugged sportsmen.

Well, that was as long as she didn't include Rook. But even her dealings with the frustratingly handsome fantasy-on-legs recently had been nothing short of polite. Yep—polite to the point of Pippa wanting to pull the hair from her head in frustration.

Every day she had to see Rook up close and personal, monitor his recovery, work with and massage his muscles to keep them from growing stiff. Yes, she had her hands all over him repeatedly, but all she got from him in return were monosyllabic responses. He was always polite, but never met her eye, never got even slightly chatty, never asked her about her day, her life, and definitely never worried about the fact he was slowly driving her crazy.

And now, as if the day's torture had not been enough, she had subjected herself to an extra dose of Rook-related misery as she watched him sidling up to a big-busted blonde bimbo.

"They can't be real—so big and perky. If he's not careful, one of those nipples will poke out his eye," she said to no one in particular. Pippa just couldn't manage to hold her tongue any longer.

"Why don't you just tell Rook how you feel, Pip? Maybe you should explain about that night, maybe apologise." Cassie shook her head, a sad smile forming. "It sure as hell can't make it any worse. I'm really worried about you, Pip. I really wish I hadn't encouraged you into getting it on with Rook—shit! I thought it would help you get over him, get him out of your system, but you are worse now than ever. You are throwing away your life… You've wanted this job for so long and yet you aren't enjoying it at all. And it's all because of Rook. God, why can't you fall for someone like Gareth? You never see him leeching onto any of the groupies. He wouldn't break your heart the way Rook has, and still does."

"You might be right, Cassie, but it's just not that easy. For starters the reason Gareth isn't interested in any of the swarms of women is because he left his heart back in Gunnedah, and until he does something about her, he won't be happy. I think that is why we get on so well. We're both broken. You know, I've been thinking about it a lot lately. I think I need to talk to Brodie. I'm thinking maybe a stint with the folks in the UK might be a good idea. Put a little distance between Rook and me."

"Oh, no, Pippa, you can't! How would I cope without you? You're my best friend, my family. Don't leave me. Don't leave the Jets—you love that team. Just talk to Rook. Gosh, if you won't then maybe I should, 'cause I don't want to lose you," Cassie cried, starting to stand up as if to make good on her threat to go to Rook.

Pippa grabbed at her friend and dragged her back down to her chair, just as Gareth and Riley came back from the bar with the drink refills. Before Pippa had a chance to ask Cassie not to mention their conversation, her best friend blurted out her worries.

"Riley, Gareth, you've got to talk some sense into Pippa. She was just telling me that she's thinking of quitting the Jets and going over to England to stay with her folks. Tell her she can't leave… Riley, do something…please."

Pippa just wanted the ground to open and swallow her up. Just behind Cassie, as she was pleading to Riley and Gareth, stood Brodie and JT. And it was obvious by the stormy look on the giant men's faces that they were not happy. Now she was the centre of attention and very uncomfortable, what with all the glares she was receiving. Pippa tried to stand, thinking that it was definitely time to use the flight mode of her fight-or-flight adrenaline boost.

"Not so fast, young lady," Brodie boomed as he took hold of her hand and dragged her back to her chair. "This has gone on for far too long. JT and I thought that you two would get it together by now and stop moping around each other, but obviously you are both far too immature or stubborn, or a mixture of both, to do that." Brodie continued his lecture, his voice becoming more serious. "But if this problem you and Rook are having is going to affect my footy team, then as coach I think it's time I step in and sort it out."

"Oh, Brodie…"

"Don't interrupt me, Phillipa Rodgers. I'm not finished." Brodie resumed speaking, his voice cutting her off abruptly, not letting Pippa say a word in her own defence.

"I'm calling a meeting. I want you and Mitchell Harris in my office at ten a.m. sharp tomorrow morning. No excuses from either of you. JT, can you go and tell that thickhead his presence is required tomorrow, and while you're at it, strongly encourage our Rook to leave that girl alone and get back to running his bar."

"Sure thing, Brodes. I'm all over it." Pippa didn't miss the ear-to-ear grin on JT as he took off, headed in Rook's direction.

"Now do I have your assurance that you will be at my office tomorrow, Pip?" Brodie was staring her down, making Pippa feel like a five-year-old getting a stern talking-to from her father. He had always been a bit of a bossy boots, Pippa thought, wondering how Caitlin put up with it.

"Yes, Brodie, I'll be there. But I'm not sure this is a very good idea. I think I need to speak with you privately first. There are some things you should know — things I've done, things that were none of Rook's doing."

Pippa was trying to stop the tears from overflowing. She hated the thought of coming clean to Brodie, hated the fact that she was about to prove she could not be trusted. About to let the man who had treated her like his kid sister, or even daughter, know that she had let him down.

"Tomorrow, Pippa. We will sort it all out tomorrow. I'm off home to my beautiful wife and gorgeous children. I think all of you should head out too." Brodie's gaze fell to cover all at Pippa's table. "Gareth, I'll see you at training. Riley, I think Caitlin is expecting a visit from you and Cassie soon. Don't let your sister down. And Pippa, stop worrying." With that Brodie strode off towards the club's exit and, as if on cue, JT stepped up next to him as they both sauntered out of the door.

Pippa smiled despite her problems. It was a bit creepy the way those two were joined at the hip. Her thoughts were interrupted by the sighs — probably of relief — coming from her friends as they all deliberated on what the events of tomorrow's meeting might achieve. Cassie, Riley and Gareth made Pippa feel even more embarrassed. Such drama! It reminded her of a television soapy, and unfortunately for her, she was the star.

Chapter Twenty-One

Rook couldn't help but feel a bit relieved that JT had broken up his tryst with the blonde. The minute Rook had sat next to her, he'd known he had made a mistake. But he hadn't wanted to seem rude, and so had made some small talk with the awestruck groupie.

God, he had forgotten what it was like to be around obsessed fans, women just wanting to add another footy player to their list of sexual conquests. It never failed to surprise Rook that women could be just as sexually permissive as men in that area. Blondie hadn't cared what he liked or who his favourite band was — no, she'd just wanted to hear when he would be back on the field and info about other teammates' relationship statuses. She'd even had the hide to ask if he was still able to perform with a dud leg — shit, he'd done his knee, not been castrated! — and hinted that she was quite happy to take the lead as she'd crudely sucked her finger in and out of her mouth. *Subtle.* And for Rook, the sight had held no attraction at all. It had not even raised a flicker of sexual interest in him.

Nope, nothing happened in that department these days unless he was around one Pippa Rodgers, he thought miserably.

Blondie had obviously picked up on his disinterest, because as soon as JT had joined them she'd had the audacity to flutter her fake eyelashes at him, oohing and ahhing at what a big boy he was. *Yeah, never heard that before*, Rook thought as he took the opportunity JT had presented by asking for a private word. He struggled to his feet and steered himself and JT away from Blondie's flirting.

Even though he was glad for the interruption, Rook could not help but be a little worried over the reason. What did Brodie want to have a meeting with Rook about that couldn't just be said tonight? Hell, they had been standing next to each other at the bar not long ago — surely Brodie hadn't taken offence at his angry outburst.

And what was with sending JT to deliver the request, or was that more of a summons? Why hadn't Brodie just asked? What was with all this cloak-and-dagger stuff?

Rook's stomach rolled as a terrifying thought took root.

"No fuckin' way. Surely they're not gonna pull my contract because of my knee?" He murmured the words under his breath as Rook's worst-case scenario — the end of his career — started to seem all the more imminent. A million thoughts raced through his mind. *But I'm getting better! Every day, I'm stronger... My God, what has Pippa been saying?* What had she been reporting to the coaching staff?

"So tomorrow then, Rook."

Rook noticed Brodie walking away from where Pippa and Gareth were sitting and heading towards the door. He felt JT slap him on the shoulder as the big guy said goodbye before heading off in the same direction. Obviously the coaches had arrived together and were leaving the same way.

"Yeah, tomorrow," Rook finally managed to mumble, but way too late for JT to actually hear it over the noise of the club.

Rook hobbled over to the bar and sat down before the sheer weight of his troubles took him to the floor.

"Hey, boss, you okay? You're lookin' a bit shaky there. What's wrong? Didn't the blonde go for it?" Mick set a fresh beer down in front of Rook and tilted his head in a questioning way.

"Yeah, just hunky-dory if you don't count my bung leg, and the fact I've been summoned for a meeting with the powers-that-be tomorrow, probably to tear up my contract on the grounds I'm a goddamn gimp who fucked the club physio and broke the club's rules... Yep, I'm just peachy!" Rook simmered before taking a long pull from the beer, rubbing at the ring of condensation left on the bar. "Think I'll just head on upstairs, try and get hold of my agent, see if he's heard anything. You right to finish up here?"

Even though he knew he shouldn't look, Rook couldn't help searching for a last glimpse of Pippa before he headed on up to his apartment. His eyes combed the darkness of the club's interior, but he couldn't find her or her entourage anyplace.

"She just left, with Gareth. Not long after Brodie and JT left." Mick's tone held a slight touch of humour in it. He raised an eyebrow in Rook's direction, while still managing to serve at least three customers at the same time.

Rook just glared back at the barman, ignoring the smug look on Mick's face, before he turned and, with the help of his crutches, walked away without forming a reply.

* * * *

Pippa hadn't been able to sleep. She had struggled with the urge to ring her dad and get his advice on what she should do, how she should proceed with her life. Should she 'fess up, resign her position at the Jets and look for something else, maybe overseas with her dad and mum? It had its positives. But she had wanted this job all her life, and did she really want to leave Cassie behind? And what about Rook? Was she strong enough to move on, get over him? Pippa didn't think so.

If she hadn't moved on since she was fifteen, what made her think she was going to be able to now? Perhaps she should just tell him how she felt. Tell Rook that he was her fantasy man, that his silver eyes haunted her dreams. That he made her pant with desire, her heart race at the mere sight of him, her core clench with need, drip moisture into her panties at the sound of his voice. She should tell him about the torture of rubbing her hands over his skin and having him show nothing in response.

Yeah, that would be a fine idea... Humiliation was something she knew where Rook was concerned, and Pippa didn't think she could handle the mortification of him rejecting her again.

Nope, resigning her position seemed the only answer.

No matter what angle, what scenario Pippa conjured up in regards to the meeting she was dreading, it all ended with one of two outcomes—either she would resign, or face humiliation once again at Rook's rejection.

And the high likelihood of watching the embarrassment show on Rook face when Brodie broached the subject of her desires was not going to be the highlight of her day, either. It would be so much easier if she didn't love him. Not that loving him was going to do her any good. The undisputed fact was that she didn't even earn a blip on Rook's radar. Nope, he was all about the fake, busty blondes, as proven again by his choice of woman at the club last night.

God, it made Pippa nauseous to see him with those shallow women, but what could she do? Rook had been a playboy from the get-go. The women had flocked around him from the very beginning of his career. Pippa should know—she had been there too, the coach's young daughter. *Pipsqueak*—God, she'd hated that nickname—had had to watch them maul him, an awkward fifteen-year-old with nothing womanly to offer him at all. They were awful memories. Pippa much preferred her more recent ones—the time spent with Rook in his apartment, the way he had made her feel, had played her body with a maestro's touch. *And why wouldn't he?* she lamented. *Rook has been with enough women to know how to make one half-innocent come alive.*

She sat staring out at the brickwork of the building that housed the Jets' offices, gym and medical rooms—the same building that her father, as the Jets' coach, had spent so much of her childhood working in, the same building she had not been allowed to enter post-match because she was female. That was probably the reason she had worked so hard to become a sports physiotherapist—to beat that rule and be invited into the footy inner sanctum.

She hadn't noticed Rook approach her car, so she literally jumped, startled, when he opened the passenger side door and joined her, sitting down next to her. It was as if all the oxygen had been immediately sucked from the air. Her smallish car seemed to shrink inwards. Pippa could feel the heat emanating from Rook's body as one of his wide shoulders almost touched hers.

Pippa swivelled her head towards him, at once captured in the depths of his silver eyes, unable to draw her own away. She sighed, or perhaps it was more like a little moan—she wasn't sure. All she did know was that this man sitting beside her, only a slight movement away from touching her, did things to her heart and soul that no other did. And in a split-second Pippa decided that she was going to do herself a favour and give it one more go. She was going to tell Rook of her feelings towards him. Hey, what was the worst that could happen? He might walk away—she was used to that.

But if she didn't try, just once more, before she gave up and walked away, she would never be able to forgive herself. Pippa had to know, had to make sure that there was no chance for her and Rook. Then, and maybe only then, she could get on with her life. Maybe, as Cassie always said, 'find a nice man and settle down'.

Chapter Twenty-Two

He had been sitting in his car, working up the nerve to head into the building that had been such a big part of his life. For close to a third of the years he had been on this earth, Rook had been part of the Jets team. It was a family of sorts, and for a man with hardly any family, it was an important part of his being.

The thought that his life might be only minutes away from changing was not a happy one, but oddly it was the lone figure sitting in another car in the same car park that had him the most distracted.

He had really messed up, had really managed to do absolutely everything wrong when it came to Pippa. Rook was still appalled that he had not recognised the dark-haired beauty as the girl he had spent so much of his youth dreaming about. The blonde curls might now be coloured black, and the girlish curves formed into a toned and fit womanly body that oozed sex appeal, but she was still Pippa. The blue of her eyes alone should have clued him in — it was just that he hadn't figured on seeing her again. Especially at Jetstream.

Rook had heard that her folks were over in the UK, her dad coaching again, so had just assumed she was there. He had certainly never expected her to waltz back into his life — maybe if he had, he might not have stuffed it up so royally!

But Rook thought he could try to make it right. He could walk over — *hobble* over — and apologise, explain why he had walked away from her. Walked away because he'd known he hadn't been good enough for her, back then. Perhaps he still wasn't, considering that he knew of Gareth's intentions towards her and yet he was still going to try to steal her from him. Hell, if he was going to be kicked from the team anyway it wouldn't matter if he and Gareth came to blows over her. And *yes*, she was definitely worth fighting for, Rook finally realised — right now, meeting be damned.

He managed to seat himself in her car with a modicum of decorum, bad knee notwithstanding, and now she was facing him. Startled at first, her eyes were now drowning him in their depths. A little gasp or moan escaped her perfect lips, lips that Rook wanted to kiss more than he wanted his next breath. Finally managing to get a grip on his wayward thoughts, Rook took a deep breath and began to form the words that he hoped would help her understand, help him maybe convince her to take a chance on him, let him compete with Gareth for her affections. He needed to let her know that she had always been in his dreams.

"Mind if I join you?" Rook smiled hopefully.

"Seems you already have." Pippa's answer, Rook noted, was not much above a whisper. Her eyes never left his.

"We need to talk… I need to tell you what you do to me, Pippa, what you've always done to me. My God, woman, you fill my dreams. Have for as long as I can remember. It just took me a while to realise that the woman who has starred in all my dreams was you. I remember that night in your family's backyard. I've revisited that night in my fantasies many times, wishing I had acted differently. But no matter how much I wanted you back then—and I did, Pip, you have no idea how much—I did the right thing walking away. Not because of the warnings from your father and Brodie to keep away from you if I wanted to keep my contract with the Jets. That wasn't what made me ignore what I wanted. It was knowing I wasn't good enough for you. Pip, you were just starting your life, and you were so smart…and I was just a footy player from a single-parent home. I couldn't take advantage of you—you were so young and beautiful, so tempting, but I had nothing to offer you…"

Rook ran his fingers through his hair, trying to control the build-up of emotion that threatened to overwhelm his confession as he remembered that night. The pain and sorrow he had felt. "I was unworthy of someone like you…"

Rook took a steadying breath.

"Pippa, I just wanted to apologise and explain my behaviour. I never meant to hurt you. I was protecting you, baby… That night at the club, I should have known it was you, it was…beyond words. I've thought of little else since then. You mean so much to me, Pippa. I've been acting like an idiot…it's just that I don't understand why you pretended to be someone else. I just want you to know that…you are amazing and I really hope we can be friends, no matter what happens from here."

What on earth was Rook saying? How dare her father and Brodie warn him off her as if she were some object to be protected? Or worse, used as a threat. No wonder he had fled from her—his career would have been over if he had not.

But how could he honestly think he was unworthy of her? Young or old, Rook was a good man. As if she cared that he didn't know his father! It was his father's loss, not knowing Rook. Pippa could feel the hysterical giggle forming and could do nothing to repress it—she actually snorted trying to stop the sound from coming. Which, of course, just made it worse and before she knew it, she was caught up in an uncontrollable case of the giggles.

Pippa wasn't even sure why she was laughing. Truth be told, she should be crying over the lost time, the emotions that she had wasted by pining over Rook when all this time they could have been in the midst of passionate lovemaking instead. Thoughts of their one night together flooded her mind, and her giggles were replaced by longing. Talking time was over—it was time for action. She turned the key, still in the ignition of her car, and listened as the engine of her car came to life. Seeing the hesitant look from Rook, she smiled.

"Oh, Rook, shh! Stop talking and kiss me. Or you can wait till we get home to my place—your choice. But as of this second I'm kidnapping you, taking you home to my bed, where I intend to prove to you for once and for all that you are way good enough for me. In fact, being with you is all I've ever wanted."

Pippa was a little surprised when Rook sat back. He seemed to be pulling himself as far away from her as he could get, considering the confines of her car. She began to panic, thinking maybe she had been too bold, sounded too forward. It would be just like her to blow this before it had even got started. She was so busy silently chastising herself that she nearly missed Rook's question.

"That sounds amazing, Pippa, wonderful, the words I've dreamed of hearing…but what about Gareth? I don't want to cause you any trouble with the Jets. Hey, they might be about to toss me but I don't want any drama for you. Don't you want to talk with Gareth first, maybe put everything on hold for a while?"

Now she was very confused, wasn't really sure what Rook was saying. She hadn't heard anything about the Jets cutting ties with Rook, and what needed to be put on hold with Gareth…?

"Oh, Rookie, there is nothing going on with me and Gareth. He is just a friend, and there is that whole 'no fraternisation' thing and all," she added with a sly grin. "And more importantly, why do you think the Jets are tossing you? This meeting with Brodie had nothing to do with that. Um, this is going to be really embarrassing." She continued, her voice a mere whisper, dropping her gaze from Rook's and fiddling with the threads of cotton that had broken from the stitching in the leather cover over her steering wheel, "It was a meeting to sort us out… Brodie was going to try and match-make."

Chapter Twenty-Three

Rook could not stop laughing. The idea that *the* Brodie James, once the nightmare of opposing forwards and coaches alike, had taken on the role of matchmaker was hilarious, and without a doubt the most wonderful news Rook had ever heard. Truth be told, Rook had always thought if he could pick out a man to be his father Brodie James would have been streets ahead of the competition. So to hear that this man he so admired was not about to cut him from his football family, but wanted to sort out his love life, was priceless.

"Princess, if I kiss you now I won't be able to stop, and I want to show you how much you mean to me. I want to go slowly, take my time, and maybe we can even try an actual bed this time. Not that the floor, bath or even a car wouldn't be just as enjoyable—it's just that I think if we don't go now we may have an audience, judging by the little group that is forming in front of your car."

Rook laughed some more as he watched Pippa take note of the group of Jets staff watching them—Brodie and JT included. He was more impressed, though, when she gave them all a little finger-wave, threw her car into gear and, after checking over her shoulder that it was all clear, took off. Glancing in the side mirror, Rook watched as a smiling Brodie turned away and walked towards the building's entry.

In Rook's opinion, the fact that Pippa still lived in her childhood home brought them full circle. As she explained to him that Cassie shared the house with her now, and that her parents had moved away, all Rook could think about was the moonlit night in the garden, when he had caused her so much pain. He hoped he could make it up to her, put the past to rest and forge a future. But first he needed to know about the marriage proposal—he had heard Gareth, and as much as he wasn't about to give up this chance with Pippa, he did want to know why she thought that there was nothing going on between them.

"Last night, at the club, I was coming over to speak with you, pretty much to say all the things I just told you." Rook hesitated.

"Why didn't you?"

"Well, that's the thing, princess. When I heard *Cowboy* ask you to marry him, it took the wind outta my sails. Can't begin to tell you how bad it felt when I heard your reply—it was along the lines of, 'It's a deal, love you too', wasn't it?"

"Oh, Rook, it's not like that. Gareth has his own heartbreak story. He knew how I felt—feel—about you, so it was more of a pact between us losers, really. A promise that if we both ended up alone we could keep each other company, sit in our rocking chairs and reminisce about lost chances and broken hearts."

Rook could not fathom how one day could change so quickly, from the depths of despair to almost perfect in a matter of minutes. He not only still had his football career but even better, Pippa wanted to kidnap him. *Although it isn't much of a kidnapping when the victim is just as eager,* he mused. But as much as he wanted to feel Pippa writhing beneath him again, and soon, Rook wanted more. He wanted everything. This thing, whatever it was, with Pippa was long term — he didn't want to waste any more time apart. He wanted Pippa to be his. Rook just hoped he could convince Pippa that she wanted it, as well.

* * * *

She was delirious. Her head was floating in the clouds. Not only had Mitchell 'Rook' Harris walked her to her door, but he had done it while ravaging her mouth, backing her up her own path, devouring her to the point of insanity, oblivious to the spectacle they were making. She wasn't even sure how they'd managed to get the door open, but they must have, considering she was now standing in the living room and tearing at his clothes.

Pippa heard buttons ping as they hit a hard surface — maybe the wall or table. She didn't care. All Pippa wanted was Rook naked and filling her. She was thankful that it was mid-week and therefore Cassie was teaching, otherwise it could have been quite embarrassing for her housemate, because Pippa was not stopping until she had completed the task at hand. *Rook naked – pronto.*

"You have too many clothes on, Pippa," Rook groaned in her ear as he nipped at the sensitive spot of skin behind her lobe.

She could rectify that problem easily enough, she thought, and grabbed the hem of her sweatshirt, pulling it over her head while at the same time trying to shuck her shoes off. All she managed to achieve, though, was to trip herself up in the scramble. She would have fallen if not for Rook sweeping her up into his arms.

"Which way?" he said.

Pippa knew Rook was asking for the way to her bedroom and nodded her head in the right direction, then latched on to his mouth with her teeth, gently tugging and nibbling on his lower lip. She felt so feminine being carried—he seemed to be holding her so effortlessly, right up until he bumped into her bed with his bad knee.

With a grunt and a surprisingly eloquent use of profanity, Rook fell. They ended up sprawled in a tangle of limbs on her bed.

"Whoops, I forgot all about your injury. Great physio I make." Pippa giggled. "Are you okay? Do you need me to kiss your boo-boo?" she said, pursing her lips together teasingly. But Rook didn't answer. Pippa was starting to become alarmed that maybe the strain of carrying her, then the knock he'd received, might have actually done him some serious damage.

"No, really, Mitch—are you okay? Say something. You're starting to worry me, maybe I need to have a look—"

Before she could finish her next word, Pippa found herself flat on her back, a familiar pair of silver eyes staring back at her, eating her alive with their intensity.

"You called me Mitch… My God, it sounded so sexy, hearing you say my name. Oh, Phillipa, I'm fine—the knee is good. I was just taking a few seconds to savour the moment, enjoy the fact that I'm finally in bed with *Pipsqueak!*"

Rook chuckled, the sound of his amusement so endearing to Pippa that it made up for his use of her teen nickname. But she couldn't let him get away with it, she thought a little evilly.

"Do not *ever* call me that again, Mitchell Harris. How I hate that name. It reminds me of the years I had to watch you hook up with all those other women, and it's not something I want to think about while I have you nearly naked on my bed."

"Baby, I'm sorry, I didn't mean to upset you. I've done enough of that in the past. I never want to hurt you again. I promise you with all my heart that I will make you happy. I want you, and only you, Phillipa Rodgers. I think I always have and just so you know, I'll want you forever. I love you, Pippa."

She couldn't stop the tears from tumbling down her cheeks at Rook's heartfelt words. She had just been teasing him again. She didn't care what he called her—Pipsqueak, Princess, Pip—but she hadn't been expecting him to say the 'L' word. It caught her off guard. It was like a dream and she was a princess finally getting her dream prince.

"Oh, Mitch, I was just teasing you. I understand why you walked away—really, I do—and who knows, but it was probably not the right time for us, back then. I was so young, so naïve, and yes, I was hurt—but imagine if we had ruined any chance of what we could have now by rushing it. I love you too. You are my heart and I can't think of being with anyone else but you."

"Yeah, well, we've still wasted too much time, and that ends now. Get your pretty little lips back here on mine."

Pippa loved the feel of Rook's mouth on hers. His tongue danced with hers, a mating ritual that had her burning, frenzied with want.

"Rook, please…"

She heard herself beg, felt his hands move over her now naked breasts. He rubbed and pinched her turgid nipples, the sensations rippling down to her clit through that invisible wire that connected her nerves. She needed to feel him buried inside her. Struggling with the ties of his sweatpants, and very pleased that he was wearing them so she could ease them over his injured knee, Pippa shoved them over his hips. Breaking free from his grasp, she managed to remove them from his toned, muscled legs completely.

She lovingly massaged a journey up his sexy limbs. "If you only knew the torture it was to touch your body and not make love to it, Rook. I love the feel of you under my fingertips, the warmth of your skin, but there is one place that I've been very remiss in touching, one place I have never been allowed to touch.

"Remember when I had to help you shower? It took all my strength not to fall to my knees and worship you. I'm supposed to be a professional, but you were naked in the shower, water cascading down your body. The temptation to grab the soap from you and lather it on my hands, soaping and cleaning every damn inch of your body, was overwhelming. It didn't matter that you were injured. All I wanted to do was ravish you, comfort you, love you. But you showed no reaction to me at all—hey, I would have been able to tell. Nothing about you was hidden from me that day. It was cruel and unusual punishment to have to see you wet, all muscles and hardness, and not be able to do anything about it… It made me so wet, I had to go change my panties. And Mitch? It wasn't the water from the shower that did it. But I have you at my mercy now…"

"You don't know how wrong you were, baby… I wanted you something fierce that day. The lengths I went to to distract my mind from you were painful, I promise…"

Pippa licked her lips as she crawled up into the V made by Rook's spread legs, her actions disrupting any further admissions or conversation. Softly, she finger-walked up his erect penis, rimming the edge of the bulbous head before encircling its circumference entirely in her hand. Drawing her fingers up and down its length, she pumped languidly, forming a slow-paced rhythm.

"You're killing me, babe…"

"Like not being able to touch you when you were all nude and wet killed me?" Pippa crooned.

She did show mercy at Rook's anguished words, though.

Pippa lowered her head and lightly blew onto the now glistening tip, then stretched her lips wide over the head of his cock. She took his length into her mouth, sucking at him until he bumped the back of her throat. She couldn't stop from making purring sounds, loved the taste of him in her mouth, the satiny feel of the skin covering his shaft so in contrast to its swollen, rigid form. She was just thinking that she could make love to him this way all night when she felt his hands on her shoulders, urging her to let up.

Pippa let Rook's penis plop from her mouth, and showed her displeasure at having to stop by forming a moue with her lips, making sure Rook noticed her unhappy pout.

"I wasn't finished with you yet."

"It's my turn…" Rook said just before positioning himself between her now naked legs and attaching his talented lips to her wet and willing pussy. When he sucked on her sensitive clit, she nearly flew up from the bed, the feeling was so intense—if not for his arms weighing down her legs, she indeed would have. Rook's fingers and tongue worked her expertly—he knew where to touch gently, where to be firm. The orgasm hit her hard and fast. The sensations were indescribable. Waves of pleasure cascaded over her, through her. It was too much and yet not enough.

"Please, Mitch, fill me. I need to feel you inside me," she whispered, her voice strained with emotion.

Rook began moving slowly up her body, paying attention to every inch of her on his travels. He playfully nipped at her hip bones before licking a circle around her belly-button. He spent so much time laving at her middle, Pippa though she would explode from the frustration. It was not where she wanted him to be. When he finally reached her breasts, sucking first one nipple, then the other into his mouth, drawing on each of the hardened nubs hungrily, Pippa was thrashing her head from side to side.

"Please, Mitch, I need more…"

"What's the hurry, Pip? I'm enjoying myself, aren't you?" He chuckled as he drew face to face with her. Rook gazed into her eyes—his, she noticed, were slightly hooded and looked as sexy as hell.

"Do I need to stop and find a condom, or are you taking some sort of contraception? I'm clean, babe. As much as you seem to think I'm a player, it's been months since I was with a woman, and you look very much like her, anyway."

Pippa loved the fact that she was the last person Rook had made love to, and couldn't help but be surprised at the same time. Yes, she had thought him a player. Mitch 'Rook' Harris was so gorgeous and sexy — and famous. She wouldn't really have blamed him, was sure he could have his pick of women whenever he wanted. But ultimately, she was glad that she had been mistaken in her opinion of Rook's morals. She had made so many mistakes, jumped to so many false conclusions where this man was concerned. But this was a new beginning. This was a chance to make everything she had ever wanted become real, corporeal. No longer just a dream or fantasy, her man was here, his body shrouding hers, his lips so close she could feel the expelled air from his mouth puff against her skin as he spoke.

"I'm safe and clear, and dying a slow death without you inside me. Please, Rook, make love to me."

His first thrust was almost enough to bring her to orgasm, his penis stroking her throbbing clit as he entered her, seating himself fully and joining them together. She began the now familiar climb towards ecstasy. She looked into Rook's face — it was a study of concentration, his lips pulled back over his teeth in what was almost a grimace, his eyes squeezed shut, an adorable crease in the centre of his forehead. She knew he was fighting to hold on, fighting to stop his own release before she had reached hers. The realisation of it, and of the fact that she was the reason for his struggle, made her orgasm peak. She was aware of Rook reaching his own pinnacle — he shouted her name as her inner walls clenched around him, and with one final surge he tensed and arched. Her own orgasmic sensations washed over her, a wave of warmth, satisfaction and a feeling of ultimate joy left in their wake.

Chapter Twenty-Four

Making love to Pippa had been monumental. Rook lay watching her sleep. She had drifted off after their third round of lovemaking, and he was enjoying just watching her, studying every delicate feature of her face close up, without the need for stealth. There was now no need to hide his attentiveness. She was breathtaking. He could see that her lashes were still blonde, the colour not completely hidden by the black goo that she had covered them with. There was a smattering of very faint freckles over her nose and cheeks. Her lips, relaxed in sleep, formed a slight smile, and her chin jutted out just a touch, begging to be kissed.

He held her hand in his, brought it to his chest, over his heart, and rubbed the pad of his thumb—lightly, so as not to disturb her—over the back of her hand. These hands had, over the last few months, wrought so much pleasure and torturous frustration. As she had tended to his recovery, all the massages and all the touches that her warm, slender fingers had inflicted on his recovering muscles, which he had not been able to reciprocate…they had driven him mad with lust. And now she was his, free to lust over whenever he wanted. Rook smiled to himself at the thought, knowing that he would be lusting often.

Rook did take a moment to thoroughly dissect his emotions, verify without hesitation or doubt that what he felt for Pippa was true. Was it possible that he and Pippa could really feel that strongly for one another? Yes—they had known each other for a long time, but most of it, until just recently, had been spent apart. They did have a lot in common, enjoyed a lot of the same things. His sport was not only his career, but also hers. His friends were her friends. She shared and was a part of many of his memories.

Rook did know one thing for a fact, and that was that his heart was so full that it felt as if it was about to punch through his chest. Looking at her sleeping form, he could not imagine being anywhere else, could not imagine making love to anyone else and sure could not bear to think of Pippa touching or being touched by anyone but him.

He was so caught up in his own thoughts that Rook didn't notice Pippa's eyes had fluttered open until she spoke. He realised she was awake and studying him, as well.

"You are so handsome, perfect. You make me melt just looking at you, Mitch. I know we haven't spent any time together—well, apart from professionally, that is—but I do know you, Rook. You are the same Rookie who was kind to Riley way back in the days after his folks died, and he and Caitlin were left to fend for themselves. The same Rookie who used his first contract payment to financially set his mum up in her own business. The brave Rookie who saved Mandy from her vicious ex-boyfriend without a thought to his own safety, and the same honourable man who turned away a fanciful young girl before she embarrassed herself."

Rook was humbled by her high opinion of him, unsure that he was worthy of her praise. He believed that most men — or sons — in the same position would have mimicked his actions, but he couldn't not notice the warmth in her eyes as she spoke of him. A sliver of worry began to grow in the back of his mind that maybe she was only attracted to his younger self.

Pippa, as if somehow connected to his thoughts, continued on in her praise of him, and his fears began to recede. "And look at you now — matured and impossibly more gorgeous, a successful businessman as well as a well-respected member of the Jets. Captain, leader, mentor to the younger players. Gareth speaks so highly of you — well, except where I'm concerned." She giggled. "Even after I tricked you into sleeping with me you kept my confidence. You could have embarrassed me in front of the team, undermined the job I had trained for, but no. You treated me with respect. More than I deserved. You, Mitchell 'Rook' Harris, are a good person and the man I love. Will always love."

Rook was stunned, shocked and speechless. Pippa had managed in just a few minutes to make him love her even more.

She saw him in such a wonderful way. She was so generous in her praise for him. Maybe if she believed he was good enough for her, then that was enough. Rook knew it not to be true, though — she was infinitely better than him. Pippa was not only streets ahead of him in intelligence, with a degree at university to prove it, but she was also gracious and caring. She had friends and family who had stuck with her throughout her whole life, and she made more friends every time she turned around. Rook had his mum and Trevor, and perhaps some of his Jets teammates, to call family. New friendships for Rook were often tainted by who he had become, and not who he was.

And she was sexy as hell. And she was his.

"I love you, Pippa. I always will. I will marry you, Pippa, and I will get down on my knees and beg you to say yes, but first I need to have a conversation with a few people. Your dad, Dave, for starters, and then Brodie, JT and Gareth… Probably should throw Riley into the group while I'm at it—pretty sure the kid will have a few choice words to say about it all. But first I need to love you some more."

And Rook made good on his threat, smug in the knowledge that he had made Pippa fall apart in his arms more than once before he gave in to his own desire.

Epilogue

Three months later…

Pippa was so proud she thought she would burst. Not only had her fiancé successfully returned to the playing field — knee fully recovered — but Rook had carved up the opposition as well, scoring and setting up tries left, right and centre. She could tell by the grins on the faces of her friends — Brodie, Caitlin and Riley, JT, Mandy, Cassie, standing there beside Laura and Trevor — that they were all as relieved as her that Rook had made it through his first game back from injury safely.

Her dad — the coach who had signed Rookie to the Jets — and her mum had made a flying trip from the UK to visit. They stood beside her as Rook, with his arm possessively wrapped around her, yet still managing to sign autographs for his adoring fans, was analysing the game with Gareth. Rook eagerly included her dad in the footy conversation, so honest in his respect and admiration for her father that it just made it all the more perfect a moment for Pippa.

Life had given her everything she could possibly have dreamed of, and still more. Pippa no longer needed her fantasies—she had the real deal standing beside her in all his sexy-fleshed, toned-muscled and strong-boned glory. Rook had given her his love and she would love him in return, forever.

About the Author

Sydney-born Donna Gallagher decided at an early age that life needed be tackled head on. Leaving home at fifteen, she supported herself through her teen years. In her twenties she married a professional sportsman, her love of sport—especially rugby league—probably overriding her good sense.

The seven—year marriage was an adventure. There were the emotional ups and downs of having a husband with a public profile in a sometimes glamorous but always high—pressure field. There were always interesting characters to meet and observe, and even the opportunity to live for a time in the UK.

Eventually Donna returned home a single woman, but she never lost her passion for watching sport, as well as the people in and around it.

Now happily re-married and with three sons, Donna loves coffee mornings with her female friends, sorting through problems from the personal to the international. But she's on even footing with the keenest man when it comes to watching and talking rugby league.

Donna considers herself something of a black sheep in a family of high achievers. Her brother has a doctorate in mathematics and her sister is a well—known Australian sports journalist.

An avid reader, especially of romance, Donna finally found she couldn't stop the characters residing in her imagination from spilling onto paper. Naturally, rugby league is the backdrop to her spicy tales of hunky heroes and spunky heroines overcoming adversity to eventually find true love.

Donna Gallagher loves to hear from readers. You can find her contact information, website details and author profile page at http://www.total-e-bound.com.

Total-E-Bound Publishing

www.total-e-bound.com

Take a look at our exciting range of literagasmic™
erotic romance titles and discover pure quality
at Total-E-Bound.

www.ingramcontent.com/pod-product-compliance
Lightning Source LLC
Chambersburg PA
CBHW021517240626
47154CB00002B/668